the
hidden
twin

also by adi rule

Strange Sweet Song

the
hidden
twin

adi rule

🐇 St. Martin's Griffin ⋈ New York

THE HIDDEN TWIN. Copyright © 2016 by Adi Rule. All rights reserved. Printed in the United States of America. For information, address St. Martin's Press, 175 Fifth Avenue, New York, N.Y. 10010.

www.stmartins.com

Designed by Molly Rose Murphy

The Library of Congress Cataloging-in-Publication Data is available upon request.

ISBN 978-1-250-03632-2 (hardccover)
ISBN 978-1-250-03631-5 (e-book)

Our books may be purchased in bulk for promotional, educational, or business use. Please contact your local bookseller or the Macmillan Corporate and Premium Sales Department at 1-800-221-7945, extension 5442, or by e-mail at MacmillanSpecialMarkets@macmillan.com.

First Edition: March 2016

10   9   8   7   6   5   4   3   2   1

the
hidden
twin

one

We look like two ordinary girls. No more than eighteen. She with a sun-yellow cap, my face half-hidden by dark goggles. Legs dangling, our hair swirls in the Caldaras City mist, long locks intermingling. Our arms weave through the dawn-lit metal railing of an old aviary high above the square. Up here, Jey and I might look similar to anyone below whose gaze happens to find us. We might even look like sisters. But no one could accuse us of the truth. We are too far away for anyone to know we're twins—for anyone to realize only one of us is human.

A handful of the priests of Rasus have gathered at the fountain in the center of High Ra Square for morning meditation. A few citizens sit near them on the white marble flagstones, heads bowed deeply. Some hurry by with only a passing nod.

"King Rasus, we thank you for the light," Jey whispers along with the distant murmurs of the priests. She crosses her wrists, palms forward, and stretches out her fingers, symbolizing the sun's rays.

"We really shouldn't do this anymore," I say quietly, but I don't mean "we." The outside world poses no danger to Jey. She is free to exist.

Jey slides an admonishing glance my way until I finally make the reverent gesture to the godking and mutter, "Thanks." My sister likes to share religion with someone, so I come out of my shadows for one dawn each month. I like the view—the way the purple- and blue-robed lesser priests fan out from their black-clad mentors like the brilliant leaves of a night cabbage—but mostly I come for her.

I rest my cheek against the warm, rusty railing. In the distance, beyond the edges of our tilted city, the great volcano Mol looms and frets black clouds. "Not that I don't enjoy getting out of the house once in a while," I say, "but a little exercise and change of scenery are hardly worth getting boiled alive."

"You haven't been caught yet," my sister says.

Yet.

The priests below continue their meditations, calling forth the glowing spirits of the past. From here, the spirits are little more than gleaming patches of fog clustered at the edges of the fountain.

"That one's victory," Jey says. "I think."

I nod, even though I can't tell the spirits apart the way she can.

I don't have enough formal Temple education. Or any formal Temple education, for that matter. I'd be welcomed about as warmly as the monster Bet-Nef, whose ancient, cursed bones still lie sizzling at the bottom of Lake Azure Wave.

But my sister watches the priests with shining eyes—with my eyes, only dark and lovely, not hyacinth blue. It's easy to see that as being the sole difference between us, my only flaw. I try not to think of the hidden differences—the spiderweb of red scars crisscrossing my back. My blood.

I don't watch the priests. I don't want them looking back, no matter how much sunlight and mist and distance separate us. Instead, I study the imposing statue that guards the Temple door on the other side of the square. An obsidian man with broad shoulders and strong, muscular arms who casts a severe gaze on the people below. Sharp teeth, wild hair, terrible bulging eyes. And wings, four of them, delicate and curving like a dragonfly's.

Redwing. A creature of twisted soul with the vengeance of the ancients burning under its skin, the result of an unholy union between a human and an Other. I stare at him, this monstrous stone prince, searching for something of myself in his face.

Morning meditation ends, and I no longer feel as though Jey and I are normal twin sisters distinguishable by eye color. She is human, and I am a dark creature of mythology come to life. *Redwing.*

Me.

"Well," she says, "I'll . . . I'll see you tonight."

"Study well." I flash a half smile. "Try not to succumb to distraction. And if you do, well—make sure he's devastatingly handsome, or at least charming enough to make you believe it."

She gives a weak laugh, but doesn't say anything more. I watch her clamber down into the recesses of this half-forgotten old building. We know how to find our way up here without disturbing the little shop or the apartment above it that have claimed the better sections of the lower floors.

I wait a few minutes, then descend, but I will not follow my sister to the college today or any day. I must return home through the city's murk and dark ways, and conceal myself once more.

When Jey and I were born, somehow my parents convinced themselves we were both human. They even let the local priest of Rasus into our house to perform the holy branding on our splotchy little foreheads.

But our mother was an Other, a princess of light and virtue straight out of a fairy tale. Jey and I are the forbidden product of an Other and a human—always twins, one human and one redwing. A redwing is supposed to be drowned by its parents at birth, but mine thought I was special. *You just looked so much like a baby,* my father says.

Of course, the moment the priest's razor nicked my skin, the wrong blood came oozing out, black as the world through tight-shut eyes. I cried, the priest gasped, and my mother exploded into a fireball that took our house and the priest with it. The fairy tale was true after all.

So Papa, Jey, and I left the purple lin fields of Val Chorm for Caldaras City, a clockwork place of cogs and gears and *clank-clank-clanks.* The burning, choking volcanic fog I can now breathe like real air stung my tiny insides when we first stepped off the train. My father carried Jey, swaddled in our best linen, at his chest, and me at his side in a basket. I was wrapped in a tablecloth, hidden under bunches of rotten linstalks, with a handkerchief tied around my mouth so I wouldn't make noise.

And so my life began. I have been tucked away, invisible, for the last eighteen years. I may look like Jey, but my blood betrays a different kind of soul.

My father says I'm a good girl, and he's right. I've never so much as stolen a piece of cake or killed an ash beetle. I've never wished harm on anyone, not even the priests who would damn me to Eternal Drowning. I don't allow myself to angrily claw the walls, to scrape the cloudy glass that separates me from the world until my fingernails peel back to black blood. That's what beasts do.

But in my heart, I know my virtue is a safety precaution. I can feel wickedness smoldering in my chest, balled up, writhing. Like the boiling water they pump out of Lake Azure Wave, solid lead pressing it on all sides until it sloshes and frenzies itself into steam, still trapped. I feel like if I did one small evil thing, I wouldn't be able to stop myself until I'd laid waste to the world.

My father says I'm a good girl, and he's right.

For now.

While Jey is starting her day at the college, I hurry through the wet city air, head down, toward the safety of our house and the glass dome I secretly inhabit. Through side streets and dirt-paved alleys I slip, the flapping frayed edges of my duster coat the only sound.

Well below beautiful High Ra Square, I emerge onto Mad Lane, a modest street that flirts with one of the seedier corners of the city but manages to remain respectable. People go about their business; most of the adults are dressed in plain but good clothing, and most of the children appear to belong to someone. I pass a few unpretentious office doors, boardinghouses, and the Pump Room, a busy tavern, before setting my sights on a little alley that connects to the next street I need. While I may not have explored all of Caldaras City on foot, I often visit it on the printed page. Sometimes I feel as though I have navigated the entire world through the maps and books my father brings home for me.

The sounds from Mad Lane are muffled in the alley, and the farther I walk, the quieter it becomes. The cobblestones give way to packed black dirt that deadens my footsteps. The fog has collected here, softening the edges of the rusty walls and barred windows. A wild raptor bird watches a couple of scraggly pigeons from on high. Steam rises from buildings' back pipes, disturbing the alley mist, and I breathe hot air laced with coal and decay.

The raptor turns her head suddenly, a lightning movement, and stares in my direction with unflinching yellow eyes. I have lived with raptors all my life. Those eyes, reflections of a fierce heart that fears almost nothing in this world, flash *danger*. I start running.

The people—two, I think—who quietly followed me into this misty alleyway cry out in alarm and are forced to take up the chase instead of simply grabbing me from the earth like a snaproot.

With jagged breath, I run. And they run. Muggers, or worse, guardsmen. The mist swirls. I don't look back. It doesn't matter why these people are after me. I must not be caught. I must not be seen.

I glimpse solid black bars through the mist, the thud of my

footfalls and those of my pursuers the only sounds in this deserted corner of the city. The gate at the alley's end is closed.

No, no, no.

I grab the bars anyway, trying to pull myself up. I slide down once, twice, the rust scratching and slicing my palms.

Hands on my shoulders. Strong fingers digging into my bones, pulling me backwards. *Violence.* It's a new sensation. I can't say I like it.

I twist away and lunge at a metal door that booms hollowly under my fists. For the first time, I catch sight of my attackers. A vision of blue.

Priests of Rasus! Burly, sweating with exertion, each wider than the other, they look more like common thugs than holy men. They both brandish flared black pistols, which is a little disappointing, since it seems to me that, by rights, priests should smite their enemies directly with the white rays of the sun.

"Hello! Help!" I call at the closed door, but no one answers. Scrabbling for another solution, I turn to the priests. How did they find me? What do they intend to do?

Do they know what I am?

"What do you want?" I lunge away as they barrel forward.

"Surrender to the godking," one says, a little out of breath. "Rasus will judge you." He lurches toward me, but I give a kick to his liberally draped midsection and he stumbles back a step.

And then I am staggered by a twisting at my center. A hot *potentiality* at my core, just above my stomach. I stop, a hand flat against the flaking doorframe, holding still, trying not to breathe. My feet burn.

Something in my brain tells me that if I just breathe in, take the long, gluttonous draw of air that my instincts so desperately want right now, that balled-up potentiality will expand and devour and fill me to my fingertips. I feel as though I could rip the doorframe from its wall, and the door with it. And the wall. And the whole alleyway.

Redwing. My skin buzzes and my blood itches.

I press my back to the door and clench my fingers. "Get away, and I will leave you be."

The men advance, knocking rotten crates sideways and causing hurried little swirls in the gathered fog. The one who spoke first looks weary. The other is angrier, spitting, "Our duties were laid out by Rasus himself."

Before I can respond, a young man emerges from the fog, slighter and shorter than the priests, wearing workman's trousers and a simple gray duster. Over my attackers' shoulders, I see him take stock of the situation and start to approach, concerned. I try to wave him away before they notice, but he calls out, "You there!" and the priests turn.

"Keep back, Beloved!" the angry one says to him. "This is a Temple matter!"

"Come on, you," the other priest says, grabbing my arm. I try to wrench free, but he is tenacious and shoves me into the metal door.

"Leave that girl!" the workman says, drawing himself up to his full, unimpressive height and raising his fists.

"Get out of here!" I try to yell to him, but heavy fingers choke my words. The priest who isn't strangling me swings a heavy fist into the air over the young man's head.

Papa says I'm a good girl, and he's right. But as the priest tightens his fingers, and sparks of air-starved blackness start to crowd my vision, I let myself fight back just a little bit. I have to, I tell myself. There's no other way out. When he relaxes for a moment—possibly so as not to actually kill me—I inhale broadly, granting my lungs a greedy draw of air that electrifies my fibers.

And for the first time, I feel it—a burning, stabbing surge that shoots from the soles of my feet up through my legs, my guts, my heart, out through my fingers. The hot core of the land, the scalding blood of Caldaras itself, rises through my body, joins with my spirit. *We are one,* it whispers wordlessly. *We are everything.*

I lash out at the priest, a release, an exhalation. After only a moment, I tamp the surge of energy back down into my core, into the earth below, terrified of what I might unleash.

But now the priest is on fire.

Well. I've never done *that* before.

He rolls on the dirt, trying to suffocate the flickering red edges of his robes. His face is bloodied and charred, his pistol glowing nearby.

The other priest stares at me. "How in wet hell—?"

But I am off, running back down the alleyway. He fires his pistol; a crate explodes in front of me. But I keep running, and he doesn't pursue. He could not catch me now. I am too fast, and he knows it. I pause, ducking into a grimy alcove, and peer back through the mist.

Damn. The second priest has turned his anger on the young workman who foolishly tried to help me. *Damn, damn, damn.* The workman tries to protect his face with his forearms as he backs away from the heavy swings of the priest's fists.

I creep toward them several paces, careful to keep to the grungy, dark edges.

"You have no idea what that *thing* was you just helped escape!" the priest yells. The workman staggers as a blow connects with his jaw. I cringe at the crunch. "You half-boiled, featherless son of a dead stritch!" He lands a wallop, and the workman collapses, blood running over his chin.

I have spent my life trying not to be noticed. It would be wise to turn back down the alley to Mad Lane, to try to salvage what safety I can and escape these priests and their Temple duties, to forget the exhilarating rush of violence.

But a swell of nausea seeps into my stomach as I watch the bloodied face of the workman, who can't be much older than me, his eyes squeezed closed to fight the pain. The blue-robed priest is kicking him now, shiny boots landing blow after blow on the still body on the ground. He is being beaten for trying to help me.

The workman manages to get his arms up over his face, but the holy man keeps striking. The sounds are sickening—dull thumps and cracks and strangled cries. "Who in wet hell do you think you are?" the priest growls at him. This gives me pause. It is a question I have never been able to answer successfully.

Redwing. A creature of evil and menace, who doesn't care if some workman gets battered to death in an alley.

Other. A being of strength and light, who stands against injustice.

Human . . .

Ver's ass, the priest has noticed me. I am still too far away for him to have a chance at catching me, but he reloads his pistol. The workman writhes on the ground, smearing his own blood on the dirt. I swallow.

The priest peers through the thin mist. "Have you decided to submit to judgment?" He fixes me with a beady gaze. He's brave, I must credit him that.

"No," I call out.

He puts a hand on his hip. "Then what in blazes are you doing?"

I gesture to the bleeding heap at his feet. "Well, I'm not beating a man to within an inch of his life." I step forward. "Yet."

What the hell *am* I doing? Being a hero? I put my hands back into my pockets to hide their trembling.

The workman lies motionless. The priest raises his pistol. He stands chest first, his other arm hanging away from his body. Simian. Our basest selves, as the hungry, leathery creatures of old are to the graceful raptors of today.

But my blood is different from his. My blood whispers power and lava. It roils in my gut and dances in my fingers. It calls out to the hot blood of the land.

"She's dangerous!" the other one calls hoarsely from the ground, but I can see the priest working himself up, convincing himself he can take on the monster all alone. My lungs twitch, pleading for the lavish intake of air that will feed the ball of furious energy at my center.

I do not wish to hurt this man, I tell myself. Wishing harm on others is wicked. I do not want to be wicked—but it felt so *right* when I cast the other priest away and bloodied his face.

No. No more violence. I intend to walk away—until the mangled workman lets out a wet gurgle. Until the priest breaks his focus on me and says over his shoulder, "Still here, scoundrel?" Until he kneels behind the workman, grasps his hair to raise his battered head, and presses the flared end of the black pistol against the underside of the prone man's chin.

It is only then that I allow the *potentiality* at my core to escape from my fingers in the slightest flick. Just a flick, that's all. I don't ball my fist. I don't pull back my shoulder. I just need to stop one man from killing another. There can't be anything wicked about that, can there?

A jet of fire lashes the back wall of a decrepit building, melting it. The burned priest on the ground groans and tries to slither away from the puddle of molten metal.

I stride toward the prostrate workman as the other priest watches, frozen, no longer a threat. He has dropped the pistol, and his eyes dart every way, scrambling to find an escape. Terrified.

I attack him anyway. I breathe from the tips of my toes, a wave of burning air that slams him into the iron gate at the back of the alley with such force that he doesn't come down. He is wedged, unconscious and quickly purpling with injury. He may be dead. They may both die. I don't know.

What have I done? Protected myself, protected this brave young man. But it was too easy. Too thrilling. Righteous justification thrums in my chest, but something else pulses, too—something that stings as I gaze at the motionless, battered men. What else might I justify with this newfound fire?

The workman opens his eyes as I approach. I feel his rapid breathing as I pull him up against the wall. He watches me fearfully as I sweep a lock of light hair out of his eyes, my senses assaulted by the rush of power and the nearness of the dark red gash across his cheek.

"I've never seen someone . . . do that," he croaks.

"You don't say," I mutter, and he makes a gurgling sound that might be a laugh. "Are you all right?" It is an idiotic question; the answer is all too evident. What I need to know is who will care for him, whether he can stand, where he needs to go. But I look into his weary gray eyes and ask if he is all right.

He smiles at me. His voice is a whisper. "I'm fine."

"I am a monster. I'm sorry. I—I wasn't certain of that until just now, to be honest." I don't know why I say it.

But the workman just closes his eyes and leans his warm, bloodied head against my shoulder.

Voices. Our scuffle has attracted attention. Through the alley fog, I see the distinctive shape of two city guardsmen's tall helmets.

"Are you able to rise?" I keep my voice low. "Friend, can you rise?" The workman comes around, and I help him to his feet, the tendons in his neck straining with his effort. "We'll have to try these doors quickly. Don't want to be caught murdering priests."

He gives another strangled laugh, as though our punitive public boiling would be hilarious.

"Come on, fella, keep it together," I mutter, pulling his arm across my shoulders so he doesn't collapse.

"My name's Corvin Blake," he says. "And those priests aren't dead. At least, the one stuck in the gate isn't—he's still breathing. That other one, well, he's a little crispy, but he's moving."

It's true. There is life in the burned priest, though he doesn't rise from the dirt. He may die yet. The guardsmen are coming. "Yes, well, we still have to get out of here quickly." I steer Corvin toward the edge of the alley.

He twists, wincing, and says, "That one. That's where I was going." We stagger over to a sturdy, flaking door, and he pulls a key from his pocket.

When we are through the doorway, I spin the hefty locking mechanism behind us. Corvin is growing heavier. I wrap an arm around his waist and half drag him down a narrow hallway into a small, dark office with a curtained doorway at the back that hints of industry and space and more people on the other side. Paper is stacked and strewn everywhere, as well as all manner of paraphernalia, from letterhead and grainy photographs to pencil nubs and stray metal bits that might be associated with the machinery I can hear in the back. A dingy portrait of a stern gentleman stares down a well-worn map on the opposite wall, and a woman with perfectly tamed red hair sits behind the desk, writing.

She leaps to her feet when we enter and rushes over to us. "Oh, Rasus, Corvin! What happened to him? Get him to the sofa."

We carefully rest him on her worn silk sofa. Through the window, a bright sign hangs over the sidewalk:

CALDARAS CITY DAILY BULLETIN
Items of Import and Interest to All Citizens

The damn newspaper. This is *just* what I need.
The woman kneels beside him, her hand on his cheek.
"I was being accosted by some ruffians in the alley," I say.

14

"Corvin was brave enough to step in and got the worst of it, I'm afraid." I open my eyes wide at him. *Please, friend, don't mention my fire trick.* I am not out of danger yet. This place means exposure—I have a face here.

The woman sweeps a straw-colored lock of Corvin's hair aside, the one that just won't seem to stay put. "Then that *was* a gunshot I heard. The guards will have heard it, too. Corvin, if they've hurt you—"

He puts his hand over hers. "Dear Nara," he says. His smile stretches the gash on his cheek in a way that makes me wince. "I'm all right. A little banged up, that's all."

The woman turns to me, taking in my appearance but not in the appraising way I would have expected. Facts without judgment. A reporter, then. "Who are you?" she asks.

I sense no hostility—or warmth—from her. My answer comes before I can think about it. "I'm not sure."

The woman raises her neat eyebrows. "I see. Well, thank you for—" A sharp rap from the back hallway silences her.

"That will be the guard," Corvin whispers.

"I'll take care of them." She rises, pats her prim suit, and strides away.

I look at Corvin. "I should—"

"Shh." He puts a finger to his lips. "Not the front door. More guards will be watching this street. Best to wait it out."

I blink at him. Awfully knowledgeable about these sorts of things for an average good citizen. I hear Nara's voice raised; if the guardsman wants entry, he'd better have signed permission from the Commandant's proper authorities. I decide I like Nara.

But the office is stuffy, and the sun is getting high. I must get home. How long until it's safe for me again outside?

I cross the room, squinting at the window I dare not approach, my attention snagging on a copy of what must be today's *Daily Bulletin* on the desk. An impossible headline stares up at me.

COMMANDANT: "ARE REDWINGS REAL?"

My breath catches. My skin prickles. It must be a joke, right? The one thing that has kept me safe and hidden has always been that, to most people, I am a fairy tale.

"Something interesting in the *Bulletin*?" Corvin says. I turn toward him, expressionless. He cranes his neck, peering at the paper on the desk. "Ah. Our bedtime stories come to life." I say nothing. Corvin watches me with curious eyes. "Do they scare you? Redwings?"

I smile. "The people of Caldaras may fear redwings, but no one really *believes* in them, do they?"

He leans back. "I don't know."

"Surely not."

He glances at me again. "We're very modern. In so many ways. But fear and hope are eternal. Every morning, the people gather in High Ra Square to mouth the meditations along with the priests, dazzled by the sparkling incarnations of long-dead emotions. If someone were to ask the crowd, in all honesty, 'Do you think redwings are real?' I think most of the people would shake their heads and say something vague that sounds very much like no, but that *isn't actually no*. Most people are just waiting for the first person to say yes."

I am silent. I look down at the paper, trying to seem casual, my eyes flickering over the words. But once I start to read, I can't stop myself. My subconscious takes over like a parched throat, gulping with abandon.

> *In the Empress's name, Commandant Zan has acquired the bonescorch orchis, which was lately discovered deep within the passages of the Red Mine by fire truffle hunters. Those who believe Others still walk among us think the orchis is the key to rooting out any redwings that may be hiding in our midst. The orchis is being kept at the Copper Palace, where Commandant plans to unveil it at Crepuscule two weeks from today. Onyx Staff calls for the orchis to be handed over to the Temple of Rasus, insisting Commandant is unqualified to harness its power, and will undermine the Temple's efforts to seek out and destroy this insidious threat. Commandant responds, "Are redwings real? If so, it is not exclusively a Temple matter, but a matter of concern for the whole of Caldaras."*

The words overpower me like Mol's fire. *A bonescorch orchis.*

I have heard of these delicate plants before, in children's stories. They are said to burn brightly in the presence of redwings, useful for tracking them down. They are also, like redwings themselves, said to be a myth.

Perhaps Commandant Zan believes the legend of the orchis to be a fraud, that he can show the people of Caldaras City once and for all that redwings do not exist.

How unfortunate for me that at least one does.

It was too much of a coincidence for the priests to have found me on the one day I'm out of hiding. They must have known exactly where to look.

This bonescorch orchis told them.

Corvin tries to sit up. His breath has grown shallow. I leave the paper on the desk and go to him, unsure how to be of help. "We need to get you to a doctor," I say, my hand itching to smooth back that lock of his hair again.

He shakes his head. "I will be fine. I've had worse than this."

I frown. "But—"

"Listen," he says, leaning toward me, his voice conspiratorial. "You should tell her."

I straighten up. "What? Tell who? What are you talking—?"

"Nara," he says, and reaches for my hand. His fingers are cold and my palm stings as he lightly brushes his thumb across it. "You should tell her."

"Tell her what?" My mind sparks and sputters—how to explain the fire? I had a weapon—a fire gun—grenades—Corvin was hallucinating—anything other than the truth.

He doesn't say anything, but gently turns my wrist. I look down at my upturned palm and gasp. I felt the old iron gate digging into my hands as I tried to climb it, but I didn't realize it had actually cut me. It isn't bad—little more than a scrape—but it has been seeping; my hand is stained with my blood.

My black blood. A redwing's blood. There's no explaining that away.

I jerk my hand back and look at Corvin, the color draining from my face. "You're mistaken. I—"

"She can protect you."

I stare at him in silence for a moment. Finally, I whisper, "I highly doubt that."

The groan of the back lock spinning into place heralds Nara's return, her footsteps crisp and purposeful along the hallway. "Upstairs," she barks, and at first I think she means me, but she extends a hand to Corvin. "Can you walk? To bed with you. I'll have Orm come up and look you over." She seems to have regained control of her authoritative self. I'm beginning to think the worried, tender Nara I encountered earlier is a rare beast.

"All right, don't worry. I'm going." Corvin rises, shuffling unsteadily toward the curtained doorway at the back. He turns and smiles a strange mixture of sweetness and pain that catches me off guard. *She can protect you.* I don't believe it.

Nara watches him go, then turns to me, businesslike. "You should be in no danger leaving through the front door now." She gives me a shrewd look. "Unless there is something else I can do for you?"

I have questions, and she senses it. She waits, arms crossed, and here I stand, electric with curiosity. I must be careful; it is dangerous here. I mustn't give too much of myself away.

But I need answers, and Nara looks like she has a lot of them.

I gesture to today's *Bulletin*. "You've seen this article?"

She doesn't look at the paper. "You hear the presses back there? I wrote that article."

"Could it be real?" I ask. "The bonescorch, I mean."

She shrugs. "The Commandant and the Onyx Staff certainly think it's real. I haven't seen it myself. Why the interest?"

My nerves give a jolt, but I remind myself she is a reporter.

Gathering information is what she does. It's her nature. "Just curiosity." I give her what I'm sure is an unconvincing smile.

Nara's face is impassive. "I'm surprised this is news to you. It's been the talk of the city. Are you from the Temple?"

I almost laugh. "No. No, I most certainly am not."

"That was emphatic," she says, fingers twitching. Is she thinking about grabbing a pen?

Ver's ass. I shouldn't have given so much away. I smile, babbling, "Oh, you know. History never really interested me. And the whole celibacy thing." My face flushes. Right. I'm clearly a woman of the world, as evidenced by the fact that a word that means *the opposite of sex* is making me blush.

But all Nara says is, "I see. I just thought you must have been somewhere secluded not to have heard about the bonescorch."

"We, uh—we don't read the *Bulletin* much." Not lately. It seems my father has been protecting me again.

"No matter," Nara says evenly.

Too much. I've given her too much. "Thank you for your time," I say with as much composure as I can manage. "Now I really must go. I'm sorry about your—husband."

She snorts. "Brother. He can take care of himself. Usually." Her voice softens. "I do appreciate your helping him."

I turn to go, but when I place my hand on the door handle, Nara is behind me.

"Take this," she says, handing me a small card: NARA BLAKE, EDITOR. Startled, I look up and am transfixed by her fierce, clear eyes. "In case you need anything else."

I step into the street, stumbling a little, and slide into an alley.

As I hurry home, I flick the corner of Nara Blake's business card with my forefinger.

ARE REDWINGS REAL? The *Bulletin* sings its sensational print in my mind over and over. Am I an insidious threat, as the Onyx Staff says? The fact that I do not exist has always kept me a little safer. Or maybe it has kept others a little safer from me. But just now, those priests in the alleyway, the fire I called forth—

Today is the day I became real.

two

The sky through the glass walls of my high room is the bright white-gray of the fog that drifts down from Mol, the great volcano. It's the clean, pale color of the steam that hisses from the copper release valves of the pipes curling through the streets of Caldaras City. It's washed-out clouds, about as close to *blue* as this sky ever gets. Raptor birds roost in this rooftop garden with me, coming and going as they please on dark feathered wings that cut the city mist like razors through silk. In here, hidden from the world, I am a connoisseur of books, green life, and ash-sky.

I lean back in my chair at my pockmarked metal desk as my father rustles leaves and taps little irrigation pipes behind me.

"Toad-hat shrub's looking a bit dry," he says. I hear the

tinny creak of metal tweaking metal. "That might do it. Keep an eye."

"Thanks," I say. In this city of brick and stone and copper, things that grow green are my joy. The haphazard collection of flowers and vegetables in the Dome has fallen mainly to my care, and even through the settled ash and gray days, my garden flourishes.

My father shuffles over to my desk, his stiff metal leg scraping the wood floor. "They're all doing well. But keep an eye." He means the plants. Sometimes I think he means something else, too, when he talks about plants, but I'm never quite sure.

I want to talk to him about the bonescorch orchis and the priests who almost got me. But I know he'd immediately scoop us up and take us away to keep me safe, leaving his prestigious position as a master gardener on Roet Island. He'd lop off this city like a dead branch, and I can't do that to him. Not again.

But he's clumping his round-shouldered way toward the trapdoor that leads to the rest of the house, and there's *something* that wants to burst out of me as strongly as that jet of flame this morning. "Papa," I start, without knowing what comes next.

He turns, woolly eyebrows raised. "What is it?"

"I . . ." I stop. *Breathe.* "Did you know I have fire inside me?"

His eyes are half moons as he smiles. "I have always known that." And then the trapdoor is open and he is clambering down, shoe to metal, metal to metal, *thud-clink-thud-clink,* until the top of his bushy head is gone, and I'm unsure if he really knows what I asked or if I really know what he replied.

The next day I rise in the dim predawn to take a brief, life-giving amble to the mailbox at the end of our little walkway. Anyone awake this early would see only the vague figure of the person they believe to be their neighbor's only daughter through the fog. This is my favorite part of the day.

This morning our street is as quiet as can be, the merchants just rising, the shift workers at the boilers not yet trading places, the well-to-do still enjoying a long sleep. I flip open the mailbox at the end of our tiny front lawn and find a single letter addressed to Occupant, 162 Saltball Street. Probably a general call to make more offerings to a certain god or patronize a new shop. I always open "occupant" letters. For the first time in my life, however, I am astonished to find the letter is intended for me.

> *To the one who doubtless reads letters that most would discard unopened. Meet me in Angel's Glade Park this noon. I know what you are.*

"Do you?" I wonder aloud. "Because that is something I would dearly like to know, too."

I sit on a metal bench in Angel's Glade Park, nervous, wincing at the noise of the artificial waterfall that doesn't quite make up for the park's lack of vegetation. I shouldn't have come. But what else could I do? Whoever wrote that letter has already found me.

Angel's Glade is on the edge of town and quite exposed to the elements, so most of the people enjoying the morning here wear bandannas to keep out the ash particles. I have tied a square of linen around the lower half of my face and watch the world suspiciously. The clouds are at their brightest for the day. The letter writer should be here soon.

A cold shiver slices through the fire inside me. What if this is a trap, and I am going to be murdered? While I'm not eager to have my throat slit, there is something attractive about the simplicity of the idea. Getting ambushed doesn't require much thought or effort on my part. Or maybe I am to be blackmailed. That's a bit trickier. I haven't much to offer other than old books and healthy plants.

Through the fog, I catch sight of a spotless red duster. Though she wears sunglasses and a linen bandanna like everyone else, Nara Blake hasn't made much of an effort to disguise herself. I feel my shoulders relaxing. And when she arrives with delicious fruit drinks for both of us, the scene is almost pleasant. Almost.

"Here," she says curtly, shoving a glass bottle at me. I have rarely tasted any beverage other than the warm water that runs from our kitchen tap, and I watch Nara sip first so I don't behave like too much of a glutton.

"First of all, stop asking people about bonescorch orchises," she says, putting her drink down and adjusting the bandanna over her mouth again, red to match her duster.

"Excuse me?"

I can't see Nara's eyes through her gold-rimmed sunglasses, but I know the exact exasperated look she is probably giving me. "You asked *me*—the bloody *editor* of the *Daily Bulletin*—if I thought the bonescorch was real. As though you're worried about redwings."

"Oh!" *Redwings.* That word, out loud. Out here. "Curiosity, I guess," I say more casually than I feel.

"Curiosity, my foot," she says. "I'm not stupid."

My stomach reels. *How much does she know? How much have I told her?*

We sip our drinks. A group of children play a ball game under metal trees nearby. I look for escape routes. Papa is on Roet Island, Jey at the college; they have no idea I even left the house. Nara Blake could have accomplices everywhere.

"Nothing has given me the slightest impression that you're stupid," I say. "But why the cryptic note? And please don't say you belong to a centuries-old secret organization dedicated to the slaughter of eighteen-year-old girls who ask too many questions."

Nara's bandanna creases in a smile. "Absolutely not," she says.

I sit back. "That's a relief."

"My centuries-old secret organization has only ever killed priests. Mostly. Although we do try to avoid that."

A cry escapes me as my bottle falls to the ground, cracking on the paving stone under the bench.

Nara gives me a stern look. "There are children playing right over there. I'm not sure their parents would appreciate them coming home with that language."

"You kill priests?" I whisper.

She blinks slowly. "Well, that's not exactly in the mission statement, but it does happen. Not that you'd know anything about something like that, of course."

I answer in a hard voice. "Of course."

"Anyway," she goes on, "I'm sorry if homicide bothers you, but I think you of all people should agree that Caldaras City should be protected from those who would do it harm. Like the monster Bet-Nef, for instance."

I pull down my linen bandanna. "The monster—? What the hell are you talking about? A thousand-year-old legend?"

"Ah, legends," Nara says with a cold smile. "Bet-Nef and Dal

Roet, humans and Others. They have woven the fabric of Caldaras, have they not?"

I huff. "Most people don't even believe in Others."

"Most people don't." Nara's matter-of-fact voice is punctuated by the splash of the waterfall behind us. "But you and I do. Don't we." It isn't a question.

I study the intricate form of the nearest metal tree, the light through its burnished leaves dappling the park's barren ground.

I know what you are.

My fingers are cold, a strange sensation in this burning, humid city. I open my mouth to speak, but I can't think of what to say.

Nara leans back against the bench, the light reflecting silver off her sunglasses. "Look, the bonescorch is real. As real as you are. But I can protect you. If you will help us. We . . . need your help."

I swallow. I can fix this. Or I can run—follow the railroad tracks down into the plains, hide out in a barn somewhere. "Protect me?" I raise my eyebrows. "What are you talking about?"

Nara looks toward the park. I can see her eyelashes in profile behind her glasses, stiff and prettily curled. After a moment, she says, "It might occur to you that I have far more reason to fear you than you do me, if the stories are to be believed."

I clasp my hands. "If you're accusing me of something, I wish you'd spit it out." Everything is so raw here. Too much open space. Too many people.

"Did you think I wouldn't follow you?" Nara looks at me through blank, silver lenses. "I'm very good at my job."

I stare back, just as blank. "Are you implying that *I* know something about Others and redwings? I'm afraid I've outgrown fairy tales."

"If you come with me, I can offer you protection," she says, "from those who would do you harm."

I stare into the distance. "I don't know what you mean."

"Stop lying to me." Her voice is steely now. "I know what you are."

That phrase again. My jaw tenses. "I'm sorry," I say, "I don't think we have anything more to discuss."

She rises abruptly, patting her duster. "The point, Miss Fairweather—for I assume you do not have a first name, nor a last for that matter, but I will assign you the name of your family—the point is that if we know you are here, it won't be so very long before *they* know you are here. Possibly they know it already. And they will kill you. I promise you that. And if you die, it's entirely possible all of Caldaras City will die with you, including your father and your sister. But I will not take up any more of your time. Good day, and breathe easy."

"Breathe easy," I say, though my own lungs are tight.

Her golden sunglasses shine. "May you always walk under the fog."

It's dark enough for me to venture out to Jey's garden and take stock of its brown, dry little prisoners. I prune here, water there, weed, and pinch the dead faces of flowers. The pale clouds I can just see in the fading light will reappear tomorrow morning, but soon they will darken into a black shroud that will cover all of Caldaras for a year.

The Deep Dark. Our one dark year out of every thousand, this

Deep Dark will be the first since the War of the Burning Land. I have found myself tending to our gardens more lately, not just my charges in the Dome, but also Jey's house garden, and even the sad flower beds near the street. Maybe it's because everyone else is doing something. The rest of the world is busy harvesting, storing, drying, salting. Making candles. Going over the boilers and pipe joints and valves and turbines. His Holiness the Salt Throne—highest priest of the Temple of Rasus and more powerful, some say, than the Empress herself—has decreed that the Deep Dark is a test from the gods to determine our worthiness. That everyone is to work together as sisters and brothers to endure the coming night.

Everyone except me, of course. I press my hands to the crumbly dirt, press myself to the living ground. My skin tingles from head to foot. As the Deep Dark approaches, my blood is changing. The scars on my back have started to burn, and my lungs are so ravenous, I feel as though I could inhale all the mist in Caldaras City and send it hissing back into Mol's Mouth like the scalding steam from a burst pipe. I am afraid of what I will become.

ARE REDWINGS REAL? the headline of the *Bulletin* shouts at me again as I dig my fingers into the ashy soil.

I don't know, I tell it. Was it a redwing who melted bricks and mortar with her passion? Was it a redwing who elicited such fear and panic in that alleyway? Was it a redwing whose cursed existence drew Corvin Blake into the fight that almost killed him?

Was that really me?

The bonescorch orchis has exposed me, and I hate it. I have never hated anything green and meek in my life, yet if I found myself face-to-face with that plant, I would rip it out by its traitorous roots. But the orchis is being kept at the Copper Palace in preparation for its unveiling, and I must remain on Saltball Street in preparation for nothing but my eventual trip to the Eternal Garden. If that's where redwings go.

"There you are."

Jey pokes her head around the side of the house. I pat the dirt from my hands onto my old trousers. My sister float-dances over to me and sits on the edge of a raptor-poop—encrusted rock like an Other princess alighting on an alabaster throne. Warm light from the kitchen window illuminates several strands of her dark hair that have escaped their bobby pins and lounge against her cheeks.

She tips her head back and rests a beatific gaze on the grime-covered buildings across the street. Even with an identical face, I don't think I could ever look that soppy.

She sighs. "You will never guess—"

"Your young man," I say wearily. What is this new one's name again?

She turns to me, smiles. "Did I tell you he's been selected to introduce Master Fibbori himself at his upcoming lecture on root vegetables at the college? Bonner knows so much about root vegetables!"

This she says completely straight-faced. Jey in a nutshell.

"He certainly seems to have many talents," I say. Jey's young men always have amazing talents, according to her. Wine tasting, art appreciation, philosophy. Introducing lecturers. "Speaking of root vegetables," I say, "these poor snaproots are begging for a quick death."

"Oh, snaproots! Never mind them!" She kicks at some wire

fencing. "Listen," she says in a low voice, "I need your help. To-morrow. You see, I'm going to meet Bonner in secret."

I cross my arms. "So Papa doesn't approve of him."

She looks away. "He did at first. But Papa can be so judgmen-tal. You know how he is." Her eyes reflect the light from the kitchen window. "He thinks Bonner is too concerned with reli-gion." She turns back to me, dreamy-eyed again. "Isn't that silly? Bonner's just very devoted to the Temple. There's nothing wrong with that!"

I'd say there are several things wrong with the Temple, start-ing with the Salt Throne's prime, albeit symbolic, vow to protect the citizenry from redwings. And ending with the two priests who jumped me in an alley yesterday.

But I don't dare mention this to Jey, so I just shake my head. "You know I don't think it's wise to get involved with the Temple."

"The godking protects us and watches over us," she says, as though Rasus is likely to intervene on my behalf should the priests decide to execute me.

I sigh. "Why can't you meet your boyfriend some other time? You're not supposed to—"

"I know, I know," she says, throwing up her hands. "I know I'm not supposed to do *anything*."

Poor thing. I bite my lip until the words slide back down my throat. Then I say, "Besides, tomorrow's Restlight. You have to help Papa on Roet Island." As caretaker of this sad little house gar-den, Jey needs the education. She needs to know about soil and light, to walk among the rainbows of petals and vines and leaves in the place people call the Jewel of Caldaras City. So my father says.

"Yes, that's the point. I have a plan, how I can meet Bonner without Papa knowing. I just need your help." She has a wild look in her eyes I recognize, and it makes my heart buzz. Memories of brief snatches of freedom, scattered sparkles on a vast gray sea.

It's bittersweet. "Jey," I say, "we can't. Not anymore. Not with a bonescorch in the city." *Not with priests of Rasus looking for me.*

She swivels to face me. "How did you—?"

I cross my arms, a hint of irritation coloring my voice. "I saw a copy of the *Daily Bulletin* on my way home today. Why didn't you tell me?"

A shrug. "Papa didn't want you to be worried over nothing, I guess. But, listen, I only need you to switch places with me for a few hours. Papa won't know! He won't even be there—I'll be dusting the peonies by the front gates and he'll be all the way around back in the private greenhouse."

It's a game to her, the secret me. And I used to feel that way as well, on those rare, special days when it was Jey who stayed home and I who ventured out into the burning mist of the city, clutching Papa's hand. *Don't speak,* he'd say, buckling my leather cap tight, fitting his enormous black goggles over most of my face. *Don't draw attention to yourself.* Those outings were dangerous. But Papa never wanted me to be a prisoner. We'd go to a tea shop or an art gallery, and I couldn't help laughing at all the new sounds and smells, and beaming at all the people.

But under Papa's black goggles, my eyes were as vibrant as the sun through purple-blue stained glass, not brown like his other daughter's. And what Papa never said, what I know now, is that if an acquaintance had noticed his daughter's eyes had mysteriously changed color, if I had cut one of my clumsy, little girl fingers on a broken teacup and strange black blood had come oozing out of me, then all those smiles—from the man on the street with the tall hat, from the crinkled old lady in the shop who sneaked me a candy—would have disappeared.

Jey leans in. "You *know* you're dying to see Roet Island." And she tosses me what looks like an old rag.

I look down at the yellowing thing in my hands—the peony from the glass bowl on my desk. When Papa brought the bloom home for me, it was milk white, and its fragrance filled the Dome to bursting. Now all I can smell on its dry petals is the earthy combination of books and bird.

The lush gardens of Roet Island—a green paradise only half a lake away from our gray city on the Empress's private estate. Who wouldn't want to see them? But at the risk of my life? Ridiculous. I would never put myself in that much danger just to see the gardens.

But to find the bonescorch? To rip its leaves off and toss its lifeless husk into the boiling water of Lake Azure Wave before it could truly betray me? To be safe forever?

I . . . am thinking about it.

Jey doesn't know how risky her plan is, but she knows I'm considering it. There's something else, though, that disturbs me—a desperation in her face I've never seen before. Her eyes implore me to help her, to risk everything for this new boy. I don't like it.

Now the night wind changes. It must bring some enticing news with it, because all the raptors—four of them right now—abruptly spring from the window of the Dome above us and launch into the darkening sky. I try to follow their dark wingspans against the clouds, but I'm distracted by my reflection in the kitchen window. The ghosts of purple-blue eyes look back at me: redwing under glass.

My sister is carefully silent.

three

Jey would never be seen in this coat. I close our iron gate behind me and step from the gravel path of our tiny front yard onto the cobblestone street. Everyone wears dusters in Caldaras City and, by default, the rest of Caldaras. Here the fashion springs from necessity. The ash that swirls down from Mol's Mouth clings and smudges, and stylish tweed trousers and silk jumpsuits must be protected all the way down to one's toes.

Jey follows fashion—stiff, embroidered collars up to the tops of her ears, ribbons and silver hooks down her front. Each of my coats is as low-collared and plain as the other, with dull brass buttons and hems that, rather than flirting with the ground, actually sweep it. But it would be pointless for Papa to waste money on flashy garments for his invisible daughter. It is Jey who would look unstylish in a too-long duster with old buttons.

I'm not Jey yet, I remind myself. I could be anyone. Just arrived on the train from Drush to visit my aunt, or a new student at the college, or a daughter of nobility come to hobnob with the Empress and the Commandant and their reputedly beautiful family.

Well, maybe that last one is a bit of a stretch.

Saltball Street is lively for a weekend. It shimmers with smiling couples carrying bright umbrellas, haughty ladies with haughty parakeets perched on their arms, and grim laborers grasping their toolboxes with scabby fingers. Tall stritch birds, their stubby wings and long necks draped in vibrant linen, carry their riders and cargo in long strides, leaving behind the occasional cloud-soft feather, a puff of yellow sunshine on the gray cobblestones.

I am vigilant, watching for robes of a vibrant blue—to most, the color of virtue, but to me, only danger. Luckily, I see no priests. The crowds will protect me today, I hope. Holy brothers and sisters wouldn't attack an unarmed girl in the middle of the street, would they?

I swallow. *Would they?*

The city leans and I head up, dragging my fingers along the gritty bricks of the buildings that hug the street—a good tenement house, a grocery, the hissing corner of a long factory. The cobblestones slope away into sunlit, ashy mist so bright, it makes me squint to look ahead.

I can see the outside world through the glass of the Dome, but it has been years since I've actually walked Caldaras City in full daylight without Papa's dark goggles on. The city without shadows, without tinted glass dulling its colors and edges, is thrilling. A middle-aged couple greets me with quick, warm smiles. Two young boys carrying paper bags rush around me, one on each side, like I am a tree in a river. I don't know which excites me more, being acknowledged as though I were any common person, or being ignored for the same reason.

High Ra Square is one of the highest points in the city, where the oldest and most beautiful buildings stand against the cloudy backdrop of Lake Azure Wave. Jey and I know it well from our perch on the rusty aviary, but I have never walked the wide flagstones. It is more open space than I am used to. My nerves prickle.

The flat, white expanse—a marvel in this sloping city of ash and coal dust—is lorded over by the massive Temple of Rasus, an ancient structure whose features are dimmed by the bright fog behind it. To my squinting eyes, it is a great bull's head in silhouette, curved horns jutting into the bleak sky—a colossal creature that could swallow the entire mass of people swirling around the square in the late morning heat.

Someone bumps my arm, and I'm lost in the new, strange feeling of being jostled. There are so many human connections here! Shoulders and elbows sliding across me, children bouncing off my legs, long hair brushing my face, replacing the scents of smoke and poison with those of flowers and soap. I just want to stop and stand in the middle of High Ra Square and revel in all these sensations.

I am excitingly conspicuous in the middle of this sea of clean-swept flagstones and undulating crowds. So many eyes—the opaque goggles of furnace workers and high society, the naked eyes of everyone else. Some have brown eyes like my sister.

Yet my eyes are blue. Wrong. *It is not unusual to have blue eyes,* I tell myself, but I lower my lids, searching for a more secluded vantage point. I could linger in the shadows of the giant obsidian redwing that watches the square, just for a moment. A normal girl on her way to leave an offering at the Temple. A girl who *is*.

A stritch's bony hip knocks me solidly, and I stagger a couple paces before tripping over the hem of my duster. My knees hit the marble flagstones hard. They throb as I scramble to get upright again. A hand finds my elbow and steadies me. An elderly man with kind eyes nods and pats my arm before moving away. Other people pause in a brief moment of concern, their gazes tracing me up and down.

"Oh, I'm so sorry, young lady," comes a voice from above. An elegant woman atop the stritch leans down. "Are you all right?"

I struggle to find my voice. "Yes, thank you."

Now the square is too much. The white stone, the daylight, the mist, and especially all those eyes, taking me in, giving me substance—it is all too much.

I scuttle across the square, brushing in and out and around, to the long, deep shadows of the Temple of Rasus. I place my palm flat against the towering redwing statue as though the gesture will steady me, tether me away from the throng. The smooth stone is cool and so is its shadow. I breathe.

Here and there, the lesser priests with lowered eyes and vibrant blue robes push wide brooms, sweeping ash and dust from the marble slabs into gutters. Papa has told me they do this all day long to keep the square miraculously white, always. I think of Bet-Nef's frothing bones at the bottom of Lake Azure Wave, their otherworldly scorch the miracle that keeps the water boiling. No one really sees the black volcano that cradles the lake in its fiery stomach. No one really sees the blue lesser priests and their wide brooms here in High Ra Square. They see only white bones and white marble.

One of the priests shuffles toward me. People clear a respectful path for her broom and the dark, dancing granules before it. The priest does not look at me, or at anything except the end of her broom, but she moves closer and closer to my shadowy harbor. My body tenses. Is she hiding a pistol under her robes? Has she been sent for me? I press my back against the stone, veins pulsing.

Then she turns, swish-swishing in a gentle arc, and cuts a path back toward the gutter on the far side.

I exhale, tingling. In the middle of the square, the priest's course bows outward, hugging the curved edge of an elaborately carved fountain. At its center, Dal Roet, the hero of the War of the Burning Land, stares serenely over the colorful masses of people, a helmet under his muscular arm, one bare marble foot perched atop the spiked shield of his enemy. He gleams even in this diffused sunlight, a brilliant contrast to the massive black stone redwing at my back.

I step out from the base of the redwing and look up. I can see the obsidian priests now, half the size of the main figure, stretching their hands up almost as high as his winged shoulders. Odd, to have a creature so hated and feared guarding the very door to the Temple. But he gives me a strange comfort. Whatever the mythology, here is a redwing out in the open in High Ra Square, where everyone can take a good look at him. Part of Caldaras City. Part of society.

My gaze lingers. Take away the teeth and the protruding eyes, and this redwing is handsome, not monstrous. File down the claws on his hands and feet, and he could almost be an Other. He is half Other, after all. What would he say, this giant stone prince, if he could address the crowds of High Ra Square?

Would he know me?

"It is only stone, Beloved."

A voice jolts me back. A man in white is looking at me. He leans on a luminous dark walking stick that spirals into the air above his white hair. His eyes are pale and sunken into his gaunt face. Several lesser priests hover around him, their eyes everywhere, their posture submissive.

My voice sticks in my throat. I know who this man is. How impossible that he is here now, talking to me on my day of freedom—the second most important priest in all of Caldaras after His Holiness the Salt Throne. This man could, with a word, send countless people to their destinies or their graves.

The Onyx Staff.

People nod or bow as they pass us. I bow, too, not knowing what the protocol is. Papa has never told me how to address high priests, only to stay away from them.

"Your Benevolence," I croak, remembering the dialogue from a funeral scene in one of Jey's novels.

"The statue troubles you, Beloved." The Onyx Staff gestures to the great stone redwing. "But we keep that primeval monster at our door to show we are not afraid of it. That is all."

Be normal. Be normal. What is normal? The Onyx Staff looks into my eyes, and even though I know he has no reason to recognize Jey in me, I feel the rawness of everything that is wrong.

"Yes, Your Benevolence," I say. "Thank you."

I wonder, suddenly nauseated, if the bonescorch has marked

me in some way. But the Onyx Staff only nods and says, "Breathe easy, Beloved." He turns with his entourage and they disappear up the marble steps into the Temple.

I slink back into the shadows, farther in this time, until my back rests against the Temple wall behind the redwing statue. The thud of my heart in my ears, the sound of my own fear, blocks out the hum of the square.

Was that a close call? Close to what? I feel as mythological as the ancient statue in front of me. Surely the primeval monster the Onyx Staff spoke of has nothing to do with me and my tatty duster.

I remember the purple face of the priest I struck down in the alley. Compelled, I look up again, and my stomach lurches. I am behind the statue now, and from here I can see the true story. The monster's great insect wings are not attached to his body. They have been severed and are being held up to his shoulders by the wicked little priests who surround him. And his relaxed posture is not due to meekness or kindness, or even the calm dignity Other princes are said to possess. In the detailed relief of the back of the statue, I can see where his spine bulges, all the way up to his neck, from the great spike on which the priests have impaled him. The great redwing of High Ra Square is dead.

four

The Jade Bridge is one of the most famous sights in all of Caldaras. Its polished green archways and railings become almost translucent under the gleaming clouds in the sky over Lake Azure
Wave. The lake's perpetual mist does not allow a view of the far
side of the bridge, so it seems to rise into oblivion. It's a sight so
wondrous, it could easily stop the breath in my lungs—if I weren't
so distracted by the dead body, that is.

A small crowd has gathered, but the people have not circled
so close as to obscure the limp figure splayed on the sandstone tiles
outside the bridge's cityside guardhouse. At first, I might have mistaken it for a pile of gray rags, but for the fact that a hand extends

from the jumble. It looks like a strange pale animal resting on the ground, with curving fingers that beckon even in their stillness.

Against my better judgment, I step closer, peering between elbows at the lifeless heap. It is a new discovery—people are not yet fully reacting. A chill ripples through me, despite the warm day. A man of forty or fifty, strands of wet hair stuck to his contorted face, dead in the street.

The crowd grows. Mutterings turn to shouts.

"Guards! Murder!"

As soon as one onlooker takes up the call of murder, others join in. Two guards rush over from the direction of High Ra Square; a third crossing the bridge hears the cry and quickens his steps toward the growing assembly.

"Citizens!" one of the guards shouts over the noise of the crowd. "Who was a witness to this? What has happened here?"

"Look at his face!" a woman cries. "Shock and horror!"

"That's a boilerman's jumpsuit. What's he doing up here?" a man says, pointing.

The swelling masses press in on me and I back up against the old guardhouse, unused now except for its convenient privy. Inside, I'll find Jey's ash bucket and petal brush, but I don't slip away just yet. Something keeps me.

Then, across the jumble of coats, hats, and hands, brilliant purple emerges. A priest of Rasus, tall and smooth, her small mouth drawn into a frown that echoes the concern in her eyes. "Guardsmen," she says in a calm voice that cuts through the noise of the confused gathering, "I saw what happened."

Now the people gathered on the Jade Bridge are no longer a crowd—they are an audience. Silence falls. The guardsman who spoke awaits the priest's testimony, notebook in hand, eyebrows raised matter-of-factly.

"Beloved," the priest says. "Wicked times are upon us, for what lies prostrate on the Jade Bridge is not only a dead man, but a fairy tale come to life."

I hold my breath, pressing my palms against the rusty guardhouse door.

The priest surveys the crowd and speaks with authority, as though she were addressing the faithful within the Temple. "When I found this poor man lying here—inexplicably!—the monster that brought his death had already vanished. But I knelt, hoping to bring him peace as he began his journey to the Eternal Garden." People nod. Some touch their neighbors' shoulders protectively.

The priest gestures to the heap of rags. " 'Beloved,' I told him, 'Rasus will welcome you. Let the Long Angel guide you to your destiny.' But instead of peace, there was fear in his eyes, and he clutched my arm." She grasps her own arm violently in demonstration. Several people gasp. The priest goes on, her testimony more and more like a performance. " 'Holy priest of Rasus!' he cried. 'Warn them! Tell the people that I have been killed by a redwing!' "

I blink. The crowd explodes into declarations, screeches, dismissals, but the guardsman with the notebook isn't writing anything down.

I study the dead man as well as I can from the back of the group. No redwing is responsible for this death, at least no redwing like me, and as far as I know, I am the only one. I watch the crowd. It's all so theatrical, so outrageous. *Do they believe?*

Not yet. Not entirely. But enough to make this city vibrate just a little more.

Now the purple-robed priest is gone. I don't know if she had anything to do with this man's death. But she has planted a seed of fear.

I inhale, stepping away. Being at the scene of a newsworthy event is even more dangerous now that the editor of the *Daily Bulletin* knows my face. And murder or no, I have made a promise to my sister and to the vile bonescorch orchis. The rusty guardhouse door opens with a good shove. I find Jey's ash bucket and petal brush in a corner striped with light from a slatted window. Per my instructions, I leave my duster on an old shelf and step back out onto the street wearing only my sister's spare green gardener's jumpsuit. No one notices me.

I try to step with purpose—I am Jey now, and she has traveled this bridge many times. I stay to the side, running one hand along the warm, glass-smooth railing as I walk, and in my other hand, I can feel moisture building up on the handle of the ash bucket. By the time the bridge reaches the shore of Lake Azure Wave, the road has risen so high into the air that the lake is only sporadically visible through the haze below, flashes of aquamarine and dancing light. Even up here, I can feel its heat. Like everyone in Caldaras City, I am used to heat, but the damp warmth that rises from the boiling lake is intense enough to make me rub my forearm across my brow.

The bridge is quiet compared to the bustle of Caldaras City proper, but it is not deserted. A man in a green gardener's uniform like the one I'm wearing rushes past, but doesn't acknowledge me. It's for the best. Two city guards stroll by, heading back toward High Ra Square; they have not yet heard news of the murder. I keep my eyes on the sandstone tiles in front of me. I have never been this high before, not even in the aviary, and I don't want to appear as dizzy as I am beginning to feel.

As the bridge begins its downward slope, I get my first glimpse of Roet Island and the Copper Palace at last.

More jade, of course. An archway like the one cityside, with Mol and Ver and the Long Angel in high relief on its carved surfaces. I follow the sandstone road off the bridge to the arch, where tall stone walls wing off on either side, protecting the palace grounds from the tangled jungle that hugs the island. I can make out the brilliant copper domes of the palace at a distance through the mist—thinner here—and though I can't see it, I know a particularly impressive glass dome behind the main structure houses the Empress's private garden.

Through the archway, I pause, awestruck.

Blue. There is *sky* above Roet Island, with a bright sun in the middle of it whose rays drape around my skin like a blanket. The blue of the sky is impossible, almost obscene in its clarity and conviction. How is there sky here? Where are the clouds? No doubt the Empress, with the latest technology at her disposal, has had some device fashioned to keep the mist away. My eyes stray to the palace, bulbous copper edifices that crowd together like mushrooms, shining gears running up and down their outsides that turn in a graceful, orderly dance.

And green. I knew it would be here. I knew grass existed, and that the palace of Roet Island was surrounded by it. But so much of it! I can *smell* it. It stretches away from me on both sides like velvet, a thousand different greens cradling spiral beds of robust flowers in bold pinks, yellows, and blues.

Fip-fip-fip-fip-fip-fip. A worker pushes a device into my field of vision, two wheels on the end of a shaft with a spinning cylinder between them. I watch him curiously for a moment. The spinning cylinder before him is made of blades; he cuts the grass to keep the lawn down to the length of a luxurious carpet. This is why the leafy fragrance is so strong. The cylinder throws up bits of grass as it goes, and the worker, fingers on the handlebars, follows with an unconcerned gait. Instead of a gardener's jumpsuit, he wears everyday gray trousers, rolled-up sleeves, a rust-colored waistcoat, and no goggles—a house servant, perhaps. If Jey were Head Gardener, she might have given him this lawn-cutting task in order to admire his long torso and unkempt dark hair. And I can't say I wouldn't have done the same.

The scent of the lawn and the decadence of all this color radiating before me push the murdered man—truly, everything but earth and sky—from my mind. It is all I can do not to tear off Jey's dark goggles and stare, even as the vividness of this place makes me light-headed and shortens my breath.

"Miss Fairweather!"

The voice reaches me across the expanse of clean air. I freeze.

A young woman in a gardener's jumpsuit has popped up from a bank of flowers and hurries toward me.

I shrink into the shadow of the archway. *Oh, Mol on a muffin, she must know Jey.* The lawn-cutter has stopped at the edge of the grass and looks over with a bemused expression as the young woman waves at me.

"Miss Fairweather?" She reaches me, a little out of breath. "I'm so sorry. I was a bit early, and I just wanted to have a look at those amazing yellow pyxies—have you ever seen anything like them? I swear, I didn't touch, not really—there were one or two dead heads, you know, that I may have pinched—you won't mention it to Master Fibbori, will you? Oh, sweet Rasus, it's just it's my first day and—"

I put a hand to her shoulder. "I beg your pardon, Miss—?"

She inhales, her round, freckled face deadly serious. "Onna. I'm so sorry. Onna Twill. You're teaching me the dusting today. I mean, you're meant to. If you wouldn't mind. I mean—sweet Rasus, you *are* Miss Jey Fairweather, aren't you?"

I blink. "I'm teaching you the dusting? You mean the peonies?"

She nods, eyes wide.

Apparently Jey forgot to mention she was supposed to show some novice the ropes today. Ver's green ass, I don't even know where the ropes are. Onna watches me expectantly, so I peer over her shoulder, scanning the grounds for the masses of peonies that supposedly stand guard at the edge of the Copper Palace.

To my great relief, there they are, sprawling rows of them on the other side of a boisterous flower bed.

"Come on, then," I say. "Bring your bucket."

Swish, swish, swish.

The petal brush is as soft as my hair after a soapy bath. Jey's gardener gloves rest crumpled in the pocket of the jumpsuit, and I let the sun lie on the backs of my hands as I work. I could swear I feel the weight of its beams.

On another day, I might enjoy this. *Swish, swish, swish.*

Onna is mercifully silent, intent on her brushing a few feet away. There wasn't much to explain, thank Rasus. Mol's ash doesn't collect here much. Not like at home, where the edges of our little house garden are continually clothed in gray-blackness.

The depth of the ash in the bucket increases almost imperceptibly as I brush, but the difference my small strokes make on each flower is as profound as if I were painting its petals over a dull gray canvas. I am like the lesser priests pushing their brooms through High Ra Square, brushing clarity into this world of dust. I bury my face in a cluster of clean blooms and inhale deeply. Glorious.

"They're my favorites, too," a voice says from behind me.

I jerk my head up. The ash bucket falls to the grass, its contents escaping in a puff. "Damn it to wet hell!" I say before I can stop myself. Onna gasps.

"I'm sorry," the voice says, hiding a laugh.

I don't speak. Jey would speak. I should speak. What would Jey say?

"Go away," I say.

"Did I startle you?" the voice says.

I turn around. "No, sometimes I just decide to throw things and then swear about it."

It's the lawn-cutter, standing at a respectable distance, not actually as close as his words seemed in the quiet air. He smiles and raises his eyebrows. His eyes are blue like mine. Well, not just like mine, but blue all the same, the blue of the impossible sky overhead. "I'm sorry," he says.

"Ack. No. It's quite all right." I try to wave him away. I smile, or snarl—something involving lips and teeth, at any rate. Why is this so difficult? Jey knows how to talk to people. And this person is talking to Jey, not me.

Funny how it *feels* like he's talking to me.

He looks over at Onna and holds out two brass cups, smiling. "I thought you might be thirsty."

I realize that Onna hasn't said a word yet. Her mouth is open and her brown irises are ringed by white as she extends a hand to take one of the cups. "Thank you, sir," she says in a shaking voice.

The lawn-cutter smiles and holds the other cup out to me. "Tell me, have you ever had ice water?"

I mustn't make a friend, I tell myself. But all the same, I can't stem my curiosity. "Is that a type of cold water?" I crane my neck just a little at the sparkling liquid in the cup. "My father says the Copper Palace has some taps that run cold."

"Yes," he says, taking a step toward me. "And it has bits of real ice in it to make it even colder. You can't imagine the sensation. It's incredible. You can feel it going all the way down your throat into your stomach."

The cup chills my fingertips. Polished stones of white ice bump gently against the sides.

The first sip makes me shudder. He's right. I can feel the slice of the ice going all the way down. He laughs as I look at him with astonishment. "It's exciting," I say. And it is—the fragrance of the peonies, the magically cold water under this bright, hot sun, and a handsome young man looking at me as though I am the most delightful puzzle he's ever seen.

He gestures. "The peonies are something special, aren't they?"

A sip goes down wrong and I cough. "I like peonies," I say. "Since you asked. I—" I am about to say, *I've never seen so many,* but I remember just in time that Jey sees them every weekend. I snap my mouth closed.

Onna squeaks, "I—I can't, sir, I mustn't—it's—you're too kind—" She's holding the brass cup out, eyes lowered.

He turns to her. "Onna, is it?" He takes the cup and she blushes.

"If you're not thirsty, would you mind . . . dumping out these ash buckets on the other side of the wall?"

"Yes, sir." She grabs the buckets, scooping up as much of my spilled ash as she can, and hurries away across the sunlit lawn.

Sir. That would explain why he's out of uniform. Could he be a master gardener?

Rasus's bloody nubs, could he be Master Fibbori himself?

My blood is sloshing around so much, it's making my fingers numb. Whoever he is, he doesn't seem to be treating me—Jey— like an acquaintance, so he is probably not Master Fibbori. I take a risk and ask, "Do I know you?"

He smiles and tilts his head, a reaction I can't interpret. "No, I don't think we've met. I apologize." He extends a hand, and I curl my fingers around his in greeting the way my sister taught me. "Zahi," he says.

"Jey. Fairweather." It feels strange giving myself a name. I hope he doesn't say it back to me. "Anyway, excuse me, but I've got to get back to dusting." I pause and, taking another risk, add, "The grounds have to be perfect for Crepuscule, with the unveiling of the bonescorch. You understand."

"I do," he says.

A swell of boldness—or stupidity—rushes through me, and I add, "Speaking of the bonescorch, you wouldn't happen to know—?"

I'm interrupted by a tinny chime emanating from the pocket of Zahi's waistcoat. He pulls out a pocket watch—expensive if it has a bell in it—flips it open, and frowns. "How the day flies." He looks at me and winks. "Well, at least—here." Now he pulls something long and silver from one of two identical leather sheaths at his hip. To my questioning stare, he says, "Mower blades. Never know when I might need them, right? It's a big lawn." Then, with a leisurely motion, he swoops a slice at the flowers, severing one fat bloom from its stem. He holds it out to me.

My muscles go rigid. "You just cut one of the Empress's flowers!"

He tilts his head again, which is getting annoying. "So I did."

Papa still tells the story of the bloom he brought me, the one now yellowing in a glass bowl in the Dome. A careless mechanic had dropped an oilcan from his perch on one of the Copper Palace's walls, and it snapped the head of one of the peonies below. My father desperately tried to save the flower, but it was a lost cause. However, the Commandant's head attendant happened by and was impressed by his efforts, so Papa was allowed to take the bloom home.

The mechanic was never heard from again.

My eyes search the grounds frantically. No one. I snap at the lawn-cutter, "You—featherbrain! What if you had been seen?"

His eyes widen for a split second, mischievous. "I would be in trouble, surely. The Empress doesn't look kindly on those who disturb her gardens. So I suppose you could say I've just risked my freedom—perhaps my *life*—to give you a present. Now, are you going to take it? It's really the least you could do."

He is still holding the bloom out, with an arrogant smile. My heart thumps. *No one saw,* I tell myself, trying to believe it. But I'm frozen.

Zahi lowers his hand. "Well, that wasn't very successful. I didn't think you— Never mind. First girl I've ever seen who dusts without gloves, and shoves her face into the flowers like a glutton, and grins at the landscape as though it's her best friend in the world, and what do I do? Make an ass of myself." He sighs, and tosses the peony bloom into the row of plants, where it disappears among the leaves.

I draw myself up. "Yes."

He gives me a weak smile. "I'm sure you're giving me the most scathing look behind those goggles."

"Perhaps."

"You should take them off so I may better appreciate your scorn."

Now I feel the danger. This lawn-cutter is too curious. That's the problem with hiding—it makes one more interesting. "No," I say. "Out of the question."

Zahi rests a hand on his hip. "So will you tell me what color your eyes are, then, or shall I just imagine them?" I think of the gaunt mechanics and hunched miners who occasionally pass my window in Saltball Street. He does not move like them. He is straighter, more comfortable in the air and the light.

"They're brown," I say.

He inhales, peering. "Are they, really?"

I take a step back and awkwardly bring a hand to my face. "They're brown." He wouldn't slice his mower blade through my goggles strap, would he? The panic that has been flirting with my heart lands heavily in my chest. I don't know what unsettles me more, his sharp edges or his soft ones. Jey would know what to do with him. And I'm pretty sure he would know what to do with Jey. But a redwing?

The tinny chime sounds again from his pocket and he sighs.

"I have somewhere else to be. And it's the end of your day as well, isn't it?"

The end of my day already? My father will be emerging from the private garden dome any moment, and I'm no closer to finding the bonescorch than I was this morning.

Zahi gives an apologetic smirk. "I'm sure you're very disappointed."

I don't know what to say, so I hand him back the brass cup. Then I bow low, remembering what politeness looks like outside my own house. "Nice to have met you. Breathe easy."

He looks at me again with that delightfully puzzled expression, and for a moment, I feel like *me* and not *her*. "Breathe easy, Miss Fairweather," he returns, matching my bow. Only I'm not breathing easy. My lungs are tight and my heart pulses in my ears, and I wonder for the first time if I'm capable of an expression as soppy as Jey's.

five

The Others of legend are dazzling creatures. The stories tell us they are gone—wiped out by the monster Bet-Nef a thousand years ago—but we keep them close to us to this day in our temples and palaces and colleges. Ethereal, beautiful things, they stare silently from sandstone eyes, threadbare tapestries, and brilliant stained glass. We carve them, paint them, speak of them as though they are listening, worship them in secret as much as we do the actual gods.

And yet it's said that, because humans are weak, it's the Other parent who must deal with the arrival of a redwing. The Other is the one who puts the brand-new baby in a sack and holds it under the water until the wriggling stops. Others are beings of light and justice, so it is only natural they feel no remorse in destroying creatures of evil destined to seek the destruction of all humans—creatures who fought alongside the monster Bet-Nef when he battled Dal Roet in the War of the Burning Land.

Not that I'd have the first idea of how to bring about the destruction of the human race even if I wanted to. Beside the fact that I don't even *know* every human, I can't imagine how I would go about killing them all. It would be such an undertaking. If I were Rasus, I could pop the humans out of existence one by one with my lightning bolts. As Mol, I could suffocate everyone in Caldaras with lava. With Ver's insidious influence, I could send a plague and they'd all vomit themselves to death within a week. And if I were the Long Angel, I would just whisper their names as they drifted off to sleep, and they'd never wake up.

My own fire is small scale; I know that. Singeing a couple of priests in an alley is hardly the sort of thing that could topple nations. For widespread slaughter, I think I would have to use poison. In the mist, maybe. It would have to be a new, terrible sort of venom; there's poison enough drifting down from Mol's Mouth already, and over the years, the inhabitants of Caldaras City have learned to breathe it.

If I did have the powers of Rasus or Ver or Mol, I would probably use it to get rid of all this damned poison fog, not kill all humans.

But I am not a god. Redwings are not gods. Only gods can

get enraged on such a grand scale as to want to exterminate an entire species. I never get angry. Almost never.

Jey's spare gardener's jumpsuit is folded neatly in the trunk at the end of her bed, but up in the Dome, I have yet to put on my own worn tweed. I am caught—as I haven't been in years—by my reflection. Beyond the black spiderweb cracks beneath the surface of the old mirror on my wardrobe door I see yet another spiderweb—a pattern of angry red ridges crisscrossing my back, as though I'd attempted to roast myself on a grate.

Redwings bear the scars of their ancestors.

According to legend, redwings in alliance with the monster Bet-Nef were the most brutal part of the War of the Burning Land. They systematically slaughtered Others—including their own parents—and when Bet-Nef's armies reached Caldaras City, they struck down priests, civilians, and even children. Legends don't do anything halfway, after all.

Then Dal Roet came to the city's rescue, riding in on some kind of magnificent beast, no doubt—maybe a flying stritch with flaming wings, why not? Bet-Nef was tossed into the lake, his terrible armies were driven from Caldaras forever, and Dal Roet himself gave each evil redwing one thousand lashes. From that day forward, one of the ways you could supposedly tell a redwing from a human was by the thousand red scars on his back. Is the story true? I don't know. But the scars are real.

Born with scars. Isn't that a kick in the pantaloons, as Jey would say.

I stare, transfixed by my own ugliness. My scars don't hurt, but lately they are intensifying, their color becoming more vibrant. Is it because I am getting older? Or because the Deep Dark is approaching? There is no one I can ask.

I don't think there are actually a thousand scars there, but my neck is stiff from angling to look in the mirror. Once again, I give up before I can count them all.

The face of the handsome lawn-cutter, Zahi, flashes through my mind. A human girl could have let him know with her uncovered eyes that she liked his uncombed hair and rust-colored waistcoat, could have smiled, flirted.

But who am I trying to fool? I was unsupervised in the city for only two days, and on the first I almost killed two men. Two priests. Priests!

"Soup, soup, soup, soup!" comes an off-key song from below. It pulls me out of my daydreams, and I descend to find Jey attacking some horrible tomatoes with a kitchen knife and singing all the while. The tomatoes from our house garden stare up at me from their basket like the tiny heads of sick old people, grumpy and brownish.

She looks up, her knife clattering to the floor. "I think I'm getting the hang of cutting tomatoes!"

"Excellent." I retrieve the knife and rinse it off in the sink.

The door opens and Papa stumps in, carrying the scent of the gardens with him. "Mmm. Soup!" Jey beams. Papa looks at me. "And how was your day, my girl?" He places his work boots on the grass mat by the door.

"Fine," I say, avoiding his eyes. He is already shuffling by me to change into his evening clothes, his metal leg clacking across the floor. On the way, he pats my head with a big warm hand.

I open the spice cupboard and pull out a few precious glass jars, then examine the little pots of herbs on the windowsill.

"Does this look right?" Jey holds up her dripping knife. Liquid of a suspicious color glints in the slanted light that pokes through our lace curtains. She tips the cutting board, and bits of tomato ooze into a big pot.

"They're . . . different," I say.

"They're a little icky." She sighs. "It's the poison air. It gets in the soil." And she's right, of course. It is much more difficult to raise plants in the open air of Caldaras City than in a greenhouse. "What we ought to do," she says, "is throw out the whole bunch of them."

Papa shuffles back into the kitchen in his comfortable old linen shirt, its smooth fibers a last remnant of the farm Jey and I don't remember. "Throw out what? What are we throwing out?"

We both know it's hopeless. Not because we can't afford to waste a few disgusting vegetables now and again, but because—

"The salt miners in Drush would love to have those tomatoes, pretty or not," Papa says, crossing his arms. "Whole families living on half a pound of salt a day."

A ludicrous story. Anyone on that diet would meet their bloated death far too quickly to be much use as a miner. But that's the end of it, and we cook the soup anyway, Jey singing tunelessly and Papa trying with all his might not to offer too much advice. Sometimes it's hard to tell what expression his tangled beard is hiding, but his eyes usually smile.

Now the three of us sit at the table, trying to consume our creation as quickly as possible so we can forget it ever existed. The soup tastes like gutters and woe, like the disease-ridden end of the world. Jey thinks it's hilarious. And it is rather funny, us sitting here eating this disaster like it's any normal supper. I hold my nose and slurp. Jey bursts out laughing.

"I will never successfully raise a plant," she says.

"Maybe you've cultivated an entirely new breed of tomato," I offer. "We could call it the Brown Beauty."

Jey grins. "Or the Rotten Delight!"

"Or the Caldaras Upchuck!"

Papa's beard shudders as he pours the brownish slime into his mouth. He snorts a chuckle. "This soup is nothing to be ashamed of. When you can raise red tomatoes on Saltball Street, you'll be ready to garden for the Empress herself. And I noticed you did an excellent job with the peonies today, Jey."

The peonies. I remember their fragrance, an emotion more than an actual memory of the scent. I see the velvet bloom I refused to accept slipping out of sight among the leaves.

A knock at the door freezes us.

Knocks are never good. When it's just Papa and me outside, even a friend might be convinced I am my sister if something seems suspicious. But in here, there are two of us. *Twins,* with no holy scars on our foreheads to mark us as human. There's no explaining that away.

Papa pauses with his soupspoon in the air. I am already throwing my half-finished supper in the mulch box next to the sink and scrambling up the ladder to the Dome, my heart hammering my insides.

I don't usually have to hide long. The knocks are mostly Jey's friends coming to collect her, or a delivery of new gloves or shears for our father. Still, a minute behind the false back in the armoire can feel like an hour. Pieces of panic sting my mind as I wait in the blackness, a hundred things that could have given me away. Reasons the knock below could be a guard come to haul me to jail. No—more likely, to the Temple of Rasus.

> How I fought the priests with fire.
> How I stared at the obsidian redwing.
> How I spoke to the Onyx Staff.
> The questions I asked Nara Blake.
> The way I smelled the grass.
> The way I loved the peonies.

But as suffocating as the blackness is, I survive. I always do. Jey's *thock thock* with the broom handle on the ceiling under my feet soon signals it's safe to come out.

She is running hot water from the tap into the sink when I descend. Papa stands by the door reading a message. It was a courier, then. Nothing to be alarmed about. Probably instructions from Master Fibbori.

Papa's face says otherwise, though. I pause behind the ladder to the Dome, its cool metal surface between me and the kitchen. He looks to me, then Jey. My breath quickens.

"Well," Papa says.

Jey looks up, detecting the same unsettling note in his voice that keeps me lurking behind the ladder. "What is it, Papa?"

Papa blinks slowly and folds the message up. "Jey." He sighs like a rumble from Mol himself. "Sit down, my girl."

Jey lowers herself into a chair as I come out from behind the

ladder and join them at the table. I keep my fingers tightly en-
twined on my lap, but Jey is not used to controlling her own
body and allows her nervous hands to tap the rough wooden surface of the table.

Papa sighs again, putting the folded paper down on the table.
"Jey," he says, but doesn't seem to know how to continue. I try to
keep my gaze steady even as my blood throbs in my ears.

"Papa," Jey starts, and I shoot her a warning glance. She shuts
her mouth. If he's going to accuse us, let him do it. There's no need
to volunteer anything until we know what's in that message.

Papa reaches across the table and pats my sister's hand, which
surprises us both. "I know . . . I know you're not a little girl anymore. I know it is exciting to talk to young men. You will even
fall in love someday."

Jey, who falls in love every other week, forces a feeble smile. I
will her to keep her response short and vague. We don't know yet
if Papa has found out about her secret meeting with Bonner.

"Hopefully!" she says, too loudly. Good enough.

Papa grasps the message again, as if he isn't certain what he is
supposed to do with it. "But, Jey, dear one, you know what the
rules are. You can't speak to anyone there. School, yes. The tea
shops, yes. But there—it just isn't safe for your sister. You must
know that, my girl."

Jey frowns. "Papa? I don't—"

"There's nothing to do now," he says. "You must decline.
Whatever you did, whatever you said, it got his attention, so you
simply must not go."

"Go?" Jey says. "Go where?"

I can't take any more. "Papa, what is the message?"

He seems to notice me for the first time. He is silent a moment, then hands it to me. The paper is heavy with a gold coat of arms embossed at the top. A sturdy wax seal has been broken, and a gold tassel dangles off the back.

Miss Jey Fairweather, 162 Saltball Street
Her Imperial Majesty the Empress of Caldaras
and
The Esteemed Azizi Zan, Commandant of Caldaras City,
Protector of the Nation
humbly request the Honor of your Presence
at an afternoon's Entertainment
to be held next Restlight
at the Copper Palace on Roet Island,
at the specific request of their Devoted Son,
the Admirable Zahi Zan.

I gasp. *The Admirable Zahi Zan?* The Empress's son? I thought he and his brothers were away, getting university educations in the snowy mountains of southern Caldaras. Questions and confusion stay my voice, the most vibrant of which is, Why in wet hell was he mowing the lawn?

How was I supposed to know? And now he has invited me to a private party at the Copper Palace!

Correction: He has invited Jey.

But neither of us is going.

six

The face of the dead obsidian redwing of High Ra Square finds me in my sleep, haunting me because he doesn't look like a redwing. Because he looks human, as I do.

I stare at the outlines of the stones in the wall next to my bed. My mind refuses to drift into unconsciousness; it swirls with memory and rapture and worry. I follow the slow progress of a beam of moonlight, and when it reaches my face, I give up on sleep and swing my legs out from under the blanket.

I leave the impression of my body in the hay mattress as I clamber out of bed, black fog pressing against the glass walls of the Dome. I spark a candle stub to life, eliciting feathery rustles from the perches above me, and reach up on tiptoe to the top of my armoire.

The old metal wrench-box I find there takes some coercing before it slides jerkily off the edge and into my hands. It came from Val Chorm, from the house that is now only the green memory of ashes. Inside is a ragged square of linen tablecloth, carefully folded, and a small collection of soft-worn pages from the penny pulps Jey brings home. Each page is from a different story, with lurid titles like "Taken by the Monster," "Duplicate of Evil," and "Bride of the Blood Prince." All the stories contain redwings in their most depraved and brutal manifestations.

The pages I've saved are the illustrations, usually melodramatic line drawings of beautiful people unfortunate enough to be terrified and lose large swaths of their clothing at the same time. But, gorgeous, frightened, and scantily clad as these people are, my interest lies elsewhere. Each illustration also depicts a redwing.

Hairy, most of them. Wild eyed. A lot of teeth and claws. I pore over them again, trying, straining to see myself. My hair is long, but I keep it brushed. My fingernails are filed and my teeth clean. The eyes that look out from my mirror seem placid enough.

It's ridiculous to think that someone who has never seen a redwing could write a story about or draw a picture of one. It's ridiculous to think there could be anything of me in these sensationalist tales.

But we know the truth of monsters by their actions, not their appearance.

Why do you keep them? Jey would ask if she knew. What could I tell her? That as horrible as these fictional redwings are, they are a family that I could belong to, if only I looked like more of a fiend?

Or maybe I take my comfort from *not* seeing myself in these pictures. I could just be a normal girl, hidden away from society, but not a danger to it. Someone who, if things were different, could go to a tea shop, attend school, meet a boy, go to a fancy party, and the world would just keep clanking along as if nothing were amiss. I could be a regular person who didn't have the power to vaporize a man's head with her fingers. Maybe some part of my brain didn't believe in redwings, despite years of seeing my scars and knowing my blood runs black. Even after my hands unleashed deadly fire upon those priests.

I didn't believe until this morning, when I saw my ordinary face in obsidian in High Ra Square, and I knew. Whoever carved that redwing, that half-Other prince, had *seen* him. Us.

It is the day of Zahi Zan's garden party, and Papa is leaving. A wheat blight has infected the east, which is just about the worst thing that can happen mere weeks from the Deep Dark, when nothing will grow for a year. The Empress has called her most respected horticulturists and botanists to help the farmers save as many plants as possible, so our father must go.

"Be well, my girls, and breathe easy." I hear the words he doesn't say. He means we are to be wary. Jey, quiet. Me, invisible. And for all his worry, he has no idea how much trouble I'm already in.

Seen.

It's that damned bonescorch orchis. The air in my lungs steams. We've always been so careful. What do I do now?

I watch the door close behind my father and listen to his boots crunch away down the gravel path to the street. Through the window, I can see Jey waving good-bye from our tiny front yard, her dark hair uncovered, her shoulders bare.

I run my fingers through my hair. No one can see me through our lace curtains, can they? Didn't Jey test them out, peering in from the yard, when we first hung them? Didn't Papa put me high in the Dome so I couldn't be seen from the street? Nothing seems certain or safe anymore.

I still haven't talked to Jey about what happened in the alley or in the gardens. I wouldn't know where to start, or what I would want her to say. The only thing I know is that it is more important than ever that I get to that damned bonescorch orchis.

Jey comes back inside, shutting our heavy door against the midday glare. "Well," she says, "that's that. Poor Papa, always getting shuffled off to solve everyone's problems. How long will it be this time, I wonder?"

I start to tie my hair back with a piece of string. Jey comes to me automatically, tugging, fluffing, and straightening.

"I'd guess enough time for you to go to that party." I don't know why I say it.

"Isn't that something?" she says, and I hear the smile in her voice. "To be honest, it did occur to me just to go. What's the harm? I mean, I've never even met anyone from the royal family, and from what I hear, I'd be sure to remember if I had."

"Why do you say that?" I keep my voice steady.

Jey gives my hair a final yank into position and swings me around to face her. Her eyes are mischievous. "Have you heard nothing about Zahi Zan? He's supposed to be quite a thing of beauty, you know. Although he apparently lives the life that goes with it." She leans in. "A different young lady every week—and sometimes more than one!"

"You read too many penny pulps," I say flatly.

"What's the matter?" Jey reaches for my arm, but I'm already at the ladder ascending to my quiet room. "Hey!" she calls, but I'm already shutting the trapdoor. As if a closed trapdoor could deter my sister.

"Here's the thing, Jey," I begin moments later. She has seated herself solidly on my table and leans forward, staring me down like a raptor on the hunt. "It's all to do with when we switched places."

She straightens up and puts a hand to her mouth. "Oh, Rasus! It was *you* who met him, wasn't it? When you were doing the peonies for me? I'm such an idiot."

I rub my forehead. "Well, yes, it was me, but that's not really the whole point."

"So you should be going to that party, not me," Jey says, which causes my insides to flop around. "You poor thing."

My sister takes my hands in hers. Her face is a tapestry of concern and love and understanding. The same expression Papa wears. The one that stopped being comforting when I started wanting more of a life than I was allowed.

"Look, Jey," I say, "you don't understand. It was a mistake for us to pull a trick like that, and now I'm *real*." It made more sense in my head.

Jey looks puzzled. "What do you mean, 'real'? Of course you're real. You've always been real."

I look at my neat row of books. "Then what's my name?"

Her concerned expression flickers and she lets out a frustrated sigh. "I'm not arguing about this right now." And in a huff, she thumps off down the ladder.

I sit on the floor next to the trapdoor and listen. After a few minutes, I hear the splash of the washbasin, the creak of bureau drawers, the rustle of the pink silk suit that is probably the most expensive object in the house—billowy in the legs, tight at the top, with a neckline that caused Papa to raise one bushy eyebrow and say, "No." I hear the crisp clack of shiny shoes on the floor and bits of song sung quietly to oneself. My sister is trying on her best party clothes.

But, for all my invisibleness, what would she do without me? I matter to Jey. And she to me, which is why I can't let the priests take me. I can't end up a heap of rags on the Jade Bridge. Not yet.

"I'm sorry, Jey," I say to the empty air. "I've got to get to that orchis."

I put on her spare green jumpsuit and tie a square of linen around the lower half of my face. I slide down the ladder, find her goggles on a nail in the kitchen, and hang them around my wrist.

She comes out of her room, hands on pink silk hips. "What are you doing?"

"Gardening," I say.

"That's my uniform." Is it the slanted light through the window that makes her expression so inscrutable?

I inhale and put a hand on her shoulder. "Jey, I—I have to go to the party. On Roet Island." I say it with as firm a voice as I can manage. Will she fight me?

Her face falls, and for just a moment, she wears the same expression she did when Papa told her I couldn't go with her to her first day of First School. But we are not five anymore, and she quickly shrugs it off. She scrunches her nose. "Like *that*?"

I laugh. "Your face will get me in the gates. But your uniform will get me where I need to go. It's important. More important than I can say. I'm sorry. I know you wanted—"

"Don't worry about that. It's you I'm concerned about. What are you up to?"

"I—" *I'm going to kill the only known specimen of the rarest plant in Caldaras.* I almost tell her, but something stops me. "This might be the only chance I ever have to see the Empress's private garden."

It's difficult to lie to Jey. It's worse when she believes me. She smiles. "I suppose you have a point. Well"—she pulls me into a hug—"have a good time."

And I step out once again into the hostile world.

East of High Ra Square, dingy metal-shingled pumphouses hug the hissing shore of Lake Azure Wave. Copper and lead pipes elbow their ways down into the aquamarine depths, collecting, heating, or recycling the water that powers our volcano city. The street runs parallel to the lake here as I make my way toward the bridge, and scalding waves slosh gently against the pilings below my feet. Two workers, black clad and covered with coal dust from the boiler fires, sit on a jetty, eating their lunches as the lake bubbles beneath them. As I pass, one of them tosses a gnawed poultry wing into the water, and my eyes follow the ripples to where a tiny bit of shore sticks out below the jetty. There, the black sand is littered with the bones of old lunches, all of them gleaming white and clean, any flesh that remained having been blistered away long ago.

I cross the street, no longer enthralled by the Lake Azure Wave's beautiful, deadly water.

The Jade Bridge, however, is just as glorious as ever. The afternoon is getting on, touching the light green edges of the bridge with glowing warmth. I soon come to the arch that marks the shores of Roet Island.

"No dusting today," one of the guards at the gate says. They have the well-armored look of the city guardsmen, but shine like new coins.

"I'm a guest." I hand the invitation over.

The guard looks at it and hacks a derisive laugh, but his partner points and says, "Fairweather. She's the daughter of one of the master gardeners."

"Yes, my father is Ring Fairweather," I say, sticking out my chin just a little.

"All right, all right." The first guard steps aside. "Not what I'd wear to a party, but suit yourself."

I ignore him and stride through the arch. The lawns Zahi Zan was mowing the morning I met him are spotted with well-dressed people, including what seems to be an exorbitant number of pretty girls. They dot the grass like enormous flowers in bright, puffy fabric of every imaginable color; servants flit amongst them, insects going about their pollinating. For a moment I am transfixed. Everything they do drips with ease. I watch them eat and drink, play ball, mallet, and hoop games I am unfamiliar with, and sit lazily at the edges of elegant fountains.

I hunch behind a bed of pale yellow embergrass, hoping my posture and outfit will convey "gardening" to anyone who casually notices me even though I do not have any gardening tools.

This part would be easier in stylish clothes, but this uniform is my best hope of getting access to the bonescorch orchis.

Then I catch sight of Zahi Zan emerging from a set of grand doors that can only be the main entrance to the Copper Palace. With his hair pulled back and the buttons on his jacket shining, I can't believe I didn't realize he was nobility. He oozes it.

A group of girls, each in different-colored silk but otherwise rather interchangeable, accosts him as he steps onto the lawn, and he gives them a graceful bow. I hear giggling. One girl—buttery yellow—detaches from the group and takes his arm.

Enough. I am here to find the orchis, nothing else. I scan the grounds from behind Jey's dark goggles. The bonescorch may be the rarest plant in all of Caldaras, but it is a plant. It needs light and care. The Empress can't be hiding it in a vault somewhere.

A sparkling glass dome, mottled with the muted colors of tree-tops within, rises behind the coppery swells of the palace. This must be the Empress's personal garden, the place that has stolen my father so often. This is the reason my robust little garden of all colors carries with it a wistfulness, for I know buttonleaf and tomatoes and stick beans are peasants compared to its marvels. I peer across the lawn, wondering who those precious, leafy beings are who require so much more of Papa's attention than I do.

The bonescorch has to be there.

I keep to the edge of the lawns, moving past the peonies, which drape their fragrance over me like spiderwebs. I head toward the glass dome along the wall, moving with purpose but never too quickly. Even in shade, I am captivated by the sun and the sky. If I had to be forever invisible somewhere, I think Roet Island would be my prison of choice.

The dome is guarded by tall, arched metal doors made of heavy golden vines. Not the sort of door that would yield to discreet jostling. Discouraged, I halfheartedly try a scrollwork handle, and to my astonishment, it turns with a smooth click. I slip inside, and at last set eyes on the garden I have dreamed about since I was a child.

Trees stretch into the glass sky, leaves of green and yellow and blue casting a kaleidoscope of beautiful light over the gravel paths and mossy embankments of the garden. Songbirds I can't see chatter and whistle from their branches—I recognize snatches of individual melodies, but I have never heard so many at once. Water cascades down the sides of the dome, its glittering rush making me dizzy, as though the whole place were shooting up into the sky. Massive flowers laze about, sprawling their tendrils, flaunting their spirals and colors and scandalously passionate scents. Black everlasting, pyxie, ring anemone—I can name only about half the species I see, and many of those are only guesses based on half-remembered drawings in my father's books.

There cannot be another garden in all the world so wonderful.

A path littered with brass stones beckons me. The garden is deserted except for the songbirds and spotted fish in shining pools, and the scattering of voices on the lawn outside fades as I move away from the golden doors. I pull my goggles up over my hair and tug my bandanna down around my neck, and the colors and scents are even more alive. When I come to a particularly fine dodder bush, I close my eyes, drunk with the fragrance of it. I might pass out. And I wouldn't mind at all.

A gargantuan toad-hat shrub waggles its long, hairy leaves at me, and I nearly laugh. I've always been proud of my own toad-hat in the Dome, since they are notoriously difficult to grow, but that one would seem positively scrawny next to this monster. Papa says the really big ones have blue roots instead of purple. I duck amongst the leaves and crouch down to take a look. Yes, there's a hint of blue popping out of the soil underneath—

Crunch.

I freeze.

Crunch, crunch. Footsteps. Careful ones. Not the footsteps of someone who wants to be overheard. I remain still, crouched amongst the giant leaves.

"So what have you found, my dear?" A man's wheezy voice seems to come from below me, and I realize I am situated on the edge of a mossy embankment. On the other side of the toad-hat, a gravel path runs along the bottom of the depression a few feet down.

"Hello to you, too," an icy female voice answers.

"Oh, I do apologize." The wheezy voice has an edge now. "Greetings. How are you? I'm fine. One of our agents got his throat slit, and the Beautiful Ones are spreading rumors about red-wings."

The wheezy voice speaks with an oily, upper-class affect, while the other sounds more naturally refined. I try to inch farther into the leaves to get a look at them, but I don't dare make any noise.

"One of our—? Who—?" the woman breathes.

"You don't get to know. Now, what have you found?"

The woman answers with a hint of venom. "What have I found? That's a good one."

"Don't be flippant with me," the wheezy voice says. "Remember, you are expendable."

Rasus, what does that *mean?*

"I'm not flippant, I'm realistic," the woman says. "Look, the Commandant has no secrets, all right? Everything you see is everything that's here. I'm telling you, it doesn't exist."

There is a louder crunch of gravel now, and his voice turns severe. "Don't be stupid. It is not your job to question its existence, it is your job to find it."

"But they say the Black Thorn—"

"If he is real, he is a human being who pops when you squash him, just like everyone else," he snaps. "We are getting impatient. If we don't find the heart soon, the Beautiful Ones will. Or shall I report back that you are unfit? I'm sure the Empress's son knows where it is, and I know someone who would be more than happy to squeeze it out of him."

"No!" The young woman sounds nervous now. "There's no need for that, please. No, I'll—I'll keep looking. I'll find it."

I hear more crunching of gravel as the two people move off in different directions. Is Zahi in danger?

When I'm certain they're gone, I step out of the toad-hat and stretch my spine. I am still puzzling as I step off the path of brass stones and back onto the main gravel walk through the garden. Maybe that's why I collide with a young man with puffy skin and watery eyes who looks like a turnip.

"Hey!" he growls, even though he is easily twice my size and I'm the one who was just bounced off into a patch of giant bluelets.

"Sorry," I mutter, at least having the presence of mind to pull my goggles down over my eyes.

"Frigging servants," Turnip Face says, straightening his foppish blue waistcoat and feathered hat.

"I'm not a servant, I'm a gardener," I snap, even though it would be better to keep my mouth shut.

"Well!" he says, "Isn't that—? Hang on, it's *you*. What the hell are you dressed like that for?"

I turn away as though I have business on the other side of the garden. "This is my uniform, sir. Sorry to bother you."

I try to step away, but he grabs my shoulder and turns me around. "What are you playing at, Jey?" he says.

Jey!

"I don't appreciate your tone. Or your hand," I say coldly, shaking him off. *Sweet Rasus, what is going on?*

"Sneaking around in here, in disguise?" Turnip Face says. Sweat glistens at his temples. "What are you doing? Are you working with *them*? Have you abandoned the cause? You little sneak!"

He grips my shoulders and pushes them together as though the information he wants will come shooting out of my chest if he squeezes hard enough. It hurts my bones, and the scars on my back sizzle. My lungs yearn for that one decadent pull of air I won't allow them, the one I know will release the power I feel writhing at my core. But I remember the bloody men in the alley and try to keep my breath shallow.

"Mol's flaming socks, I'm not in disguise!" I say. "I'm a gardener, you featherless oaf!"

"No more of your lies, Jey!" he spits, smacking me across the face with an open hand.

It stings. Even worse, it knocks my dark goggles to the ground. I scramble to retrieve them, but it is too late. The young man has frozen, his gaze transfixed on my face. "What the hell—?"

"What's going on? Is something the matter?" A voice speaks up from behind him. My back cools; my shoulders ache.

"Everything's fine," Turnip Face says, though he looks a little shaken. He turns, and we both set eyes on Zahi Zan. "Your Excellency!"

Zahi bows, Turnip Face bows, and I'm not sure what to do, so I end up nodding rather violently.

Turnip Face is all smiles. "You've met my lady friend, Miss Jey Fairweather?"

My lady friend. This must be Bonner, then. Mr. Root Vegetables. Oh, Jey, you could have your pick of young gentlemen! Why this goon?

"Certainly, we've met," Zahi says, his face blank. "It's good to see you, Miss Fairweather. I'm glad you could attend my little gathering." He extends a hand and I curl my fingers around his briefly. Then his features lighten in the faintest hint of a smile. "It seems I must apologize, and admit my utter embarrassment that you took my invitation as a request to work in the gardens today."

"Oh, no," I say, forgetting Bonner for a moment. "I just . . . I really like the uniform."

Zahi laughs.

"I apologize, Your Excellency." Bonner takes my arm a little roughly. "I'm taking her home to change right now."

"As she wishes," Zahi says, "though, really, my friends, it is unnecessary." He glances at me. "I thought I heard shouting."

I try to look baffled. "Shouting?" My best chance is to steer him away. I cannot hope for help, and I certainly can't risk exposing my identity to the Empress's own son. I can deal with Bonner on my own.

"No shouting here," Bonner says. Flaming lout.

"Well, I'll let you two enjoy the garden, then." Zahi gives us a polite nod and takes his leave, joining a group of enthusiastic young ladies on the shady lawn outside.

I look daggers at Bonner, whose little eyes are wide.

"You're . . . you're not her," he says.

Damn. No, no, no. I try to keep my voice steady. "What are you talking about?"

"You're not Jey Fairweather," he says.

"Of course I am." I swallow. "Look at me. Who else would I be?"

"You have *blue eyes*."

"Don't be silly," I say calmly. "I've always had blue eyes, don't you remember?" Tamping down my revulsion, I put a hand to his face in a gesture of affection, but he pulls away sharply.

"When she said she had a sister, I—"

My chest gives a jolt. "She said she had a sister?"

"You are a bloody twin," he cries, gaping at me like a fish.

My brain boils. "What did she tell you about me?"

"Where is your mark, twin?" Bonner snaps. "Where is the priest's scar on your forehead? Don't lie to me."

My heart is racing. I look into his eyes. "Please," I whisper. "For Jey's sake, please forget you ever saw me. Okay? I'll leave town. I'll never come back. I promise. Please, I would never hurt anyone."

He blinks at last, and frowns. *Please, Rasus, let me have won him over. I'll never ask for anything else again, I promise.*

When Bonner speaks, his words are low and careful. "I'll keep your secret from these good people here today. What you need to do now, girl, is put your goggles back on and pull up that bandanna."

I do so, relief flooding my veins. "Thank—"

"Now, you come with me," he says, grabbing my arm. "And if you disappear, I'll go to your house tonight and break your sister's neck while she sleeps."

seven

When Bonner and I leave the grounds of the Copper Palace, we pass Zahi Zan and one of the pretty girls—the one dressed in buttery yellow—sitting on a stone bench next to a fountain. She laughs and throws her head back; he is making stupid faces. Neither of them notices us.

It's not as though I'm being kidnapped or anything.

The trek back across the Jade Bridge is a mixture of trepidation and annoyance. Bonner doesn't say where we are going, but all I have to do is ask myself, *Where would I take a redwing if I captured one?* So of course we are heading straight toward the crowds of High Ra Square and the Temple of Rasus.

Bonner squeezes my arm with his sweaty fingers as though

he is physically controlling me. Even without my redwing blood, I could shake this bloated slug off me. But I cannot run—he knows where we live, where Jey goes to school. I can't watch her every minute when it's impossible for us to be together in public.

We veer off wide Ver's Way, navigating damp alleys and side streets peppered with dark-windowed shops I would hesitate to explore. We pass a few little brown street gardens whose meager harvests look even more unappetizing than Jey's tomatoes. Bonner pulls me along, breathing heavily. For all his bravado, I can tell he is afraid.

He chooses to take me along the back ways of Caldaras City rather than the crowded routes—the actions of a guilty man trying to hide his crime. But the result is that we are now alone in the spiderweb of run-down, forgotten lanes, and he doesn't know what I am capable of. I don't entirely know myself.

A raptor gleams in a little patch of sunlight, watching me with lazy interest. Scientists tell us raptors and great stritches and little parakeets are all strange, new versions of the terrible creatures that used to roam the land before human beings and Others, maybe even before Mol exploded out of the fiery depths. They are as ancient as the gods themselves, but they have not endured because of temples and worshippers and supernatural powers. The raptors, with their hollow bones and streamlined bodies, have survived because they adapt. They see reality for what it is, not what they wish it to be.

We're getting closer to High Ra Square and the Temple of Rasus, and I don't expect to be welcomed with open arms by the priests there. Or the guards. Mol's blood, I hadn't even thought about all the Temple guards. And there will be throngs of people in the square, and innocent worshippers in the Temple. . . .

I'm going to have to kill Bonner. Here. The realization jolts me.

He gives my arm a particularly zealous tug and I dig my heels in. We come to a stop. Four or five dirty stritches peer suspiciously from the shadows of a roughly soldered pen.

My feet burn with the power below them, roiling in the ground. The ball of energy at my core snaps and arcs.

Do I really want to do this?

"Come on." Bonner wrenches my arm. He gives me a hard look, but I see the fear beneath. He is afraid of me, and he is right to be.

"Don't do this, friend," I say, looking deep into those arrogant, watery eyes, trying to see into the soul of a person who could profess to love my sister and then threaten to break her neck. A person who could kidnap someone who has never done him any wrong and hand her over to those who would kill her.

My fingers start to tremble, tingling with fire. The stritches shuffle quickly to the back of their pen, clustered in the shadow of a grimy metal half roof. Bonner is frozen, staring, finally aware of the perilous position he has put himself in. I could dull those watery eyes for good right now, and my sister would never have to know what happened. I could boil the blood inside his veins.

Do it now, I tell myself. My fingers are so hot, I could peel his skin with a touch.

"Let's go, creature," he hisses, puffing himself out like a rock thrush looking for a fight. "Get moving."

Do it. I extend a hand. Bonner looks at it, wide eyed.

But suddenly, the dirty alley mist is disturbed by a small sound. A cough. I turn, ears prickling. There—so close, it's amazing we didn't see him—is a ragged man with shallow breath and hair like fine, junk wire. He sits in filth against a back wall, legs splayed as though they are no longer really a part of his body. A huge, ancient raptor with tattered feathers and its one eye closed is perched on the man's bony shoulder, two old friends forgotten by the rest of the world.

The man looks up at me with blank, pink eyes, all memories of fear or anger or happiness long since evaporated. But through the emotionless haze, I can tell he is waiting to see what I will do next. He coughs again, and the big raptor opens its faded, golden eye and finds me. Does he know of redwings, this man? I will be the first one he has ever seen, and the last.

Bonner doesn't even glance at them. "That's enough, you. Move along. What's the problem?"

"The problem?" I give him a stony glare, feeling three eyes on me all the while. Now I lean in close to my kidnapper and whisper, "The problem is that you're on fire."

In an instant, I grab Bonner's hands and permit a small burst of flame to pounce through my fingertips. He screeches— dramatically, I think, since it's just a small fire—and staggers, falling to the ground. "By all the—! What did you *do*?" He pats his raw hands against the greasy black dirt of this back lane.

For a moment, I think I hear more raspy coughing from the old man, but when I turn, his pink eyes are sparkling. He is laughing. I meet his gaze and can't help but laugh along with him.

Bonner rises drunkenly. "Don't—don't you dare run, you monster!"

I cross my arms. "I won't run. Not while my freedom is payment for my sister's life. So you can keep your bloody hands to yourself."

His eyes flash. "You're going to die, redwing. The Beautiful Ones are going to rip your flesh from your bones."

"If it keeps you away from my sister, let them do it," I say. "That's what love is, I suppose."

"Love!" He looks genuinely astonished. "Love is protecting innocent people from evil! As if a thing like you could know anything about love."

The skin on my face turns cold. I almost don't recognize the fearsome voice that comes from my own throat. "What I do know," I snarl, "is that I could kill you right now if I wanted. *And it would be easy.*"

We set off again, and Bonner doesn't say another word. I glance back at the ragged man, but he and his companion have closed their eyes. They sit motionless in the dirty fog, and for all I know, they may go on like that until the end of time.

Now I have complicated matters. We step into a wide, noisy street and the just-brighter-than-shadows diffusion of light that passes for sunshine here. Since I did not kill Bonner in secret, I'll have to escape once he has deposited me at the Temple, and pray I can make it back to Saltball Street to warn Jey before he realizes I'm missing. A slightly more delicate operation, I admit.

Moments later, we finally ascend the marble steps that lead to the great Temple of Rasus. The vestibule beyond the front doors is cavernous enough; I can't imagine what the actual sanctuary is like. Bonner bows low as we enter, then gives me a look. I give him a look right back, all venom. *No way. I'm not bowing.* He squints as though he should have known I wouldn't have the decency to thank the god who is about to smite me. Then he motions for me to follow him, even though that's just what I've been doing for the last half hour. My work boots clop on the clean floor, white marble tiles that gleam with patches of sapphire, gold, and ruby from the light shining through stained glass windows.

A purple-robed priest, a rank above the blue lower priests, stands near the entrance to the sanctuary, but Bonner ignores him and pulls me to the side. There we wait for what feels like an eternity. Priests and civilians come and go, but Bonner pays them no attention. Eventually, another purple priest emerges from the sanctuary—the same one from the Jade Bridge and the murdered man—and Bonner is finally interested. They speak in low tones while I pretend to give a critical eye to the celestial scene carved into one of the vestibule's sandstone pillars. The priest eyes me, then disappears through a modest door I can just catch sight of behind a large gold curtain. I wonder how long it will be before the Temple guards arrive.

It is not long.

Like any self-respecting temple, this one has a dungeon. I'm sure they have another name for it, like Righteous Correctional Detainment Area and Exercise Facility. But as someone who has read more than her fair share of penny pulps, I recognize the iron bars, dirty stone floors, and pieces of equipment that look extremely specialized without the nature of their specializations being immediately evident. The dim light from a few fat candles set in the walls creates the kind of gloom that gives rise to unwarranted panic.

Or completely warranted panic.

Bonner was ushered away, the purple priest's hand on his back, a couple floors up. The guards and I continued to descend until bright gaslight, marble, and gold velvet were replaced with yellow flickers, bare stone, and suspicious stains.

My feet still burn, toying with invisible tendrils of flame that snake up from the earth under the floor, but as far as I can tell, escape is impossible from this room. One door, one staircase leading up, and probably fifty people I'd have to incinerate between here and the outside. Not ideal. I'll have to wait a bit longer.

The Temple's one-size-fits-all iron collar is fastened heavily around my neck. The attached chain must weigh nearly as much as I do, and I hunch forward to avoid it pulling my throat back and strangling me. And I realize I may be a blight on society, but is a chair too much to ask?

The two black-clad guards, a rugged, bearded man and a skinny, hollow-eyed woman, scowl at me from under their spiked iron helmets—representative of the sun's rays, an idea that would work beautifully if the sun were black and terrifying.

"All right, what are you in for?" the bearded guard asks. "Fabrication or heresy?"

I frown. "They don't tell you much, do they?"

"Fornication?" the hollow-eyed one offers.

"Now you're making me blush." I cross my arms. "Do you really not know why I'm here? How are you ever going to torture me properly?" Jey would be proud of how completely I'm concealing my fright. Well, almost. Just have to keep that loud heartbeat in check.

Sweat drips down the sides of my face. The dungeon is stifling. But the anticipation of my punishment, the mystery of it, is the worst part. My insides feel like they're being squeezed by the very air in here.

The strange thing is how unafraid the guards are. Here they have a *redwing,* an ancient creature of evil and destruction, in captivity, and there are only two of them? As I look at their expressionless faces and spiritless movements, I sense an air of mundanity about the whole thing. According to legend, I want nothing more than the death of every human being in Caldaras, and I have the supernatural power to do it. Don't they care? Shouldn't they be terrified?

Not that I'm feeling very supernatural right now. I am hot and sticky and nervous. I have to bite the insides of my cheeks to keep my jaw from shaking.

The bearded guard says, "All right, then, off with her clothes."

"Now, wait a minute—" I start, but the hollow-eyed guard already has her bony fingers on the buttons of my green gardener's jumpsuit.

I can't believe I was ever enthralled by human interaction, ever wanted someone to touch me. Human interaction is terrible. I elbow the bony fingers off, and the bearded guard says, "Ah, don't rip your suit!"

They're planning to—to I don't know, and I don't want to think about it, and all he can say is *don't rip your suit*? Does that mean the priests would be angry if they knew what these two guards are up to?

The bearded guard goes to a low shelf and retrieves a nasty-looking stritch whip. Sweat runs in rivulets down my temples now, but I don't move.

The hollow-eyed guard puts her hands on her hips. "You want a lash across the face, miss?" she says. "Stritches are big birds. You know what a whip can do to a little thing like you? Slice your nose right off your face, or pop an eye out of its socket."

"I'm not little," I say, but the guard just puts a finger in her mouth and makes a *pop!* sound.

The bearded guard looks askance at her. "Rasus, what kind of mind do you have? Stop being creepy." He turns to me. "That said, miss, I will ruin your face if you don't cooperate."

My throat tightens. Cruelty is much creepier wrapped in politeness. I edge away from the bearded guard into the shadows between candles.

"We need you to remove that uniform, miss," the bearded guard says. "Just the top bit is fine."

"No." My hand flies to the topmost button of the slit that runs down one side of the jumpsuit's front. I take another step back.

The hollow-eyed guard sighs and gives the other one a weary glance. "I'll give her the choker." The bearded guard pauses, but then nods, candlelight flickering in his eyes.

The choker is not creatively named. My collar is designed with a clever spring and lever mechanism that someone so inclined can use to apply and relieve pressure to my throat. The hollow-eyed guard holds the trigger, leaning casually against the blackened stone wall as though she has better things to do.

She only has to squeeze once. The shadowy dungeon becomes

a haze of painful red sparks dancing before my eyes, and I know I would rather remove the jumpsuit than get choked again.

I don't give the bearded guard the satisfaction of undoing my buttons himself. I slide my arms out of the sleeves and let the top half of the suit fall. I know I should feel shy—I know about modesty and nakedness—but truthfully, nothing feels as shocking or invasive to me as simply being seen, acknowledged, clothes or not. Even now, with half the jumpsuit around my waist, what bothers me most is that these two guards know I exist.

"Turn around," the bearded guard says, businesslike. Hesitantly, I turn. I feel him approach from behind, hear the stritch whip dragging on the gritty floor behind me. Then he pauses. "Is this some kind of joke?"

"I don't think so," I say. "Unless I really don't get it."

"What's the matter?" the other guard asks. I try to turn back as she crosses to us, but the bearded guard pushes me back in place.

The hollow-eyed guard runs her hand down my back. She grabs a fat candle off the wall and brings it closer, illuminating my thousand scars. "What in wet hell is this?" she says.

Don't these people *attend* Temple? Do they know *anything*?

"These scars are old," the bearded guard says. "Look, they're all healed up."

"Damn it all." The hollow-eyed guard traces the ridges on my back with her finger.

"The problem with this organization—and I've been saying this for years—" the bearded guard starts.

"I know, I know," the hollow-eyed guard jumps in. "I know what you're going to say."

"A lack of communication," the bearded guard says.

"Would it kill them, I mean would it *kill* them to keep track of these things?" The hollow-eyed guard sighs heavily. "I was eating my evening meal, you know." She moves away from me, and I turn around, the heavy chain swinging awkwardly.

"I know," the bearded guard says, then looks at me. "All right, get dressed. Hurry now. The Onyx Staff wants to see you."

Well, I think as I start to do up my buttons, *this may have been the oddest torture session ever to take place in the Temple of Rasus.*

The fearsome high priest known as the Onyx Staff is probably the last person in Caldaras City most people would expect to find reading aloud from *Merry Mother May's Big Book of Fairy Stories for Well-Behaved Children.* But I am harder to surprise than most people. I don't even raise an eyebrow when he starts in on "The Tale of the Blind Miller" as we stand before a group of twenty or so priests of varying rank in an almost oppressively warm candlelit room.

Not that the Onyx Staff would have made a good First School teacher. There is no comfort in his deep voice as he reads to the gathering. "But the Miller," he intones, "though he could not see the two men, was not fooled by their disguises, for he heard the likeness of their voices and knew them for *what they were.*" He gives me a hard stare clearly meant to be meaningful. From his perch on a high, wooden chair at one end of the small room, the Onyx Staff reminds me of an illustration of the wild raptors on the cliffs of Drush, their white feathers smoothed against the wind, their beaks dulled by the gritty air.

For all the stairs the guards and I climbed, we must be somewhere near the top of the Temple, but the room's one meager, brown window offers little insight into the world outside. The priests, their faces obscured by bandannas, are quiet. I don't look at them, these people who have nothing better to do today than watch this nonsense. Instead, I keep my eyes focused on the face of the Onyx Staff, his white hair shining in the gleam of the small window. The light does little to soften his cruel edges.

I stand at the other end of the room with my wrists chained to the floor. Indistinct shapes crowd the room's shadows, spiky iron devices and asymmetrical structures I don't really want to think about. Behind me, the wall is carved with a relief of Rasus, the many-handed sun. "Are you familiar with the story of the blind miller, Beloved?" the Onyx Staff asks.

I clench my fingers. The iron cuffs are starting to chafe. "Yes, Your Benevolence." My voice is muffled by the still, hot air of this cramped room. "My father read me fairy tales just like everyone else's parents did. And he did the voices much better than you, although I'm certainly willing to hear your Harko the Happy Bat if you'd like another shot."

Someone snickers, but quickly stifles it. Maybe some of them will feel bad for me. *Hey, remember that girl? She was feisty, wasn't she? I mean, unspeakably evil, yes, but haven't you always wanted to give the high priest a bit of lip?*

The Onyx Staff continues to stare at me with all the warmth of a dead maggot. "The miller in this story discovers the secret the merchant and the tailor are hiding," he says. "What is that secret, Beloved?"

"I plead silence, Your Benevolence," I say, "so that I might not spoil the ending for these good priests."

Scattered laughter bubbles from underneath a few bandannas.

Nervous eyes glint in the gloom. Are the faithful starting to wonder if the Onyx Staff will raise the actual onyx staff he holds in his right hand and bash my head in with it before a verdict can be reached?

But he doesn't. Instead, he gives us all his sourest frown and says, "I do not accept your plea of silence in this instance, Beloved, and if you want to have any hope of convincing the Temple of your innocence, I'd advise you to answer all questions simply and truthfully."

My lungs expand, stretching my skin tight. The scars on my back seem to writhe like living things trying to burn themselves off my body. *Convincing the Temple of your innocence.* It's possible, then. Maybe I'll make it out of here with everyone in one piece after all.

"Then the simple truth," I say, "is that I have not been accused of a crime."

Two or three priests mutter in protest. The Onyx Staff leans forward into the light from the dirty window. "I will repeat my question: What is the secret of the merchant and the tailor?"

I grow weary of this game. Everyone knows this story. "They are twins."

"Twins?" He arches a feathery brow. "And why should that be kept secret?"

I snort in derision. "For a high priest, you are awfully unfamiliar with mythology." One of the priests in black lashes my head with a stritch whip I didn't know was there, slicing my ear. Warm blood oozes under my hair. I can't lift a hand to rub it, and its tickling bothers me more than the pain.

"Pardon me," the Onyx Staff says lightly. "I didn't catch that."

You don't have to enjoy this, you wicked old beetle. I don't say it aloud. Instead, "The merchant and the tailor are not human twins, and so do not bear the mark of a priest on their foreheads. They are the offspring of a human being and an Other."

"Ah, fairy tales," he says to the others. "Children's stories. Isn't that what these are, Beloved?" He holds the storybook up as the group murmurs hesitant assent. "Drivel with no place in a court of law."

This isn't a court of law. For one thing, there is no judge, jury, or scrivener. There is no list of charges signed by an officer of the Commandant. There is only the Onyx Staff.

The high priest lets the storybook fall to the floor with a thud. "Yes, as children, we all heard the old stories of Other princes and princesses, and as adults, we abandoned them. After all, this is the modern age, one of machines and locomotion and equality. Surely we have outgrown fairy tales. Yet . . ."

At his pause, the priests shuffle their feet nervously.

"Yet," the Onyx Staff continues, "to this day, twins are marked with a priest's razor so that we may know them as human and good." He turns to me. "Beloved, what is a redwing?"

"It is a type of flower," I say, "that can cure forty-seven different ailments."

My answer is technically true, but the priest in black flicks his stritch whip again anyway, now across my back. The *crack* is more impressive than the injury this time, but I don't want to press my luck further. Next time it could be my eyes.

"You are absolutely right to scorn such a question, my dear. I doubt these learned people need such a thing explained to them." The Onyx Staff takes a step, his white robes catching patches of brown light. "Of course, everyone knows redwings do not exist. The beings known as Others have not lived in Caldaras for a thousand years, isn't that right?" He spreads his arms and smiles at the gathering. "In any case, surely no one who gave birth to a creature as monstrous as a redwing would allow it to live."

"Surely not," I say darkly.

"But," the Onyx Staff goes on, his voice suddenly quiet and eerie, "despite what 'everyone knows,' there are those of us who remember a different story. We remain vigilant, beautiful in the eyes of our god."

The Beautiful Ones.

Now the Onyx Staff addresses me. "You do not bear the priest's mark, Beloved, and we know you to be a twin." A few contemptuous exclamations rattle the thick air. The Onyx Staff looks to one of the purple-robed priests. "Brother Bonner, would you step forward, please?"

My kidnapper detaches himself from the shadowy group and slouches toward me. Not too close. I resist the urge to spit at him.

The Onyx Staff speaks in a calm voice. "This is the brave young man who discovered the unmarked twin in our midst—the monster." He turns to Bonner. "All of Caldaras owes you a debt of gratitude, Beloved. Now, if you could do us one more service."

Bonner nods. "Anything, Your Benevolence."

"I would like you to answer a question," the high priest says. "How can we identify a redwing?" Bonner's eyes flick to the black-clad priest with the stritch whip, but the Onyx Staff chuckles and says, "Do not fear, Beloved. You have done nothing wrong. I am merely giving you the opportunity to prove your case to our brothers and sisters."

Relief floods Bonner's face. "Scars," he says.

The Onyx Staff looks at me. "If you would be so kind as to kneel, Beloved," he says gently, and in a split second, I'm struck again with the stritch whip, this time on the back of the legs. I fall hard onto the floor, smashing my knees. The chains around my wrists jerk, making terrible clanking sounds that fill the quiet space. I am coughing when the Onyx Staff says, "Are you prepared to provide the evidence for this, Brother Bonner?"

I can see Bonner sweating. He doesn't know if I have scars or not, and it's possible he's been wasting everyone's time. I glare at him, glad he gets to stew a little before this is all over. His turnip face glistens.

Seriously, Jey, this clod?

He approaches me hesitantly. The Onyx Staff motions for me to turn around, and the priest in black pulls on my chains. I comply, and soon feel the timid scrape of a blade at the back of my neck.

The little dirtbag, he's actually going to slice my clothes off. I hear the fabric of Jey's green gardener's jumpsuit slowly ripping. He doesn't have to rip it all the way down, but he does anyway, and my naked, scarred back is on thrilling display for the whole room.

"Behold the righteous scars forever carved into the back of every wicked redwing! Behold the proof of the gods' eternal anger!" The Onyx Staff's voice cuts the stale air as the room erupts in shouts and cheers and anger. "Now we strike for the second, and final, evidence." The black-clad priest prods me to turn and face the room again.

"Let us see," the Onyx Staff bellows, "what flows through the veins of this creature!"

One of the purple priests approaches, wielding a shiny dagger set with stones that sparkle. Bonner, eyes wide, steps aside as the purple priest takes my hand, extending my arm and pushing the sleeve of my jumpsuit up to my elbow. He rests the blade of the dagger against my skin.

"My ear's bleeding already," I offer. "I can't quite reach my hair, but you could just lift it up and show everyone if that's easier."

"Be quiet," he snaps, pressing the blade. With a quick motion, he slashes the dagger across my forearm. I feel nothing, but blood gushes out—more than I would have imagined.

Bonner steps back, horrified. "It . . . it really is black," he murmurs as the liquid drips down my fingers and pools on the dimly lit floor. I stare at my wound, slightly perplexed. It doesn't even sting.

"What did you expect?" I ask. Then, just to be nasty, I give him a good snarl. He jumps six inches into the air. I can't help but laugh. It comes out as a strangled cough.

The room is in a frenzy now. "The blood of evil!" the Onyx Staff says. "No human goodness resides in the veins of this creature! Brothers and Sisters, look upon this redwing, and look upon your doom!"

Breathe, I think. They don't know how much doom I could bring them.

And I find myself *waiting* for it. I want to lose control. I want to blame my evil blood for the mayhem I will rain down upon this sanctuary.

"I am condemned, then?" I say. "You're certain of that?"

"One does not condemn a monster to death." The Onyx Staff raises one thin eyebrow. "One only has to capture it, and give it what it deserves." He motions, a twitch of his fingers, and I hear gears clank somewhere behind me.

The places where the stritch whip struck me ache in earnest now, but I raise my chained arms as best I am able. Hot spikes of power find their way through the bones of the Temple, up through this metal floor, up through my legs. "Then I condemn *you*."

My first burst of fire almost hits home. I see a distinct flash of surprise contort the Onyx Staff's face as flames erupt from my hands. Priests dive and shout.

But before I can strike fully, I'm knocked backwards by harsh jets of water that come javelining out of what I now realize are large pipes edging the room. The torrent pushes me back against the carved wall, and as I thrash, I see the assembly regaining its composure.

Damn it to wet hell. If I'd attacked only moments earlier, they'd all be smoldering piles of righteousness by now. But I just *had* to know that I was to be condemned, that I was out of options, didn't I? Imbecile. I had to be able to *justify*. As if a raptor needs to justify its talons, or a volcano its lava.

I struggle to stand, thick jets of water forcing me ever backwards, my chains slicing into my wrists as I writhe. The Onyx Staff shouts above the din, and priests scramble to pull levers and turn valves. I've got to regain control, call back my fire.

Then, with a groan, the floor begins to tilt.

I slip, liquid over smooth metal, sliding away from the priests and the Onyx Staff. Through gasps and rushes of water, I see them illuminated by white sun instead of dingy secondhand window light. That can only mean—

I twist to find open air behind me. The mechanisms in the floor are winding it down away from the wall, a jaw opening as the priests watch from their level platform. I'm sliding toward sky.

My feet scrabble for purchase, but the floor is too slick. I wrap my fingers around the chains at my wrists, the only things between me and the high mist, as the outside pours in.

Soon the floor is gone entirely. The jets of water stop. And I hang.

Through the glare, my eyes register the delicate emerald rainbow of the Jade Bridge stretching into the mist far to my left. My gaze travels upward, into the blinding white fog behind which a sun must surely burn somewhere, then down.

I am two hundred feet above boiling Lake Azure Wave. The back of the Temple juts out over the water; there is nothing below me but bubbling aquamarine.

"Breathe easy, Beloved." The Onyx Staff leans out from the dark opening above me. "May the Long Angel guide you to the Eternal Garden." And he turns, disappearing once again into the recesses of the temple.

How long do they intend to leave me out here? My arms are already sore. I need a plan. The scars on my back crackle and burn, but I swing my legs, trying to connect with the hanging flap of what used to be the floor. I kick at it, but my boot just slides.

Maybe I can climb back up my wrist chains. I grab one and hoist with every drop of strength I can muster. The little room is only about ten feet above me. The chains grow tighter as I make what little progress I can, closing the distance.

Then another metallic creak sounds from near my head, and the manacles open. It is all I can do to grab a chain with my now free hands and cling.

I'm not meant to hang here after all. I'm meant to fall.

No matter. Same plan. I hang on with my left hand and reach with my right. But the chain is surprisingly rust-free and smooth, and there's nothing I can do to stop my fingers from sliding along its wet surface.

I remember the words I scratched into my journal as a child, when I first started trying to understand myself: *Fact: Redwings don't actually have wings.*

That's too bad, I think as the chain slips from my grasp. I manage to make one last grab at it before I plummet two hundred feet into the boiling water of Lake Azure Wave.

eight

"Papa, how did you meet Mother?"

Jey and I were at an age when everything required explanation. We were scientists.

Our father sat back in his not-quite-big-enough-for-three bed. The candle on his bureau guttered and rain clattered against the dark window that looked out onto Saltball Street. Every few moments, lightning would flash, but the thunder was safely grumbling in another part of the city. It was time for us to return to our own beds.

"Haven't I told you?" Papa said, tousling Jey's hair.

"No," I said, wise to his tricks, "you haven't. How did you meet her?"

He frowned, then smiled, and we knew we were going to get the truth. "Years ago, before we moved to Val Chorm, I was apprenticing with the head gardener to the Commandant. He sent me to gather fire truffles near Mol's Mouth."

"You went up Mol? To the top?" Jey's eyes were wide.

"I certainly did," Papa said proudly. "It's an amazing place. Dangerous and terrible, but beautiful at the same time."

"Like a raptor," I said. "If you were a mouse."

Papa nodded and patted my hand. "Just like that," he said. "Now, fire truffles are very difficult to gather—that's why they're so valuable. They grow just at the edges of the lava. They love it, the sulfur and ash. They thrive up there. But that's treacherous ground to walk. You must wear special clothes that keep the heat away. And if you lose your footing, or if the edge gives way, well, that's the end of it."

"I could do it," Jey said, shaking Papa's old quilt. "I'm light. I wouldn't break the edge."

"I'm sure you wouldn't," Papa said. "I wasn't so lucky, however. After hours of searching, I spotted a whole cluster of fire truffles along a little glowing stream. In my excitement, I stepped too heavily on a crust of ground, and my foot broke through onto the lava."

I touched a ridge in the quilt. "That's why you have a metal leg?"

Papa put his hand over mine. "It's not very cuddly, is it?"

"No," Jey said. "And it makes you move funny, and then people stare."

I patted the metal rod through the bedding. "But it's good," I said. "It means you can still walk."

"Yes, it does, and I'm very grateful for that," Papa said. "I'm even more grateful for your mother, who answered my cry for help. She pulled me away from the lava and called the fire off me."

"What did Mother look like?" I asked.

Papa's gaze traveled back in time then, and with a wobbly voice, he said, "She came out of the lava like a person diving into water. Only up. The air was the water, and she burst into it."

"You can't dive in the water," Jey said. "It's too hot."

"Some water is fine for diving." Papa smiled at her. "I know you don't remember the lakes of Val Chorm, but—well, never mind. Your mother came because I called her—that's the only way she could come. And as she called the fire off me and out of my skin, I spoke to her. She was very curious, just as you girls are. I spoke with her about the only subject I had any knowledge of: plants. She was fascinated. There are no plants where she came from. She wanted to see them. So . . . she did. I took her down the mountain and showed her the marvelous trees and flowers of Caldaras."

"And you loved her," I said.

I had never seen Papa cry before that moment, and I have not seen it since, but as he looked at me, his eyes shone like the morning mist off Lake Azure Wave.

"I loved her very much," he said.

nine

It would be an interesting scientific exploration to study what it is people think about as they're falling to their deaths. Some, I imagine, try a last-minute bargain with the gods. Some might spout expletives all the way down. And some might know relief for the first time in their miserable lives.

As I plummet toward my scalding demise, my father's words come back to me.

She came out of the lava like a person diving into water.

I've never seen someone dive into water, and I've certainly never done it myself, so I could never really picture it. But now is my first—and last—chance. I stretch my arms over my head, extend my legs, and wonder which end should go in first.

It's my feet. The beautiful water of Lake Azure Wave strikes the bottom of them like the priest's stritch whip. Its heat scrapes my body all the way up as I plunge from the cruel nothingness of air into strange, thick buoyancy. Being the diver doesn't give one a very good view of what diving looks like, but now I have something of an idea, at least. *This is what my mother looked like.* It is a type of comfort, I suppose.

Now I am in a churning underwater realm with no up or down. I open my eyes. Shafts of low sunlight cut through the aquamarine, and my heart twitches at the splendor of it. Shimmering bubbles trace my arms and legs as I am suspended, enthralled by this endless country of peace and depth. *Strange,* observes my addled brain, *being boiled alive isn't nearly as unpleasant as one would imagine.* The places where the whip sliced me sear as though knives are working the cuts open, but the rest of my skin buzzes with an energizing warmth.

I don't know how many seconds pass before I fully realize that I don't seem to be experiencing death by boiling. I've seen Jey boil her fair share of fruit beetles for stew—which I vow never again to be a party to—and their end always comes quickly. A sharp hiss and their little yellow legs are stilled forever. *How can we do that to them?* my soggy brain asks. *What this city needs is a . . . a . . . Fruit Beetle Advocacy Organization.*

Ver's ass, brain, remember where you are! With a mighty effort, I drag my thoughts back to the present, and the happy fact that I am not boiling.

I am, however, drowning.

Redwings cannot swim. At least, redwings who have been raised without access to a sizable body of water. Papa wouldn't even let me visit the public baths on our excursions, even though the visitors always wear rubber caps and goggles, because my scars would have been visible in a bathing suit. So now, my momentary delight that my flesh is not going to be scalded from my body is dampened by the water trickling into my lungs with a raw burn.

Move your arms. Move your legs, I think, but my limbs are unresponsive. My body is shutting down, panicking. Then peace washes over me. I become very still. I close my eyes.

The thing about boiling water, though, is that it doesn't like *down.* A boil is all about *up, up, up.* It is supremely difficult to achieve *down* in a boil, so even as I drift without aim through the bleak, lovely depths of the lake, my trajectory is skyward.

In a short time, my head breaks the surface. Now my lungs know what to do, and the air scorches me all the way to my center. The inrush sparks my body back to life; my legs start moving, and I raise my hand to wipe the drops from my eyes. The surface of the lake ripples, hot and restless, but I manage to keep my nose and mouth in the air as my instincts take over, pushing my body through the water.

Ahead I see the lakeside façades of the buildings on either side of High Ra Square, the Temple of Rasus lording over them all like some sort of bulbous, all-powerful fungus reaching its tendrils into the sky. Making my way back to the shore, a thin strip of black sand bordered by a sturdy foundation wall, doesn't seem like a very good idea. But there is nowhere else to go; Roet Island lies far away at the other end of the long Jade Bridge. So I flip onto my back and pump my legs until I pass into the shadow of the temple's overhang, then all the way to shore.

When I crawl out onto the black sand, my body is suddenly

cold—absurdly, blazingly cold, with my muscles sluggish and shivering. I inch my way to the ancient stones of the Temple of Rasus and curl up against them, the overhang hiding me from the eyes of those above. My mind turns briefly to Papa and Jey, but soon my thoughts dim as my eyelids close of their own accord.

ten

Sometimes it can be difficult to tell which side of the line between reality and myth you're standing on. Especially when things like posh parties and boiling death-water plunges start happening all in the same day.

However, when I awake, I definitely have both feet planted in reality. My ear throbs, I am covered with rotten vegetables and worms, and two grubby pumpmen are snickering at my naked butt, which is hanging out of my shredded green jumpsuit. *Good afternoon to you, too.*

I shake the vegetable remains off and twist around, glaring at the pumpmen.

"Ho, girl, good for you!" one of them says, wiping the top

layer of coal dust off his forehead with a handkerchief. "Must say, I'm a bit envious o' the night you must've had!"

At that, the other one snorts, and they both amble away smiling. Well, at least I've made someone's day a little brighter.

I tuck my legs under me and scoot back into the shadow of the Temple of Rasus, away from what I assume is its lower kitchen window, judging from the pile of food scraps beneath it. As tired as I was after emerging from the lake, I would like to think I'd have had enough presence of mind to avoid sleeping in a fetid pile of wormy kitchen slop. Apparently not.

As I gaze blearily at the world around me—black sand, the shabby rear faces of Caldaras City's nicer buildings, Lake Azure Wave stretching away toward Mol's Mouth—the events of yesterday slowly drip into my consciousness. My thoughts are still fuzzy and my body tired, but I try to sort through them.

My search for the bonescorch orchis did not go well.

I am filthy.

I need some clothes.

I was . . . Wait, was I *executed* yesterday?

I was definitely executed yesterday. Also, it appears I cannot be boiled.

Why didn't those pumpmen notice my scars?

I am hungry.

The good news, I realize, is that in all likelihood, the Beautiful Ones believe I am dead. They saw me fall into Lake Azure Wave, and it isn't as though people do that and survive. I am dead, and Jey is safe.

At last, with everything in order, I rise unsteadily and creep back toward the low window. With the pumpmen gone, the shore is deserted, but I have no way of knowing when more people will wander by. Whatever dangers the Temple holds, I can't stay out here, and any back kitchen will most likely be unlocked during the day.

It's a logical plan—my only plan—but it reminds me of a Mother May story I read when I was little, about a servant girl who escapes her cruel master with the help of a kind Other princess. Once the girl is out of the house, she goes right back in the kitchen window like a half-wit, and then the master . . . kills her? Marries her? I don't remember, but I think of that stupid servant girl as I clamber over the garbage pile and hoist myself up.

Luckily, I find myself in a dark pantry, not the main kitchen. Praise the gods and their lovely feet, as Jey would say. I slip in. As someone who has spent most of her life being invisible, I'm good at slipping in and around. I can hear voices nearby, where the light spills through the pantry's doorway. That will be the kitchen, where the evening meal is likely being prepared for the temple's residents.

Clothes. I must cover my scars, first and foremost. Getting something around my behind would also be nice. Then there's the matter of the foul layer of itchy grime that covers me from head to toe. I peer into the shadows of the little pantry, keeping an ear on the voices in the kitchen. It will take only a second to duck back out the window, but I won't have a second if I am taken by surprise.

I am not astonished to discover that people here don't store their clothing in the pantry. However, I do find a couple large sacks of flour that might do in a pinch. It will be a shame to waste all that flour, especially with the blight in the east, but I suppose that's what happens when one must scramble to survive.

"Are you just getting in, Sister?" A comfortable, middle-aged woman's voice disturbs the pantry, and I stiffen. "I'm afraid lunch is long gone, and I'm only doing the vegetables down here this afternoon. You'll have to try the upper kitchen for something more substantial. Oh, but I could scare you up some bread and pickles if you'd like."

Another voice answers, "Thanks very much, but I'll just wait it out until evening. I lost track of time studying."

Studying. I wonder if this sister was one of the faces in the sanctuary yesterday, the sanctimonious cult who sent me to my death. What could she have been studying? *How to Torture and Execute People?*

But I calm those thoughts. The Temple of Rasus is home to many priests and postulants, and whoever the Beautiful Ones are, there were only about twenty of them.

"Anyway," the sister goes on, "I was wondering if I could leave this here for Mr. Gore."

The rustle of fabric. Fabric? I take a tentative step toward the slightly open door to the kitchen. I don't dare get close enough to see, but I listen, frozen with concentration. Well, frozen until a stray mulch worm wriggles free of my hair and I flick it to the floor.

"Oh, you didn't tear your new robes!" The woman clicks her tongue.

"These are my old ones," the sister says. "A stritch stepped on the hem when I was sweeping the square a few days ago. Just if Mr. Gore has a moment."

"Of course he has a moment." Shoes clatter across the floor. "I'll set them down here next to the *Bulletin*. He always reads it first thing when he comes in, so he'll be sure to see them. He's only got the one tapestry to mend this evening, far as I know—just the edging, not the scene, thank Rasus, or none of us would get any sleep. So he'll— Oh, I've let the snaproots boil over!"

More clattering of shoes followed by the clanking of pots. I hear the sister say, "Thank you! Breathe easy!" and then a door opens and closes.

Snaproots. I like snaproots, my stomach reminds me with a grumble. I feel inordinately ravenous this morning. I suppose I did have a long day yesterday, but still.

I consider my situation from the shadows of the little pantry. If I were anyone else—Jey, for instance, though Jey would never allow herself to be covered in mulch with her ass hanging out; she would have opted to drown—I strongly suspect I could step boldly into the kitchen, where the vegetable woman would clutch her bosom and say, *Ooh, didn't you give my ticker a shock, my girl!* and right away, her heart would melt at my pathetic appearance and she would give me all the snaproots and robes and bath soaps I desired.

If I weren't me. But I am me. So my only options are to wait until the kitchen is deserted, or take this woman out of the equation, perhaps with a stealthy blow to the head. And I don't care how many times her employers execute me, I'm not attacking someone who is cooking. So I settle behind the flour sacks, hoping she has to take a necessaries break before this Mr. Gore comes in.

Waiting in the dark, there is nothing to do but sit in my own skin. I smell terrible. Like rotten fruit and festering wounds. The ear the priest slashed with the stritch whip aches and thumps, and

I feel tiny creatures—mites? maggots?—crawling all over my skin. Everything itches. I'd almost jump back into Lake Azure Wave just to relieve this misery.

After maybe fifteen minutes, I start to panic. The vegetable woman is running taps and humming and clanking pots and talking to herself like a domestic automaton, and it's looking more and more like I'll have to go with the flour sack plan after all.

I'm just about to rip a sack open and fashion the world's ugliest evening gown when I hear her mutter, "Oh, sweet Ver, I've left the cabbages in the upper kitchen! What a ninny."

As soon as the door opens and then closes behind her, I sneak out from the pantry. The kitchen is as large as the entire downstairs of our house, with a great hearth on one side and a large sink on the other. A modern coal stove—unused—sits next to the hearth, and the long central table is littered with vegetable scraps. I move swiftly to a wooden bench across the room, where a heap of vibrant blue fabric rests. The shade makes my stomach lurch as I remember the priests who jumped me in the alley, but I swallow my repulsion and grab the sister's robes.

True to her word, the cook placed them next to today's *Bulletin*. I know I must not linger, but I wonder how the city—how Nara Blake—views my capture and execution. Have I been officially charged with the murder on the Jade Bridge? Has anyone come to my defense? Has anyone spoken out against the Onyx Staff? Does anyone even believe it? I pick up the paper and anxiously flip through its pages.

Not one word. Not a mention of the discovery of a mythological redwing, here in the heart of Caldaras. Not even a passing reference. The Beautiful Ones work in secret, then. Interesting.

My glance falls across the top corner of a page, where the date is printed. I frown. That can't be right.

I was asleep for three days?

Three days?

That explains why I'm hungry. I toss the *Bulletin* back onto the wooden bench and hurry to the pot of snaproots hung over the hearth fire, but before I have the lid off, I hear footsteps clacking down the stairs nearby. Damn.

I run for the pantry, but pause, half in shadows, when I hear voices floating in through the open window. Double damn.

Are there any other ways out? A skinny door over next to the coal stove could easily be a cupboard, but I try it anyway. Back stairs, praise Ver. I pull the little door shut behind me just as I hear the main door opening and the cook returning with her cabbages. Hopefully she will be too distracted to notice immediately that the robes are missing.

The stairway is dark except for the yellow outline of a doorway one flight up. I could wait here for my chance to escape out the pantry window, but that may be a bit more complicated now that the vegetable woman is back and this Mr. Gore will be coming soon. I might be better off climbing the stairs to see where they lead.

At least I know they won't lead to the Onyx Staff. This is a utilitarian staircase. It's possible he doesn't even know about it. Servants are meant to appear and disappear like magic, without clogging up the real staircases. In fact, as I stand here listening to the clanking of pots, I feel a sort of kindred spirit with the servants of the Temple of Rasus. Up it is, then.

On the next floor, I creak the door open a few inches and put my eye to the crack. This is clearly the upper kitchen, buzzing with activity as the cooks and servants prepare for the evening meal. I close the door carefully and tiptoe up another flight, scratching at the bugs on my head.

This door opens onto heavy golden curtains edged in blue. I sense a cavernous space behind them—apparently the curtains' purpose is to hide this door—and when I venture a peek beyond, I find the vast vestibule of the temple, with its gleaming marble floor and flared sandstone pillars. Priests, aristocrats, and common citizens come and go through the large arched doors. I might be able to slip out this way once I put on the robes.

But my spirits sink when I catch sight of Bonner, the little menace, across the way, in thick with a knot of priests. I can't risk him seeing me. I'll have to wait.

It isn't wise to linger, so I ascend again, hoping to find temporary refuge above. On the next landing, I open the little door onto a low, white hallway, probably the servants' quarters. At this time of day, this area of the temple should be all but deserted, and I encounter not a soul as I take a few timid steps out from the shelter of the undersized stairwell. I press my good ear to the first door I come to, a simple tin design, and hear loud snores within.

A few more careful steps and I come to another door. I hold my breath and put my ear to it, just as crisp footfalls echo through the white hallway. Someone heading this way. There is nothing to do but dash inside, pushing the door closed behind me.

I'm met by a beautiful sight.

There is a kind of beauty that arrests all who encounter it—the Jade Bridge at sunset, the play of light in the Empress's garden. But there is another type of beauty that is the mundane made exquisite by the desires of the beholder. That is the beauty of the bathroom I now gaze upon.

I slide the bolt on the door, confident this is the one room that will not arouse suspicions if it is locked.

The white enamel bathtub—a bathtub! With its own tap!—gleams in the clean light from a tall, frosted window, and a small table nearby is set with an array of brushes and a rainbow of jars of soap powder. Along one wall, a little fireplace sports a perky midday blaze and towels puff out from a shelf next to the sink. I cross the room, entranced, to touch one of them. But I catch myself in a mirror.

Holy Mother of Mol. It is clear I have been sleeping in garbage for three days. I'm completely unrecognizable. My skin, ragged clothing, and hair are covered with slime and debris. I twist around, finding my back as unpresentable as my front; the reason the pumpmen didn't notice my scars is that they are concealed by filth. I can see the tiny bugs and worms now, crawling and sliding, enjoying the layer of grime that coats my entire body. I never thought to disguise myself with muck before, but it seems to have been quite effective.

And then there's my poor ear. It is sliced through, a huge gash extending from the outer edge almost to the center. Black blood coats the whole area, sticking to my hair and neck. Surprisingly, the place on my arm where the priest sliced me with the ceremonial dagger is completely healed.

It is definitely time for a bath.

But first I turn on the tap at the sink and take a long drink of the fresh, warm water that rushes out. My stomach stretches and my insides prickle all the way to my fingertips.

Then I run the bath. As I wait for the tub to fill, I peel off the old green jumpsuit, observe a brief moment of silence in recognition of its honorable service, and toss it into the fire. When the tub is full, I lower my frazzled body into the water. No soap right now, this is just to rinse off the major dirt, blood, and stowaways. After a few minutes, I drain the murky water and fill the tub again, this time with a few handfuls of pleasant-smelling lavender powder. Now I linger, brushing the soapy water over my skin, ducking my head under for as long as I can stand the sharp pain that splits my ear as the clean foam works its way through the laceration.

I could stay longer. I could stay all night, according to my aching body. Forever. But I know I must leave the fragrant water, dry off with a fluffy towel, and put on the detestable blue robes of the Temple of Rasus.

It takes a few minutes to work out what drapes and ties where. But after a bit of trial and error, an unremarkable sister stares out at me from the mirror. I am new.

I step out into the white hallway just as three priests in purple turn the corner and head in my direction. I pause, my hand on the door handle. I don't want to jump back into the bathroom they must have just seen me emerge from, but I don't know whether I should really be seen taking the servants' stairs, either. So I inhale and turn to face the priests, keeping my head down as I stride away from the stairway door. I pass them without a word, and they take no notice, carrying on their own low conversation.

Around the corner, I stop and lean against the wall, letting out an uneasy breath. More hallway, more doors. I listen; the priests are still speaking in the white hallway by the stairs. I wait, hoping they will disperse.

A door to my left opens abruptly, and a priest in blue emerges. I tilt my head down, examine my belt.

The priest pulls the door closed behind him and says, "I'm sorry, were you waiting for this room?"

The voice is familiar. I look up.

"Jey?" The blue of Zahi Zan's temple robes matches his eyes, which are wide with astonishment.

"Mol's cursed undies," I say.

He laughs. "I had no idea you were studying in the Temple." At least he doesn't seem to know I'm meant to be dead.

My mind sizzles. *Be Jey, be Jey.* "I'm sorry," I say. "I should really be—um—pruning something. I mean, praying something. Shit. I thought I was a gardener."

"I thought you were a gardener, too," he says easily.

"Actually," I say, trying to hide the quaver in my voice, "I thought *you* were a gardener." He gives me a puzzled look. "Cutting the lawn?" I venture.

"Oh!" He chuckles. "Well, they thought I was a little high profile to be sweeping High Ra Square. The high priests gave me permission to do comparable meditative exercises someplace a little more private. It's a glamorous life, isn't it?" Zahi tilts his head. "I must say . . . you look lovely in this color."

I freeze. "Lovely?" *Why did I say that?*

"Of course." He gestures. "Even here, in the same uniform as everyone else, you are a flower among weeds."

It's just like a line from a romance novel. It may actually *be* a line from a romance novel. But I hear myself stammering, "Thanks. You're—lovely, too." His eyes crinkle in a grin.

What the hell is going on? I'm not lovely. I'm not even human.

And Zahi Zan isn't lovely, either. Handsome, yes, sweet Rasus, he's handsome. And a bit too aware of it. My temples ache.

"I shouldn't say such things to you," he says, not meaning it in the slightest. "What would your young man think?"

"My—*Bonner*?" I had forgotten. Oh, what to say about Bonner? My mouth answers before my brain can get a word in. "He's—dead."

"Dead?"

"No, not dead." I frown. "He just . . . he looks like a turnip and I hate him."

Zahi laughs, looking pleased. "I see! Well, were you waiting for the meditation room?" He is very close to me now. I can see the fibers of his robes, the stubble on his cheek. I should step back, but I don't want to. He smells like flowers. Or is that me? I may have overdone it with the lavender bath powder.

"Yes," I say. "I mean, yes, I was waiting for the meditation room. Uh . . . thank you."

He smiles and reaches behind me, twisting the door handle. I don't move as he leans in even closer to push the door open. "Your meditations await," he says, and gestures to the little room behind us. "I've never found much in there except the memories of bored priests, but you never know."

I peep inside. The room is clean and lined with candles, and holds no furniture except a grass mat. "The memories of priests?" I ask.

Zahi nods. "Just how new at this are you?"

"I'm not new at all," I say, sticking out my chin a little bit. "I just don't meditate very often, that's all."

"I see," he says. "Well, in that case, I'd be happy to help you get started. I mean, refresh your memory, of course." And he smiles. Generations of aristocratic breeding come together in that smile, a perfect combination of serenity and confidence. Directed at me.

What I should say is, *Perhaps some other time.* What I should do is get rid of him as quickly as possible.

But maybe he could be an ally. He isn't one of the Beautiful Ones, so he must be as much an enemy of theirs as any sane citizen. And unlike most of the rest of Caldaras City, he has the ears of the Commandant and the Empress. Maybe we could help each other. Maybe he would even tell me where the bonescorch orchis is being kept.

It is a lot to hope for. But I take his hand anyway, step back into the little room, and push the door closed behind us. And I say, "Very well, refresh my memory."

Zahi sits on the grass mat amid the candles, and I join him. "Everything that happens is remembered. It takes up a space. When we meditate, we call upon the world to remember its past, and in doing so, we strengthen our connection to all times, places, and beings."

I think of the glowing shapes in the fog of High Ra Square during morning meditation. "So the visions the priests call forth are—memories?"

Zahi nods. "In a sense. They're really more like records. They are what has taken place." He straightens his spine. "You must get your own identity out of the way. Just feel."

He closes his eyes, dark lashes over his skin. His breathing slows. The high thin windows of this white room drape us in clean light as I watch his chest rising and falling peacefully under blue fabric.

After a few minutes, he cracks open one eye. "You could try this yourself, you know."

I give him what I hope is a pleasant smile. "I'd rather watch you."

He gives me a cheeky look and goes back to his meditations. "I can sense some old joy in this room," he says, eyes closed. "Here."

The air in front of us seems to take on a gleam all its own, separate from the yellow dots of the candles or the pink beams from the windows. It isn't strong, but I can definitely see *something* there, growing and shining. It lasts for a few moments, getting a little brighter as it fills the room. Then it is gone.

Zahi opens his eyes. "Did you see it?"

My voice is thin with wonder. "That was a spirit of joy?"

He turns toward me. "It was the memory of something joyful that happened here." He shrugs. "I don't know what it was. Some of the high priests can call forth very specific visions—people moving, their clothes, their faces—as though we are actually watching what occurred. But most of us are lucky to get a floating blob of some long-dead feeling."

The warmth of the room blankets my skin. "I like the idea that there was joy here in the past."

He leans closer. "There could be joy here now."

Mol's blisters, he's looking at my lips. Could he be considering kissing me? My mouth is dry. Is it possible? Has a human being ever kissed a redwing before?

"I—" I start. "Are you going to kiss me?"

He doesn't blink. "I was thinking about it. Would that be all right with you?"

I swallow. "I might burst into flames."

"Is that supposed to dissuade me?"

"Is it allowed?" I glance toward the closed door. "Haven't you taken a—a vow of—?"

He rests his mouth against my cheek. "Have you?"

"Holy Rasus," I say.

Zahi whispers into my good ear. "You don't have to take that vow until they give you the purple robes. You know that, right?"

I tingle, my mind in disarray. *I shouldn't be here.* He thinks I'm Jey. What will I do if he finds the real Jey Fairweather, out there in the world, wearing her elegant clothes? My stomach twists.

And then *growls* with the ferocity of a territorial raptor. I feel the color drain from my face. In all the penny pulps I've read, the sweeping romantic scene has never once been preceded by the heroine's stomach growling.

Zahi bursts into laughter. "Sweet Ver, are you hungry?"

I bark out an awkward laugh. "I suppose I am."

He throws his head backwards and slaps his thighs. "Why didn't you say so? Come on." He rises, fiddling with the belt of his robe. "Forget meditation. Let's get some food."

"I—" I get to my feet. "Well—"

"We're surely late for the evening meal," he says. "We'll just have to go elsewhere. Are you up for venturing out into the wide world?"

My mind fizzes. If the evening meal is under way, Bonner is no longer lurking in the vestibule. Leaving the temple with Zahi might be my best chance at remaining undetected. My stomach growls again.

"All right." And it's not just my stomach or my nerves; right

127

now, I want to follow Zahi Zan into the outside world. To eat food with him. To—

Mol's butt, he's taking off his robe. And . . . he's wearing clothes under there. The rust-colored waistcoat I can still picture against a backdrop of impossible green.

I blink. "You've got your regular clothes on," I point out helpfully.

"Yes, you can hang your robe in here." He shakes the creases out of the blue fabric. "I promise no one will take it." Now he sees my face. "What's the matter?"

"Nothing, I just—this place we're going—could I just wear this? Do they allow priests?"

Some of the candles have nearly burned down, their guttering casting sparks in the shadows. Zahi gives me that puzzled look I remember from the gardens on Roet Island. "I'm not sure I've ever seen a tavern displaying a 'No Priests Allowed' sign," he says. "But just leave your robe here and wear what you've got on under—"

I shift uncomfortably.

"Under—" He swallows. I wonder if he can see how red my face is in the low light. "Yes." He clears his throat. "I, uh, I see. I mean, I don't *see*, I—" He opens the door, wiping his hands on his thighs. "It's fine. Just wear that."

The Feather & Scuttle must, in some way, be a tavern. The bodies in the shadows—leaning, laughing, raising glass to mouth—are familiar. But it all seems just a little off. A furtiveness to the shiny eyes, a jagged edge to the music, the flutter of the nearly invisible in the veiled corners of the room.

We descend. Outside, twilight lingers, but in here, it is already night, black walls glittering in a strange orange light that pulses between fan blades on the ceiling.

I adjust my folds of blue fabric. I am certainly disguised, but that doesn't mean I don't stick out. The scars on my back itch. I mustn't stay long.

I follow Zahi to the bar, where he leans on his elbows, twisting his head toward me. "Snowflake?"

I raise one eyebrow. "Yes, darling?"

He laughs and turns back to the pale, stooped man wiping glasses with a rag. "Two snowflakes," he says. "And a private room, please. And food. Dear Rasus, get us something to eat."

"Your Excellency." The man nods. I lean back against the counter, watching hair, shoulders, arms, teeth, all pulsing in the orange light. Someone shrieks and spills a drink. A cluster of people laughs. Fashion here mimics the streets above with a sneer. Collars are high, necklines are low, and more than one person sports gauzy wings with wire frames and a naked back streaked with red.

"Are they . . . are they dressed as redwings?"

Zahi snorts, casting a dismissive eye. "Real rebels, aren't they? This place attracts them. Dark, low, hidden. Never doing anything *real* for this city. They're like bugs."

I breathe, flexing my nervousness out through my fingers. "So now would not be a good time to show you my antennae?"

He looks at me incredulously as the bartender pushes two slender blue glasses toward us. "You're not going to lecture me on how beneficial bugs are for our soil? You're flirting instead?"

"My mistake. I thought lecturing about soil health *was* how one flirted. I was trying to avoid it."

He laughs and hands me a glass. It's cold.

I feel eyes, orange in the light, follow us as we cross the room. Zahi pushes aside a generous curtain to reveal a bare table, clean, and a curved, cushioned bench against the wall. A woman with long, spidery lace cuffs follows us and leaves a tray of bread and pickled vegetables.

I devour them. My snowflake, which I think is just ice water with a bit of mint, also disappears quickly.

Zahi sips from his own blue glass. "So tell me about your family."

"I'd rather hear about your family," I say, crunching a briny carrot.

He tips his head back. "Everyone knows all about my family, don't they? I think it's actually required knowledge to graduate Third School."

I move closer to him. "I failed Third School."

"Ah, I knew you had a dark secret." He touches my face. I want to steer the conversation toward the bonescorch, maybe the Beautiful Ones. But I also want him to keep touching my face. "Well," he says, "my mother is the leader of the nation and my father commands her armies. A love story as old as time. I've got an older brother, who isn't nearly as handsome as I am, who is next in line for the throne, and I hope he lives a very long time so I never have to have any responsibilities."

"Except the Temple," I say.

"Right, the Temple." He leans in and presses his lips against mine. And just like that, everything is dull and muffled and far away except him—warm, close, real.

It doesn't last as long as I'd like, but it is a kiss the world can never take away. Zahi leans back. "I think this whole Temple thing might be a phase I'm going through."

And his smile is so pretty, and so sly, that suddenly I can do nothing but lunge forward for another kiss, which turns into two and three and more, each deeper and more searching until I realize I've worked all the buttons on his shirt open and he has his arms around me and his fingers are starting to slide the smooth blue fabric of my priest's robe away from my neck—

My scars.

I can't let him find my scars. It takes all my will to pull away from him. He blinks, relaxes, pulls back.

"I'm sorry," I say. "I—"

"No, please, I'm sorry," he says. "I must have misread your . . . signals."

We both unconsciously look down at his naked chest. And laugh.

"Oh, Rasus," I say. "That shirt's probably worth more than my whole wardrobe."

"It probably is," he says.

I get to my feet. "I should go."

He rises as well, and nods. A sad half smile flickers. "I understand."

I take his hands. "No, you don't," I say. "But maybe someday you will."

eleven

The sun is well below the horizon when I approach our house on Saltball Street. I don't mind traveling in darkness; as well as these blue robes disguise me, they are rather conspicuous. At least the hood hides my face, though it is not customary for brothers and sisters to wear their hoods up all the time.

I am surprised to find the house dark, and a queasiness slips around in my guts for just a moment. *Calm yourself. No reason to think anything is amiss.* Despite Bonner's threats, the human sibling of a redwing is blameless. Anyone who has ever read Mother May can tell you that. That child is as innocent as a sunrise and, if anything, is to be pitied and protected because of her despicable twin. Now that I am dead, Jey has nothing to fear.

She has gone out with friends tonight, taking advantage of Papa's absence to exercise her freedom, that is all. Just as I have. I must confess I am a little hurt she can be out reveling while I am, as far as she knows, still missing.

But my mind is uneasy as I walk the path to our door. Some part of it sees the overturned flowerpot, the kicked-up stones, but I don't let myself admit something is wrong until I depress the latch on our door to find it swinging from one hinge.

A strange smell hits me as I enter the kitchen. No, more like the absence of smells. Papa's earth-covered boots, the floral fragrance that clings to him, Jey's perfume, coal dust from the cookstove, the lingering scents of breakfasts and suppers.

I take in the room. The heavy table askew. A chair on its back. The door to Jey's room open wide, as she never would have left it.

No.

I rush through the doorway to find her bed unmade and her armoire full. A graceful, curving vase—a prized birthday present from our father—is in pieces on the floor, Jey's meticulously ash-grown blue daisies scattered and broken.

She is gone.

Stomach churning, I gather what remains of the daisies and bring them into the kitchen. At the sink, I fill a tin cup with water and cut the broken stems with a pair of sharp scissors. My efforts don't matter; their lives ended days ago. Still, as my nerves prick my skin and my mind swirls, it helps to do something.

I right the chair and lean forward, nausea overtaking me in little waves. The wood grain squirms as I gaze vaguely at our kitchen table.

I should have run back here.

As soon as I woke up in that pile of worms, I should have run to Saltball Street. Why did I waste so much time at the Temple? What terrible things were happening to Jey while I kissed a young man who shouldn't even know I exist?

I sit, running my hands over the table's uneven wooden surface. I've never been connected to a name before, the name this house bears, and now people know who I am—the Beautiful Ones, Nara Blake, Zahi, who knows who else? I have taken risks and exposed myself, and now my sister is gone.

But I will find her. And the first person I'll ask is that son of a stritch, Bonner.

I rise, determination burning my lungs, and take two steps toward the door. A sudden crash from the Dome freezes me. *Someone is here.*

I move carefully to the ladder at the back of the kitchen and place a hand on a metal rung at shoulder height. I cast my ears into the ringing silence. Nothing more. Probably one of the raptors knocking my books over again.

I peer up into the darkness. "Jey?" The Dome breathes only silence for another moment, then—

CLANG.

The ladder shudders as a body thumps down, two rungs at a time, landing with a jarring knock. The woman is thin-framed but formidable, towering over me in a long, tight coat as black as night fog. "There you are," she snaps; then her red mouth frowns. "What the hell happened here?"

I cross my arms. "Uh—you trashed my house?"

"Enough of this." She draws a dull-surfaced pistol from a holster around her hips.

"Mol's bulging coin purse!" I yelp, skidding across the floor toward the broken doorway.

"Damn it!" the woman yells, her voice edged with a rasp. "Get back here!"

No one in the history of the world has ever turned around in response to "get back here," especially not when it is said in a menacing tone by someone holding a pistol. However, any inclination I might have had to accede to her request dies quickly when a bone-rattling explosion rocks my ears. She has fired the damn thing at me!

I kick the swinging door out of the way and stumble out into the night. A couple of raptors take off from the pitch of a roof across the street as I sprint through the beams of the streetlamp that guards our fence, the woman fast behind me. The cobblestones push on my feet, heavy with the gardener's boots that miraculously survived the boiling lake.

The second bullet doesn't miss. I feel the piercing flame the moment I hear the shot, an eruption of pain that staggers my whole body. At first, as I fall sideways into a low stone window frame, I don't even know where I've been shot. But when I try to push forward, my left leg buckles. The ball is lodged somewhere in my thigh. *Sweet Rasus, let it not bleed very much.* This is the first prayer my brain slings forth. *Boil me, slice my ears, cover me with maggots if you will. But black blood pouring from a bullet wound—no robes in all of Caldaras would cover that up.*

I brace myself against the wall. No open doors, no busy market, no public park that might have offered a hiding place. I either run, or I—don't.

I run. Left and right, through lamplight and shadow, the tilt of Caldaras City keeping my mind slanted and my elbows flapping for balance. My thigh screams, dripping hot down my leg under my robes, but I have no other choice. I lurch past couples, ladies in deep conversation, and dapper gentlemen, some of whom look at me sideways as though I might be a purse snatcher. But my priest's attire is enough to keep the suspicious looks from becoming cries for a city guard.

The nighttime mist dampens my face. The woman in black keeps pace about a block behind me. Maybe she's waiting to see where I run to, which is a decision I need to make quickly.

I think of Nara Blake. She wanted my help, promised to help me in return, but do I trust her? If Bonner does have something to do with Jey's disappearance, my path probably leads back to the Temple of Rasus. Nara Blake has no love for priests; that much was clear. And I have to go somewhere.

The street spills out, as they all seem to do sooner or later, onto High Ra Square. Even after dark, when most citizens are indoors for fear of the rest of the citizens, the square is quietly humming with activity. Common people and priests of all ranks wander the smooth white flagstones, taking advantage of the city's version of a pleasant evening. I slow down, insinuating myself in between two groups of priests and casting a glance over my shoulder, before mustering a final effort to sprint toward the fountain of Dal Roet and throw myself behind it.

I peek out from behind the curved marble. Priests everywhere. Blue, purple, a few black, all sizes and descriptions. Gentlemen and ladies, urchins and wealthy brats, stritches, pet parakeets, and showy, fat raptors. No figure approaches the fountain in a purposeful way. Is it possible I have lost my attacker?

I straighten up, one vertebra at a time, my thigh searing pain up and down my body. The fountain spits and bubbles; people speak easily amid patches of warm fog. I chance a few steps toward the edge of the square, where a dark alley promises some small measure of concealment.

Two priests in black stop speaking and regard me as I limp too close to their private sphere. I pause and nod briskly, muttering, "Breathe easy, Beloved." The words come out a bit wincing and strangled, but I flash what I hope is an innocent smile.

The high priests' faces are inscrutable for a moment, before one returns my nod and the other follows suit. "Breathe easy," they say in unison.

At last, I reach the mouth of the alley and cast one final look over High Ra Square. Three young people sit on the edge of the fountain now, two boys with weak chins and a girl whose high-collared shirt is unbuttoned to well below her clavicle. They could easily be Jey and her friends, I think with a pang. But they are not. I know in my heart that, at this moment, Jey is not with anyone who could be called a friend.

My distraction has betrayed me. Eyes on the other side of the square flash in the light from the holy beacons set in the wall of the great Temple. The woman in black has found me.

I duck into the alley, weaving around old crates, stritch manure, and leaning sheet metal. It opens onto another, familiar alley. I press my back against a grubby wall and scan left and right.

Rubble is still strewn at the place where I melted the brick wall—I am close to the back door of the *Daily Bulletin*. I stagger to the gated end of the alleyway and yank on the door. Locked. In desperation, I pound my fists against the dented surface. "Hey!

Daily Bulletin! I'm at the back door! Hey, there!" *Bang, bang, bang.* Nothing.

Waves of dizziness wash over me. I'm unsure how much longer I can remain vertical, and the woman in black will emerge at any moment. I doubt she will miss her shot here, and I have a strong suspicion that one bullet lodged in one's flesh is more than enough.

A swell of laughter intrudes on the quiet, and I remember the Pump Room tavern—it must also back onto this dirt-packed passage. I find the door about halfway down, where the sounds from the pub start to mix with the muted buzz of Mad Lane.

This door is unlocked, and I pop it open with a clank. I close it behind me and, with much effort, shift the inside handle to the locked position. It is a bit corroded, and takes a couple good shoves with my shoulders before it creaks into place. Finally, a moment to breathe.

Or a moment to fall to the floor in agony.

Mol's blazing buttocks! I pull up my robes and examine the wound on the outer part of my thigh. It is not too bad, actually. It's bleeding, but not excessively. I poke at it a couple times with dirty fingers, but there is no sign of the little deformed piece of metal under the surface. I can remove it later, but for now I can at least get it bandaged.

Wash it first. I take in my surroundings. This back storage room is dim, crowded with barrels and crates, and the sound of the Pump Room's evening crowd filters in through a slatted inner door. I crawl over to a shelf of jugs and grab the first one within reach. The golden liquid within stings down to the bone, but washes my incriminating blood away onto the straw-strewn floor.

I sacrifice a small sack of oats for a bandage, whispering apologies to the tavern keeper and dumping the evidence behind a stack of crates. Wrapped tightly in burlap, my leg feels a bit better, and I pull myself to my feet and wobble over to the inner door.

I peer between the slats, holding my breath. At the other end of a short hallway, I glimpse a crowded room, low lights, lots of movement and sound and color. The few faces I catch are flushed and bulging with laughter. I don't see any other priest robes, but surely a place like this is for everyone. It's just a matter of sneaking in when no one is—

A man starts down the hallway toward this storage room. I give a start, backing away from the slatted door. The last thing I want is to be mistaken for a thief and handed over to the city guard.

I have only seconds. Think, think. Hide. A row of large barrels stands against one wall, and I scramble into one and crouch, wincing. It would be nice to cover myself, but there is no time. The sides of the barrel are high enough to hide me as long as the man doesn't look in.

As soon as I crouch down, I hear the slatted door open. The man saunters to the other side of the room, and after a moment, I hear the dull rasp of small wooden barrels—kegs, most likely—being shuffled around. I don't dare breathe except with shallow sips, and I hold my knees to stop the fabric of my robes sliding against the edge of the barrel.

It isn't long before the man's footsteps take him in the direction of the slatted door once again, and I hold my lungs and my hands very still. Once he returns to the noisy common room, I'll wait a few minutes and then try to slip in unnoticed. I wait for the sound of the slatted door clicking back into place.

But it doesn't come. Could the man have left the door open and gone back down the hallway without my hearing him? I close my eyes, listening.

Two thudding footsteps, and a stern voice says, "What in wet hell are you doing in there?"

I gasp, startled, and raise my head a little.

The man is looking at me over the edge of the barrel, arms crossed. He reminds me of the stout, rosy-complexioned fruit vendor my father sometimes stops to talk with when we are out together. Only he wears an expression that promises wallops rather than peaches.

"You—you mean me," I say.

"Your powers of deduction are staggering, Sister. What are you doing in my barrel?" he says gruffly. "Rather, what *were* you doing in my barrel, because you cannot possibly be sitting there *still,* even as I am preparing to call the guard and have you hauled away."

I stand. "Oh. Right. I just—" I throw my good leg over the side and try to hoist myself out, but my robes catch the edge and the barrel tips over onto the floor with a crunch. "Rasus's flaming ass!"

The man raises his eyebrows. "Not very nice language for a woman of the Temple."

Shit. "Oh—" I scramble to my feet, the pain in my leg making my breath catch. "—well, I'm only a—" I look down at my robes. "—a blue one."

The man nods. "Uh-huh." He doesn't sound convinced. "You mean a postulant?"

"Postulant! Right. I knew that."

"That gives me hope for the future." He leans back against the slatted door, eyes twinkling despite his stern expression. "What's your name, Postulant? And think of a good one, or I'm calling the city guard. That was my favorite decrepit barrel."

"I—" My mind is paralyzed. I won't give him Jey's name and I can't give him my own, since I don't have one. But he already knows I'm going to lie, so—I search my memory for a name, any name. "Nara Blake," I say. "My name's Nara Blake."

The man straightens up. "What?" His tone is no longer light, and he peers at me shrewdly. "Did you say Nara Blake?"

That was apparently the wrong name. "No," I stumble. "No, I said Dal Roet. My name's Dal Roet. After my great-great-great-great—"

The man steps toward me and puts a callused hand on my shoulder. "How do you know Nara Blake?"

I back away. "I don't! I don't know what you're talking about. I—"

"Get the hell out of here, Sister," he spits. "Before I smack your head off your shoulders."

"Sounds like a deal." I limp over to the outer door, imploring all the gods I can think of to have sent the woman in black away by now.

"Mr. Orm!" a girl calls down the hallway. "Any more gin? We've got a wedding party!"

"Coming!" the man bellows back. But something sticks in my brain.

"Mr. Orm?" I turn around. Why do I know that name?

"Well," he says. "Now you have the advantage of me, clearly. Nevertheless, I'm calling the guard in thirty seconds."

"No, I— *You* know Nara Blake, don't you?" My leg throbs and I put a hand to the warm wall, praying I don't pass out.

"I know I don't like questions." Orm scowls, but he doesn't move. He's listening.

Risking everything is getting easier. I'm not sure that's a good thing. But I have nowhere to go, and Nara Blake is the only person in this city who has offered me protection. Whatever her motivations are, she has to be a better bet than the guard or the temple. Or the gutter.

"Orm," I say as the memory slides into focus, "did you help Nara's brother Corvin after he was beat up in an alley? She was going to ask you to look in on him."

He looks down his nose at me. "And how in Ver's green land do you know that?"

"I'm the reason he got beat up. No—wait—I mean, he was helping me run off these two—um—ruffians."

"You're a damned liar."

My sight is beginning to blur. I slide down the surface of the door and look up at Orm, who regards me with an expression I can't interpret. "I need somewhere safe. I think Nara would help me if she were here. Please. My sister is missing." I leave out the part about having been shot in the leg, though he must see I'm not exactly at my best. Maybe he thinks I'm drunk. Maybe a few dips in the ale barrel wouldn't be a bad idea.

Orm doesn't move. I find his face through my hazy vision. "Nara wanted my help. She said . . . may you always walk under the fog."

Something in his face changes. "You—you can't be— Curse you, you featherless little stritchlet," he says. "We thought you were dead." He takes a step to the right and lifts a hinged flap to reveal a handle set into the dingy wall. When he rotates it, a large panel slides back with a metallic *click-click-click-click*. Iron mesh stairs descend into darkness. I feel my eyes widen with astonishment. "It's safe down there," he grumbles. "Until Nara tells us what to do with you. Now, up." He pulls me to my feet and I steady myself for a moment, then follow him through the secret doorway.

"Cozy," I say as we clink our way downward. Already I am thinking of the white-gray sky through the glass of the Dome as I remember the dank nightmare of the dungeon of the Temple of Rasus.

At least there is gas down here. I can see its steady, pure light from under the studded door at the bottom of the stairs.

"I hope you like beer and sandwiches, because we don't do anything else," Orm says. I don't ask what kind of sandwiches. Unless the Pump Room is a lot more upscale than its creaking door and rusty flooring would have me believe, the sandwiches will taste like smoke regardless of what they're made of.

"Thank you," I say. Orm takes a key from around his neck and rattles it into the keyhole, and after a moment we are stepping into the room beyond. The place called "safe."

At first, I don't see the furniture or the colors or the people. I only smell an evasive sweetness; it is thick in the air here, almost overpowering. The heat hits me, too. Of course it's hot underground, but it feels unnaturally hot here, as though a fire were burning.

I steady myself, my hand against the heavy doorframe. A fire *is* burning, in a small hearth opposite the doorway. I begin to take in the rest of this round, brick-walled room. A row of books stands neatly on a graceful-legged side table flanked by stiff arm-chairs. A handful of people dot the room—men and women, my age, older, most of them wearing the dull colors of pump workers and mechanics. Some look me over appraisingly; some keep their heads down.

"Welcome to the Under House." Orm crosses the floor. "I'll show you the bunk room. It serves its purpose, but don't expect the Copper Palace. Just through here."

He pushes open an arched door. The bunk room is long and dark, and thankfully not so hot as the main room. A few cots jut from the edges, most of them covered by thin blankets of different colors. Metal hooks adorn the walls, some hanging dusters or scarves, some empty.

"There are spare clothes in here." Orm pulls an old trunk from underneath one of the cots. "That is, unless you really are from the Temple."

I give a little cough. "I, uh—"

"Oh, for the love of the Long Angel, you're the worst liar I've ever met." He shakes his head, but smiles and heads back through the arched doorway. "Washroom is through there." He points to the other end of the bunk room.

"My sister—"

"We'll find your sister," Orm says, and for a moment his gentle, concerned face reminds me of my father. "Wash your face, put on something less goddamn conspicuous, and I'll fetch Nara. We'll see what she has to say about you."

When he has gone, I creak open the trunk and start to paw through its modest offerings. Of course, everything smells like mothballs. I pull out a tatty muslin shirt and head to the washroom to rewrap my leg. At least it's probably more hygienic than an old sack off the floor of a dirty storage room. *Slightly* more hygienic. And I do wash my face, my fingers relaxing a little as I test the fresh basinful of hot water.

Back in the bunk room, I throw my robes to the floor. The trunk's modern underclothes feel better against my skin. I pull on an old pair of pants, simple and in good shape. They are from a time not so long ago as to be completely outdated, but their sturdy black twill doesn't billow like the airy silks and light muslins that now pepper the streets. I find them a bit restrictive, but there are no other options. I button a worn shirt—why would anyone need so many buttons?—and tie my hair up, not as elegantly as Jey can do it, but in a way that at least implies *domesticated*.

A knock on the bunk room door. "Come in!" I call.

Nara Blake strides in. "Well," she says, "you got yourself executed rather more quickly than I'd imagined." She leans against the wall, arms crossed.

"That's a hell of a greeting," I say, wincing as I lower myself onto a cot. "Aren't you even surprised to see me?"

"A bit," she says lightly.

"I did get thrown into a *boiling lake*." I draw myself up. "Most people might be a little impressed."

She pushes herself off the wall with her shoulders. "I said I was surprised to see you."

"And you couldn't even be bothered to run a story about my execution?"

Nara shrugs. "Your execution was a secret. The Beautiful Ones don't even exist. I don't know about any of it, officially. Besides, what would I have said? 'Onyx Staff Offs Another One'?"

I feel my jaw drop. "What?"

She takes a step toward me, eyebrows drawn. Her mouth is— Is she smirking? "My dear, don't you know why everyone is afraid of the Onyx Staff?"

"I didn't know everyone was afraid of him. I—my father told me not to speak to high priests."

"Your father was right. The temples have a lot of power, especially the Temple of Rasus. The priests are very . . . devout. And people who displease the Onyx Staff—heretics, revolutionaries, criminals, newspaper editors who print the wrong story—they sometimes disappear. *Poof!* Like steam off the ass of an overworked stritch."

"I could have lived without that image." My leg throbs and I shift my weight. "But that's—that has to be illegal. Right? No trial, no conviction? And only the gods can punish someone for heresy. Why doesn't the Commandant do something?"

"Do something?" Nara sits on the edge of the cot opposite me. "Even if he wanted to take on the Temple of Rasus—which would be fairly insane, even for a politician—he couldn't possibly prove anything."

I lean forward. "What? Why not?"

"The Onyx Staff doesn't bellow out orders like a dictator," she says. "He insinuates, or he uses metaphor, or he talks about something else entirely. And people magically end up—well, some of them end up at the bottom of Lake Azure Wave."

I don't know how to respond. My shoulders slump back against the wall behind my cot.

Nara adjusts the front of her tidy jacket. "Sorry, does that spoil your squeaky-clean image of Caldaras City?"

I scowl. I'm pretty sure Nara Blake is on my side, if there are sides to be on. But that doesn't mean she isn't irritating. "Still. Secret or not, you did know what happened to me. And one would think your readers would have been mildly interested."

Nara smirks. "Well, look at the recluse who wants to be famous now."

I huff. "I am not a recluse, and I certainly don't want to be famous. It's just that I thought this whole thing might be a bigger deal since I'm a—you know."

Now she gives me a hard look. "No, I *don't* know. Are you trying to tell me something?"

I breathe in. Didn't I decide to trust Nara Blake the moment I asked for her help?

I put a hand to my top button. *No!* my mind yells. *Wrong! Stop!* But my fingers pull the button loose, then the ones underneath, all the way down. I stand, slipping my arms out of their sleeves, and now I wear only the short chemise from the old trunk. I turn away to give Nara Blake a full view of my bare shoulders and naked upper back.

To her credit, Nara reacts nothing like the priests in the temple sanctuary. She glances at the door to the common room, then blinks, takes a deep breath, and steps toward me. I don't move as she touches my back. "That part's true, then," she says. "The scars."

"I've got the blood, too," I say.

"So I've heard. I'll have to take Corvin's word for it, I suppose."

I put on my shirt and start to button it back up. "I'm not opening a vein for you. Don't even bother saying please."

"Well. Good. Now that we've got that out of the way," Nara says, "maybe you can do something *worthy* of a story in the *Daily Bulletin*."

"I'm a bit out of tricks. Getting boiled alive was supposed to be my big finish."

She snorts. "My friend, you don't think you're the *only* redwing the Onyx Staff has had thrown into Lake Azure Wave, do you?"

I put a hand to my forehead. "What in wet hell are you talking about? Of course I'm the only redwing he's thrown in the lake. I'm the only goddamn redwing!"

"As far as we know, yes, you are," Nara says. "And you know how rare—how impossible that seems, even to those of us who accept that real, living Others, straight out of a fairy tale, have visited this very city. But power needs fear to survive, and there is nothing in Caldaras more fearsome than a redwing. So to lend an artificial hand to his very real cause, the Onyx Staff sometimes . . . creates them."

Wait, what? "Creates—?" But I stop myself. I remember the guards in the dungeon preparing to whip my back—and stopping when they realized the scars were already there. I remember the dagger that sliced my arm before the whole sanctuary, the cut that didn't hurt and was miraculously healed when I awoke only days later, but that nevertheless produced a torrent of black blood for all to see. The cut, I realize, that was never there at all. And I remember the look of utter shock on the face of the Onyx Staff when one of his "redwings" actually fought back.

Nara rises and crosses to the door. "Well, welcome to the Under House."

"That's it? Opening your doors to a fearsome mythical creature like I'm a random tourist? Aren't you supposed to be getting the vapors or something?"

"I'd rather help you free your sister."

Relief—or is it hope?—balls in my throat. "Can you really?"

"I certainly hope so."

I speak with more emotion than I intend. "Why help me, Nara?"

She blinks, and for the first time I notice the shadows under her eyes. "You are a rare thing, my friend. Unique in ways that make you extremely important to us, and to our enemies. We need your help." She smiles weakly. "And . . . well, I wouldn't want anyone kidnapping Corvin. It would make me quite angry. I imagine you feel the same way about your sister."

"Yes. Thank you," I say.

"Very well, then," Nara says, businesslike. "But I'll be honest—I'm afraid this might be dangerous."

I smooth my hair and check my reflection in the glass of a framed landscape on the wall. "I've already been killed once."

Now she turns to me, serious. "Yes. And the fact that you're dead is the only reason you're still alive."

When Nara and I enter the common room, Orm and a woman are sitting at a long central table that holds collections of papers and pewter mugs. They rise when they see us, and the woman takes Nara's hands in hers. Nara looks to Orm and says, "How is he today?"

Orm nods. "Right as rain. He'll be here in a moment, I should think. I sent a boy to fetch him."

Nara looks at the woman now, tall and delicate with shining blond hair, and says, "Elena. This is—is—" Nara looks at me. "Well, this is she."

Now the blond woman turns her attention to me. She extends a hand, and I curl my fingers around hers.

"A living, breathing redwing!" she says, her eyes shining.

"This is a bit of luck, isn't it?" Orm winks. "And to think, I almost had you hauled off."

I shoot Nara a wide-eyed glance. Is it her intention for everyone in Caldaras to know what I am? She doesn't respond.

"Welcome, friend," Elena says, releasing Nara's hands. Her voice and eyes are soft, the opposite of Nara's steely exterior. "We are the Fog Walkers, those who leave the shelter of Mol's warm breath only to protect his city from harm. There is great danger coming, but you may just give us a chance."

I frown. "Danger?"

Nara makes a dismissive gesture. "She doesn't know anything yet. And her sister's gone missing."

Elena's face falls, the green of her shirt reflected in her eyes. "Oh, yes, of course. You must be positively climbing the walls. Come, sit."

We gather around the long table—Nara, Elena, Orm and I, and the other residents of the Under House. They smile and make room for me, offering words of welcome. All the contact makes me light-headed. Or maybe it's the pain in my wounded leg. I try to smile back, be normal. But they know what I am, these people. When does this dream end? When will I wake up, midair over

Lake Azure Wave? I take a swig from my pewter mug, which contains a liquid that might once have been beer before it was wrung out of someone's old watery stockings.

A moment later, Corvin emerges red-faced and weary from behind the studded door to the stairway. He gazes at me, astonished, then shoots Nara a questioning look.

"Sit," Nara says. "Our redwing is not drowned after all."

Still watching me, Corvin hastens to the table and lowers himself next to his sister. "You're looking well for a dead person," he says with ragged breath.

"You, too," I say, which makes him gurgle-laugh.

"We lost you on Roet Island," Corvin says, and Nara gives him a sharp look.

I lean forward. "You were *watching* me?"

Now Nara regards me dispassionately. "I told you we needed your help." There is no cruelty in her features, but I realize with a shiver that Nara Blake is used to getting what she wants. I study her carefully painted eyes, her flawless, powdered skin. Something in me knows she is good, in the way a just law is good. But good doesn't always mean right. Or kind.

Suddenly, the studded door crashes open and in strides a young woman, tall and striking, with glossy, unpinned hair and red lips, dressed all in black. On one hip hangs a long saber, on the other a pistol. She says nothing, but casts a sour glance over the room before sitting heavily at the table and pulling a mug toward her.

I jump to my feet. "You!"

She raises her eyes. "Oh, *damn it*."

"What's going on?" Elena says. "What's the matter, Fir?"

The woman—Fir—has risen from her seat and gestures violently at me. "What is *she* doing here?" She looks at Corvin. "Don't tell me you got her! I swear, if you've stepped on my toes again—"

I point. "You shot me in the flaming leg!"

"*What?*" Orm puts a palm to his forehead. "For the love of all that's on fire, girl, why didn't you say anything? I'll have you fixed up—"

Corvin stands now. "What is all this about?"

Fir looks knives at me. "She was in the house."

"In the house?" I look to Nara, Corvin, Orm. "You mean, in the house *where I live*? Who is this woman? Did you send her to kidnap me, too?"

"You weren't supposed to shoot her!" Corvin looks horrified.

"She ran!" Fir says. "My assignment was to bring her back, and I wasn't going to lose her the way you did!"

Elena speaks calmly. "You were meant to persuade her, Fir."

"I was meant to *produce* her," Fir hisses. "And when I get a job, it's because persuasion has failed."

"Enough of this!" Nara barks. "Fir, Redwing. Redwing, Fir. Now, everyone shut the hell up and sit down."

Everyone sits, and I cast a wary eye over the room. Fir takes a swig from her mug. I guess the Fog Walkers really do need my help. It's baffling.

"The Deep Dark is a week away." Nara is all business now. "That's what our priority is, to get the redwing to the Heart in time for Crepuscule. If Sunny's information is correct, the bone-scorch orchis will be a problem. But now that we have the redwing—"

"No." I slap the table. The Fog Walkers are silent, eyes on me. Nara sets her mouth disapprovingly. "'The Heart'?" I snap. "'The orchis'? 'The redwing'? I will not be an item on your scavenger hunt. Whatever it is you need of me, we rescue my sister first. And I must write to my father as soon as possible."

"The work your father is doing with the blight is critical," Nara says. "It's best for him to stay where he is. Your sister has been taken to the Temple of Rasus. She is in no danger for now."

"What?"

"She is in no danger." Corvin's tone looks to soothe my ruffles. "They are most likely keeping her for questioning, that is all."

I glare at him. "I know exactly how their questioning goes."

"In any case, the Heart takes precedence," Nara says. "Then, I promise you, we will free your sister."

I stand, even as my leg throbs. "I don't know whose heart you're so flaming interested in, or why you care about the Empress's damned party, or why in Ver's green land you need my help so much that you're willing to send *her*"— I jut a thumb at Fir— "to 'produce' me. But I'm going to free my sister before I do one more blazing thing, and if you can't help me, I'm walking out that door." I fold my arms. "Choose."

"Oh, Mol's tongue, can't you see what she's doing?" A biting voice pierces the hot air. Fir scowls at me. She has risen from her seat and gestures. "We're not seriously going to entertain the idea of a jailbreak at the Temple of Rasus!"

I rise and nod to the table. "I will take my leave, then."

"Wait!" Nara and Elena speak in unison, then look at each other. I pause, a few steps from the door. Elena continues, "Of course we will help you free your sister. And if we have to do it now"—Fir swears and pounds the table, but Elena goes on—"if we have to do it *now,* then we will. That's all there is to it."

"And then what? She decides to help us out of the goodness of her heart and be our redwing savior?" Fir stabs a finger in Elena's direction. "False hope is worse than no hope. You're a bunch of fools if you think a redwing actually exists. She's probably just another heretic with false scars."

Corvin sets his mug down heavily. "You're crossing a line, Fir."

"Show us your bullet wound, redwing," Orm says. "I'll pull that deformed little metal bastard out of there, and Fir can see all the blood she wants."

"Not good enough." Fir points at me, takes two wide steps to where I am. "I'm sick of these rebel princesses from the Feather and Scuttle seeking us out. We've dealt with their tricks before. Sleight of hand, illusion. Just like the bloody Temple. She's had plenty of time to ink her bandages."

"I saw her blood," Corvin says, resting a fist on the table. "Nara can vouch for it."

"Nara and Corvin," Fir scoffs, "and no one else." She saunters over to me. "You've got a twin sister and you're unmarked. That's all we know."

The room is quiet; even Orm holds his tongue as Fir goes nose to nose with me. I don't back away. If this is some kind of test, I'm sure as wet hell not going to let her get the better of me. I let her lean in, the sweet, sharp scent on her making my nostrils tingle.

Her eyes narrow. "You know what I think?" she snarls. I don't respond. She turns to the others. "That's *all there is to know.* She needs help getting her goddamned unmarked twin out of the temple prison, that's all. And isn't that what we're just about to do? Fools."

The people around the table erupt into mutters, throwing me doubtful looks. Elena's face is impassive. Orm looks at me as though I owe him some kind of response.

"So what's your game, princess?" Fir unsheathes her long saber in one violently graceful motion. I don't move. "Are you a spy?" she asks, soft and treacherous. "Or just a very stupid girl who thought killing priests would be fun?" Now she brings her saber to my throat. A few Fog Walkers gasp as the blade presses against my skin—just the right amount of pressure not to pierce. She knows what she's doing.

I look into her flashing eyes and I know her. She has a space here, and I am not allowed in. But to call me human? If she only knew what I would give for that to be true!

I am no human. And if I am to exist at last, let it be as myself.

"Fir!" Nara stands, hands on hips. "Stop this!"

Fir turns, instantly playful. "Just a joke, Nara." She looks at me again. "Fine. I'll rescue your dear sister. Why don't you stay here and I'll write you when I've saved the day? Only—I didn't get your name. Oh, right, your kind don't have them." She steps away, smiling sweetly at Nara and lowering her saber.

Almost lowering her saber.

I am too quick for her. I grasp the blade, still at my throat, and she staggers. She turns back, eyebrows drawn in surprise.

"My name?" I press the edge of the blade into my flesh until I can feel the blood trickling down my neck in thick, hot rivulets.

The others jump to their feet. Mugs clatter to the floor. Fir's eyes widen and she tries to back away.

I release the blade, now black with my extraordinary, unmistakable blood. "My name is Redwing."

twelve

So far, my least favorite thing is the pants.

Corvin and I stretch out on the roof, our elbows over the apex. He fiddles with knobs on his binoculars, though how he can see anything on this moonless night is anybody's guess. A streetlamp casts a murky pallor over the gated doorway of the workhouse across the street.

"It's the chafing," I whisper. "My thighs are not used to all this excitement."

"I wear pants like this every day." Corvin peers through the binoculars. "Your thighs can handle it."

I squint into the darkness. "Yours aren't so tight. And Orm did just pull a bullet out of me. Not the sort of thing you want tweed rubbing against."

"One would think you'd be more concerned with the goddamn slice you made in your own throat with Fir's saber."

A black scarf tied around my neck hides the bandage. The cut stings when I move my head, but it will heal. Besides, it was worth it.

"None of the Fog Walkers wonder if I'm really a redwing now, though," I whisper.

Corvin laughs. "No. No, you're right about that. You're out of your mind, but you're right." He looks at me. "You've got to start taking better care of yourself, Redwing. I see you've got part of an ear gone as well. You're starting to look like a half-plucked alley hen."

"Oh, *that*." I finger the ear the stritch whip sliced. "I just need a new hairstyle."

I flash him a cheeky smile and his expression softens. It catches me off guard, and for a moment, we look at each other in silence. He seems like he's about to say something, but a sound from below steals his attention.

A figure approaches from inside the gate, indistinct in the night mist. "Here she is," Corvin whispers, and we are both silent, tense. I'm still not entirely sure how this game is played or what the teams are.

The figure swings the gate open slowly and pauses, looking up and down the street. The streetlight illuminates an old woman's face. There is something shifty about her, her patchy coat and rough edges. The way her eyes squint in the dim light.

I frown and lean over to Corvin, my words the barest whisper in his ear. "Who is she?"

He leans his head in my direction. "Teppa the Fowl. We can't talk to her here. She'll just run back inside, and I'm not about to tangle with the workhouse guards. Got to get her out in the open."

Satisfied, she closes the gate behind her and hurries off. In an instant, we are up and following swiftly.

We keep to the rooftops, our black attire sometimes hiding us even from each other as we trail her. I try to keep pace with Corvin as he slips under pipes and over pitches, in and out of the darkness of gables and the striped shadows of iron balconies. The old woman moves below, winding through garbage-strewn alleys and broad cobblestone streets. I am a tiny bit grateful for the snug tweed now, as I brush against jagged edges and squeeze through openings that might have been made difficult by the fullness of my not-as-stylish-as-Jey's stylish pants.

At last the woman stops at a well-lit storefront: FLOWERS OF THE FINEST SILK & PAPER. From a pitched roof across the way, Corvin and I watch as she pulls something from the recesses of her old coat and starts to fiddle with the door. "A simple flower merchant?" he whispers. "No scruples. None at all." Then he gives me a nod and jumps down through the mist to the cobbled street. What did that nod mean? Am I supposed to follow? I refuse to jump from this height onto a recently shot leg.

Cursing under my breath, I grasp a nearby drainpipe and shimmy down, streaking my hands and clothes with rust. Corvin is already across the street, looming over the woman.

"Nope, nope, nope. No Temple jobs. Nope." The woman shakes her frizzy white hair.

Corvin nods to me as I limp over to them. "Ah, Teppa, I hope you'll enjoy meeting my new friend. Say hello."

Teppa the Fowl's vacant, staring eyes reflect dull light as she swings her head my way. "Speak, ruffian, or I'll gut you."

Corvin shakes his head condescendingly over her shoulder, but I am not so quick to dismiss her threats. She looks—potent.

"It's a pleasure to meet you, Miss—er—Miss Teppa." I hold out my hand in greeting as I have become accustomed to do, but she doesn't acknowledge it.

"'Miss Teppa,' is it?" She rasps a laugh. "Where did you dig up this one, Corvin Blake? Another starry-eyed revolutionary ready to die for the Fog Walkers?" She leans in, the scent of soot and decay wafting over me. "Just be sure you're ready, love, because die you will."

"Shut up," Corvin says severely. "Listen, I told you, we need to get into the detention level of the Temple of Rasus."

"I am not your personal lockpick, you thugs," the old woman spits, then coughs. "No deal."

"Here's my offer," Corvin says. "You can either get us in with your slippery little fingers, or I'll pick the lock myself with your bloody teeth."

I look at him in astonishment. Threats, pistols, sabers—who are these Fog Walkers?

But Teppa the Fowl only laughs and puts a scabby hand on Corvin's arm. "Ah, my Corvin Blake. If you are as handsome as you sound, then the gods truly had their vengeance in making me blind."

Fir is waiting for us in High Ra Square, lounging against the giant obsidian redwing. The square is finally deserted, the temple beacons casting a strange, beautiful patchwork of soft light on the vast expanse of flagstones.

Fir stretches lazily as Corvin, Teppa, and I approach. She saunters over to us, one hand tucked in her pocket, the other gesturing to the enormous statue. "I see it now," she says to me. "There is definitely a family resemblance."

I ignore her. Corvin says quietly, "We go in the front, take the servants' stairs to the detention level, and bring the prisoner out the way we came. The . . . new girl . . . is the priority. Fir and I will deal with any situations that present themselves."

I swallow. *The new girl is the priority.* I know what that means, what he's not saying. *The redwing is the priority. Her life is the priority. Not her sister's. Not ours.*

"Risky," Teppa says. "But it's not my skin. I was coerced."

"We can't bring the prisoner out the damned front door," Fir hisses. Corvin throws up his hands, but I jump in.

"No," I say. "We don't go out the front door. We go all the way down the servants' stairs, to the lower kitchen. There's a window in the pantry we can climb through."

Teppa hacks out a laugh. "The new girl has done her schoolwork."

Fir glares at me, but gives a crisp nod. "We enter in pairs," she says. "If there's anyone in the vestibule, we go all the way into the sanctuary as though we're there to offer prayer, all right? When the vestibule is empty, we find the staircase."

Corvin and Fir enter first, then Teppa the Fowl and me. Two high priests in black amble toward an ornate door, laughing softly at some joke as we pass through the gaping vestibule. They don't pay us any notice, but Corvin and Fir cross all the way to the large doors to the sanctuary and go inside. Teppa follows, keeping only a foot or two behind them, so I hang back.

I have nearly reached the sanctuary when I hear the groan of old hinges. I turn to find a hunched figure emerging slowly from the ornate door in front of the black-clad priests. The priests stop their conversation and move aside, bowing low—so low that through the soft pattern of night light I see their knees touch the floor.

I give a start. Someone before whom even high priests kneel? It can't be the Onyx Staff. I bite my cheeks, willing this to be true. And no, it isn't him. It is an old man, who carries not a staff, but a basket. He is dressed in pink robes, elaborately ornamented with ribbon, and he moves with small, slippered steps. The Salt Throne. The most powerful priest in all of Caldaras.

To my horror, he turns his head and fixes me with a gaze. It is too dim to see his eyes well, but the meaning of the gloved hand he extends in my direction is clear: *Come here.*

I give a panicked look toward the sanctuary. No sign of the others. I look back at the Salt Throne, who is as still as the stone pillar next to which he stands. He holds his hand out patiently.

What can I do but go to him? It would be far worse to disobey. At least now I have some small chance of coming out of this unscathed.

The high priests step back, smiling. What do they know? Am I done for? Or are they just . . . smiling?

"Good evening, Beloved," the Salt Throne says in a thin voice. "Welcome to the temple. I am on my way to offer nightkiss petals to the holy fountain."

I bow low. Something tells me this isn't an occasion for a hand-shake. "Good evening . . ." *Wet hell, I don't know what to call him.* "Good evening, Beloved," I say.

The high priests both gasp. Ver's ass, I've fouled it up; royally, by the sound of it. But the Salt Throne just looks at me. Then his wrinkled face ripples like water—a smile. "A term reserved for one's equals or inferiors," he says. "According to the Temple, that is. According to . . . me, I suppose."

I bow again, lower, touching my knees to the floor. "I apolo-gize, Your Benevolence, I—"

"'Benevolence' is reserved for the Onyx Staff," the Salt Throne says, gesturing as one of the priests helps me to my feet again, "and I've always wondered if that was a bit of a joke. Most would call me, 'Your Brilliance.'" *Your Brilliance. I knew that!* "In any case, there is no need to apologize, Beloved."

I keep my eyes lowered. "I am honored by your greeting, but I am ashamed that I did not address you properly." *Please don't have me boiled again. Or shoot me. Or slice my head off.*

The Salt Throne puts a light hand on my shoulder. "I wanted to speak with you because my heart told me you had something valuable to say. And now I know it is this: We are all beloved of Rasus, the godking." The priests make their open-palmed gesture; I try to follow suit but end up just kind of waving at them. "All of us, lowly and exalted, are equally warmed by the rays of the sun. All are beloved." He closes his eyes. "Thank you."

I don't know what to say, other than, "You're welcome."

"Breathe easy," he says, and the high priests echo, "Breathe easy."

I bow, just a bend at the waist. "Breathe easy." And the Salt

Throne and the two black-clad priests proceed through the temple doors and out into the moonlight.

With the vestibule now empty, Fir, Corvin, and Teppa come through the sanctuary doors. "What did you say to him?" Fir asks as though she is accusing me of something.

"I said we were here to break into his private quarters and draw mustaches on all the Holy Engravings," I say. Corvin snorts, but Fir shoots him a furious look, and suddenly he appears to be clearing his throat.

The doorway to the servants' staircase is hidden behind the heavy golden curtains, but I remember where it is and find it in only a few short moments. Corvin raises his eyebrows in approval, but Fir just keeps watch, her intense gaze flitting from one corner of the room to the other.

We climb, careful of our footfalls. The detention level is one floor up, a narrow hallway that curves around the outside of the cavernous sanctuary. I do not expect to find the door locked; are servants not required to clean and deliver meals even here? But the others don't seem surprised, and Teppa's tools make short work of the lock. It is clear we need her.

Fir pokes her head out first, then motions for us to step out from the little stairwell. She is brave, I must admit. The bare hallway is a stark contrast to the lush fabrics and colors of the vestibule. Fir proceeds slowly, keeping to the shadows between the few weak lamps, and we follow, silent, always unsure of what we'll find farther along the curve of the wall.

Suddenly, Fir stops, flattening herself against a darkened doorway. Teppa freezes, and I turn to Corvin, who exchanges a look with Fir and then nods. He gestures and I turn. Fir has tied a linen bandanna over her nose and mouth, and holds more out to us. I look to Corvin again, who has already tied a black bandanna just below his eyes and is pulling a satchel from his hip. Teppa and I put on our own bandannas, which smell like oil. I hold my breath as Corvin sidles past me along the wall. Slowly, he creeps past Fir, who slides back toward us, head turned to follow Corvin.

When he has almost disappeared from view, I see Corvin's arm swing—he tosses something from the satchel farther down the curving hallway. Then he retreats, and we all press ourselves against the wall.

A few minutes pass before Fir begins to move forward once again. My heart jumps as the terrifying figure of a Temple guard comes into view, the spikes on his iron helmet casting severe shadows on the bare walls. But as we approach, I see that he is slumped over in his chair.

I turn to Corvin. "Star pods!" I whisper. "That's what you've got in that satchel!"

I can't see the smile under his bandanna, but it changes the shape of his eyes. "Also known as anysleep. I'm never without them."

"They're a nightmare to grow," I say, impressed. "They're such fragile little things. And they have a tendency to knock you unconscious. You must be quite a gardener."

"He steals them," Fir whispers. Corvin clears his throat. I'm beginning to wonder if he's getting a cold. "Here," Fir says, a hand on her hip. She stands just beyond the unconscious guard in front of a solid-looking door. "There won't be any other guards. There isn't much security in this area; the prisoners here are just detainees. Your sister may have been asked to come in for questioning simply because you were executed."

"Well, they didn't ask very nicely," I mutter. I can still see our broken vase, the overturned furniture.

Fir shrugs as Teppa sets to work on the door. After a moment, Corvin pulls his bandanna down and gives the air a tentative sniff. "It's fine," he says. "Anysleep dissipates quickly."

The rest of us cautiously pull down our own bandannas, but aside from a slight bitter mustiness, the hallway seems normal.

"That means he'll be waking up in a few minutes," Fir says. "Hurry up, Teppa, you revolting old skeleton."

"Why don't you stuff that oil rag in your mouth, villain?" Teppa says, clinking a jagged metal device into the lock. "It'd probably make your breath smell better."

My eyes snap to Fir's face, but instead of the rage I expected, she seems amused. I can't help grinning. There is something about Teppa.

Whatever she has been rattling around in the lock gives a satisfying click, and she steps back. Fir turns the handle and gives the door a little shove. We wait, but nothing happens. All seems clear.

"Be quick," Fir whispers as I slide by her. "We'll keep watch out here."

"Thanks," I say. I meet her eyes when I say it, unintentionally, and it seems to throw her off a little. She gives a quick nod.

The room beyond looks more like a parlor than a jail cell. It's certainly nothing like the dank, candlelit dungeon below the sanctuary. I move with caution, taking care not to disturb the graceful upholstered chairs or the thin-legged tables set with books and used teacups.

Between a gold velvet settee and an iron coatrack is a slender door, slightly ajar. I creep over to it and snake my head around the edge.

It is a modest room with two dressing tables and a row of beds. *The prisoners on this level really have it nice,* I think, remembering my hollow-eyed guard and her choking device. The room is dim, and it takes me a moment to make out a sleeping form.

I pad over to the bed, where a familiar lock of dark hair spills from under a floral-patterned blanket. I lean down, my face nearly touching the sheets. "Jey." I touch her shoulder.

She shifts, extending her legs and sliding the blanket off her face. My sister cracks her eyes blearily, then opens them as wide as raptor eggs.

I put a finger to my lips and motion for her to follow me. Jey rises hesitantly and joins me in the parlor. I shut the door to the bedroom without a sound and signal for my sister to come with me. She doesn't move; she is in shock. I go back to her, put my arms around her, and whisper, "It's all right. I know somewhere safe we can go."

Her body feels rigid and strange, and she keeps looking at me with those raptor-egg eyes. I take a step back. "Jey," I whisper. "We must hurry."

Then, slowly and without breaking eye contact, she shakes her head.

I grab her shoulders, and she shrinks. "What's the matter with you?" I hiss. "I've come to get you out of here. But we mustn't be caught—we have to go now!"

"No," she whispers, so quietly I can barely hear her.

I release her. "What?"

"No," she whispers again. "I . . . I know what you are."

All I can do is stare at her. "What do you mean? What do you mean, you know what I am? You've always known . . . what I am."

"I know more than that. More than you think." She looks down. "You were never educated in the Temple, sister," she says.

"That would have worked out well, I'm sure."

"But I go." Her voice shakes. "I go, and I listen. I thought they were going to—to rehabilitate you. Bonner said that the Onyx Staff would cast a healing light over you."

"Bonner!" I can barely stop myself from shouting it. "Bonner is a cruel man, Jey! Listen to me—"

"No, you listen!" she says, sounding more like herself. "Do you think I wanted to get you killed? Do you think that was easy for me?"

I steady myself against an overly dainty chair. *"You* told the priests about me? That I would be coming home from the aviary that day?" The realization crawls over my skin like a thousand worms. No longer steady, my legs buckle and I sit heavily on the chair's fine upholstery.

Jey wrings her hands. "Bonner didn't say they would execute you! He said you would be cleansed. I—"

"It's not your fault," I say, trying to hide the tremble in my voice. "It's Bonner's fault. He lied to you, that—that eel of righteousness. He's a lying scoundrel."

"He's not," she says, unaware of how young she sounds. "I love him. We can't choose whom we love."

My cheeks heat up. "What you have with Bonner is not love!" I stop myself, inhaling deeply. "We have to get away from here."

"No!" She paces away from me. "No, redwing. I understand now. I didn't know before that you were a—a monster. I thought you were just like me."

"I *am* just like you!"

Her eyes flash. "I saw the priest! The one whose face you burned off!"

I open my mouth, but no sound comes out. I can still see his blood-streaked face.

"And the other one!" Her words scratch with anger now. "His arms were in six pieces! Bonner brought those men here to show me what you really are."

"Jey, they were trying to—"

"And I saw Bonner's poor hands. His hands, sister. How could you?"

Oh, Jey, why must you be so trusting? My sister's innocent faith in that vile young man has led us to this. She is safe for now, but to the unshakably righteous, eventually everyone begins to seem tarnished and wicked.

Jey's voice quiets. "I am here for my own protection." She glances back toward the bedroom. "The Beautiful Ones know you didn't die. They said I had to come with them so they could keep me safe."

"Is that so?" I clench the delicate arms of the chair. "Did you smash our birthday vase because you were so happy about being safe?"

She lowers her eyes. "I didn't want to go at first. I didn't understand."

"Yes, you did." I look at her face—my face. "You always understood."

Now she stares back at me, hard. "They said you were an angry beast. That you would come for me. And you did."

I jump to my feet. "I came to save you!"

Jey recoils. "Please! Please don't hurt me, redwing. If you ever loved me at all, if there is anything human in you!"

I can't speak. I stare at my sister cowering at the thought of leaving her prison.

"Bonner and I are going east tomorrow," she says. "We're going to join Papa. You won't follow us there, will you?" She swallows. "They said you would seek revenge against Papa, too, once—once your mind starts to go. We're going to take him away, and then you'll never find us."

Heat trickles down my face, worse than worms, worse than blood. In a fragile whisper, I ask, "Do you really believe all those things about me, Jey? Do you really want to go east with Bonner?"

She says nothing, but I can see her shaking. Jey, who has never been afraid of anything in her life, is afraid of me.

"I want to be far away from this madness," she says, sniffing. "And you . . . you can be me now."

"I'll never be you," I say. And for the first time in my life, I don't want to.

I turn and walk silently from the room. I make sure to close the door behind me.

thirteen

The cot in the bunk room of the Under House is not as comfortable as the mattress in the Dome, and it smells of beer instead of hay, but I sleep anyway, then wake in a curl under the thin blanket. I certainly don't need the blanket for warmth in this sweltering basement, but right now I need a barrier between me and the rest of the world. I pull the fabric over my face.

Murmuring from the common room buzzes in my ears, the words indistinct but the tone heated. I stretch an arm over my head, resting its weight on my sore ear to block out the sound. I keep my eyes closed.

The door opens and closes. Footsteps draw near. I sense someone sitting on the cot next to mine, but I don't open my eyes. I listen to him, the whisper of his every breath keeping me from unconsciousness.

"I brought you something." Corvin's tone is a little hesitant, almost as though he is asking a question.

I slide the corner of the blanket off my face and look up at him. "Is Jey right? Am I a monster?"

His expression becomes distant; a dullness creeps into his eyes. "You can't start asking yourself those kinds of questions."

I let my head flop back onto my pillow. "Well, *that* helps."

Corvin's focus becomes more present and his features soften. "Sorry. All of us—we can be a little . . . intense. Especially—"

"Fir," I mumble.

"I was going to say my sister. Nara." Nara. If she were here now, she would sweep that stray lock of light hair from his bruised face. "We came here with nothing, and the city held us up," he says. "She wants to protect the people here who can't protect themselves."

I roll onto my back. "They don't know to protect themselves. From—from whoever."

Corvin reaches behind himself. "Do you want what I brought you or not?"

I turn my head. "All right."

He pulls out my wrench-box, the one from the top of my wardrobe. All my penny pulp redwings, photographs of Jey and my father, my mother's tablecloth. I sit up, gazing first at the box, then at him. "How did you . . . ?"

He smiles and shrugs. "I got some of your clothes, too. I hope you don't mind. I figured you'd want your own things. I watered your garden, too, for what it's worth. All those green plants up there, in the middle of the city. It's quite amazing."

"I've got a watering system," I say. "My father designed it. And the raptor poo. The plants love it. Never could figure why the raptors have to wait until they're inside to do all their business."

"Sounds . . . delightful?" Corvin holds out the box. "Anyway, when I found this, I knew it was special."

I reach for the box, wrapping my arms around it. "It is," I say. "Thank you." I let my upper body fall backwards onto the cot. The box isn't cuddly, but it calms me.

Corvin is silent for a moment. Then he asks, "What do you know of Others?"

"I know very little of anything I haven't read about." I close my eyes. "In the stories, Other princes and princesses—they're always princes or princesses—are lovely, intelligent, kind. They admire humans enough to use their magic powers to come to the aid of lowly servants and noblemen alike." I open my eyes and study the dark metal ceiling. "They are everything redwings are not."

"Redwings are not lovely, intelligent, and kind?"

I snort. "Not traditionally."

"You don't seem very traditional to me," Corvin says. I am silent. He leans back, propping himself up on his arms. "What about your mother? She was an Other."

"She died soon after I was born," I say. "I don't remember her."

"I'm sorry," he says softly. "Do you know anything about her? What she was like?"

I inhale and sit up. Enough of this lying around. I swing my legs over the side of the cot.

Corvin straightens up. "I've offended you."

"Offended me? Certainly not," I say, color rising in my cheeks.

He nods. Then, in a gentle voice, he says, "My sister is going to ask you to do something extremely dangerous. She sees it as the only way to save Caldaras City, and maybe it is, but I want you to know that you can say no."

I don't know how to respond. Instead I rub my thumbs along the edges of the wrench-box. "Would you like to see my mother's tablecloth?"

The corners of Corvin's eyes crease in a half smile. "I would love to see your mother's tablecloth."

I click open the box, which utters a small creak of protest. The scrap of linen is neatly folded at the bottom. Corvin's gaze lingers on my stack of penny pulp redwings, but he doesn't say anything.

"Here." I hand it to him with care. "She grew the linstalks herself, and my father spun it."

"This is very fine." Corvin fingers the brown edges. "But what happened to it?"

I had almost forgotten the tablecloth must once have been large enough to cover a table. For most of my life, it has been this scrap—just enough to swaddle a secret baby. "Our house burned down," I say, avoiding his eyes. "My father saved this bit of the cloth." But no one saved her.

"Can you weave, as well?" Corvin asks.

The heat in the bunk room is starting to make me light-headed. "My mother wasn't a weaver; our neighbor did that. My mother was a gardener like my father. Linstalk can be tricky, you know." A meadow fluttering with flowers flashes through my mind—is it a memory, or did I imagine it? "You have to let the stalks rot from the inside for a long time, then you break it—smash it to wet hell—and then finally you're left with these long, smooth fibers that can actually be made into something beautiful."

Corvin carefully folds the scrap of cloth and hands it back to me. It seems old and shabby in this light. It would have shone when it was new. "Thank you for showing me," he says. "I'll leave you to your sleep." He gets up and lowers the gaslight. From the doorway, he turns. "I've seen the lin growing in Val Chorm, before it's harvested," he says. "Rippling with speckles of the loveliest purple-blue color. It's beautiful then, too."

The Under House is dark and silent at last, but I'm wide awake, swinging my legs from a decrepit balcony overlooking the alley behind the Pump Room. Two wild raptors clutch the railing, night-alert.

I have two options: go or stay, as simple as that. Simpler. Go.

I would probably like the cliffs of Drush, where raptors eat lizards until their feathers turn green. I could cultivate a little desert garden and cook for the salt miners. I could live under the sky, away from the bonescorch orchis and the Beautiful Ones.

Yet Caldaras City feels like home, as greasy and poisonous as it is. I rest my face, still hot from the Under House's roasting bunk room, against the railing of the balcony. The iron is cooler than the steamy night air, but hardly a relief. Nara told me to get some sleep, that we would talk about it in the morning. She trusts me to be here in the morning, and right now I can't find a good reason to be. *Zahi* . . . I close my eyes. No. Zahi cannot be a reason. To him, I am Jey. Not me.

The back door to the Pump Room clangs open. Nara and Elena step into the alley, their features barely visible in the dim reach of light from Mad Lane. I still my legs, hoping the women will pass without noticing me. The raptors, however, launch themselves irritably, and though they move with the noiselessness of predators, they are large birds skimming the contours of a dark alley. Nara and Elena notice.

"You're not going to sleep up there?" Nara sounds like she is three seconds from scolding me.

"I'll come down in a few minutes." We all know it is a lie. I may sleep up here. I may slink away toward the Path of Mol, the wide avenue that leads to the train station. But I'm not going back down to the Under House tonight.

"Come have a drink with us," Elena says. "You've had a long week."

"Thanks, but I'm fine."

Nara nods and starts to move away, but Elena stands her ground, hand on hip, and says, "Balderdash!"

I jerk my head back, never having been confronted with "Balderdash!" before. Elena stares up at me from the gloom like a storm brewing.

Nara looks at me with a bemused expression. "She'll stand there like that all night," she says. I suspect I was wrong about Nara being the more severe of the two.

We don't go to the Pump Room, but back to the office of the *Caldaras City Daily Bulletin*. Nara locks the door behind us and leads the way through the little curtain at the back of the office. The sizable space beyond is bright and noisy, with great clanking printing presses whirring out tomorrow's paper. People in dark jumpsuits move as precisely and purposefully as the cogs of the machines they operate. Nara and Elena pay them little notice as we make our way to a spiraling metal staircase in a corner of the room.

The apartment above the office is elegantly furnished—damask and deep colors—and Nara wastes no time decanting three small glasses of something precious and emerald green that completes the atmosphere of sophistication.

"I suppose I might have assumed you didn't live in the Under House," I say, sipping. The fragrant, minty liquid prickles my nose. My eyes start to water. So much for sophistication.

Elena assumes an ornamental pose, one elbow resting on the mantel, and Nara seats herself on a red velvet settee trimmed with dark wood.

"We've no need to live in the Under House," Nara says. "We are not in hiding."

"In hiding?"

"There are things you do not understand," Nara says.

"Thanks for that vague assessment," I say. "But it is true, I must admit. There are many things I do not understand. How to darn socks, for instance." I put a hand on my hip, cocking my head. "Do people go into hiding because they cannot darn socks?"

Elena chuckles. "I would have disappeared long ago."

Nara downs her glass. "Fine, Redwing, then understand this: Those who would betray this city in the Deep Dark don't want their plans to be known, and they have powerful friends. Once their eyes are on you, you disappear or you die, and it's better if you get to make that choice yourself."

"See, that wasn't so hard," I say, suddenly entranced by a strange canvas on the wall: vibrant reds and yellows on a field of jet black. Now I can't tell if my eyes are watering from the emerald drink or the assault of color. I blink and turn my gaze elsewhere.

Next to the gaudy, jumbled piece of artwork hangs an exquisite landscape framed by twisting brass. I fold a hand behind my back as Papa taught me to do. "Very nice."

"It's a Zan," Elena says. "Fanny. Great-something-or-other to our dear Commandant."

"Is it Val Chorm?" I take a step back, letting the green wisps and dots of purple-blue swirl in my eyes.

"It very well may be," Elena says. "Nara inherited it from her grandmother, who lived in Val Chorm."

I turn back to the room and Nara gestures to an armchair upholstered in the same red velvet as the settee. As I lower myself into the seat, she asks, "Have you been to Val Chorm, Redwing?"

"I'm from there, actually." I take another minty-fire sip of my drink. "But I don't suspect we're here to discuss my childhood."

Elena sighs and pulls a delicate coppery chair out from a desk next to the fireplace. She seats herself and says, "We're happy for people to stop by for a chat. Some of the reporters will come up, you know, or the occasional bridge club friend, but we don't get an excessive amount of visitors. So don't think that you aren't welcome. But, yes, the real reason you're here is that Nara wants you to save the world."

"Don't be dramatic," Nara says, draping an arm across the back of the settee. "Save the city, yes, and by extension, the rest of Caldaras."

"What are we saving the city from?" I ask, half wondering if this is a joke.

"Mol," Nara says.

Ah. Yes. A joke. "And how do we do that?"

She looks as though I've just asked whether underwear goes on one's ass or one's head. "We kill him."

I look from Nara to Elena. Both wear the same apprehensive, grave expression. *Not* a joke, then.

Kill Mol.

Don't they realize Mol is a *god*?

Don't they realize Mol is *also a volcano*?

I gulp down the last of the emerald green liquid so fast, it burns. "Thank you for your hospitality, friends, but I must take my leave. I'm not in the god-killing racket these days."

Nara rises, a polished finger already pointing at me, but Elena stops her with a gesture, sweeping over to a side table, where she picks up the decanter. "We will, of course, give you more of an explanation than that," she says, refilling my refined little glass. Nara sits again, and I lean back in my armchair. *They get five minutes.*

"Very well." Nara fixes me with a somber gaze. Between rich tawny drapes, the dark window behind her starts to glisten with rain. "You know about the War of the Burning Land."

This catches me off guard. "Just because I didn't go to school doesn't mean I got out of slogging through that bone-dry epic poem, you know," I say. "Twice. A bunch of flowery nostalgia about Dal Roet defeating the monster Bet-Nef and his redwing minions so everyone could live happily ever after."

"The monster Bet-Nef, yes," Nara says, "who wanted to cover Caldaras City with fire. That was almost a thousand years ago, yet there are some who worship him still."

"Worship *Bet-Nef*?" I snort. "That's lunacy. I don't believe it."

"But you must," Elena says, her green eyes glittering, "for they are within the Temple of Rasus. You've met them."

"Ah. A good place to hide," I concede. "Crazy masquerading as different crazy. They call themselves the Beautiful Ones, you know. And I hardly call getting thrown into a boiling lake 'meeting.'"

Elena nods. "Yes, well. They, like Bet-Nef, believe Mol is Rasus incarnate on this world, just as he is the sun and the stars in outer space. They want to—free him. And the Deep Dark is when they will do it."

I throw an arm over the back of the chair. "So they want to free a volcano, whatever that means, and you don't think we'll all get along? Is that it?"

"You can be as flippant as you like." Nara's tone doesn't actually indicate that I should be as flippant as I like. "But the fact is, we need you to find and destroy Mol's Heart. According to legend—"

"According to legend," I say. "What a reliable source of information."

"According to legend," Nara snaps, "only a redwing can find the Heart."

"I'm sorry," I say, "but I live in one room, and even then I can't find my pants half the time."

"The Beautiful Ones are powerful." Nara's voice is even. "They grow more powerful by the day. We have reason to believe their leader is none other than the Onyx Staff."

"That's a good theory, as he's the one who tried to poach me like an egg."

Nara frowns. "You have proof, then. That is something, I suppose. I . . . I had hoped the cult didn't run that deep."

I raise an eyebrow. "I'm sure we're all shocked that the Onyx Staff has turned out to be a dangerous lunatic."

Nara cracks a smile at this despite herself, then clears her throat. "The Beautiful Ones must be stopped. The Burning Land below Mol is the realm of the Others. It will destroy us. All of us."

"The realm of the Others?" I have never thought about what the realm of the Others might look like or where it might be. I knew only that my own mother rose from the lands below the surface of Mol.

"They say the Burning Land is not all bad," Elena says gently. The fire in the little hearth glimmers in her eyes. "They say it's a place of blazing light and utter darkness. Quietness and gentle currents." She inhales and stretches her neck, tamping down the emotion I can see anyway. "There is great beauty there, so it is said."

Her gaze flicks to the strange canvas of reds, yellows, and blacks. I study it again. Could the jagged lines and wide curves be more than they appear at first glance? Am I seeing the fiery, underground world of the Others?

I try to find Nara's cold determination in Elena's face, but there is only sorrow there. And perhaps regret. "So why do you need me?" I ask.

"When Bet-Nef realized he had been defeated, he hid the Heart on Roet Island," Nara says.

I shrug. "And?"

They exchange a look before Elena says, "We can't find it."

This is tiresome. "So get better Fog Walkers."

"We don't need better Fog Walkers," Elena says. "We need a redwing. It is not a matter of cunning or strength, but of blood."

"It always comes back to blood sooner or later, doesn't it?" I sip the green fire; it's getting easier.

"Look, we've tried stealth and coercion and threat and blackmail, and it's gotten us nowhere," Nara says.

"Sounds like I missed all the fun."

"We realized we just have to accept . . ." Nara trails off. She doesn't seem to know how to finish the sentence.

Elena is all patience. "By Bet-Nef's design, a redwing—one of his loyal followers—is the only being who can break the protections surrounding the Heart. At least"—she flashes an apologetic smile—"according to legend."

Now *this* gulp of green liquid is positively delightful. "That's me, all right," I mutter. "A goddamn legend."

"We were going to steal the bonescorch, to help us find a redwing," Nara says. "Elena was convinced there must be one in the city."

"But then you came along," Elena says. Now they're both looking at me anxiously, as though any of this is anything other than complete insanity.

It can't be true, can it? The Onyx Staff can't be so supremely cruel as to stir a bunch of naive priests into a frenzy in order to—*to burn Caldaras City alive*? I close my eyes, remembering the look of serenity on his face as one of his priests sliced my ear in two with his whip.

Mol's flaming backside.

I glance down at the empty glass in my hand and sigh. "Well, first off, I'm going to need another one of these."

fourteen

Assassinate a god. Isn't that a kick in the pantaloons.

The first part of the plan, obviously, is to visit a fancy hat shop.

"Clear," Fir says. I step out of the alcove, where I was pretending to admire some decorative metalwork. A pair of blue postulants disappears into the crowd behind us. This fine afternoon, posh Sweetrose Avenue is bursting with the noblesse and their stritches, humans and birds of burden equally festooned with feathers, ribbons, and bright draperies. Tonight is the beginning of Crepuscule, the evening before the Deep Dark. According to Nara, it is during Crepuscule that I will be able to find Mol's Heart. Now I just have to get onto Roet Island.

Fir, Corvin, and I proceed through the city mist, which is thin and sun brightened at this elevation. The structures here are designed to impress, mimicking the shining swells of the Copper Palace, just visible across the water when the capricious haze affords a momentary view of Roet Island.

Even though the residents of the Under House know my secret—and I theirs—I am still a redwing, and not fit for public consumption. The three of us are dressed to blend in. Corvin seems to enjoy the novelty of his tall hat, while I've borrowed a white cap from Nara. We have all donned smart, well-fitting dusters, silk shirts, and high-heeled boots polished like gemstones.

I can't say I'm enjoying the high heels. Fir and Corvin stride easily down Sweetrose Avenue—the wealthy district suits them—as we weave in and out of the groups of people and stritches. I hold my head up high, but wobble trying to keep up. I wonder if they were nobility once, in another life. Fir exudes health and privilege. And Corvin—I steal a glance as we pause to give way to a group of ladies exiting a high-end tobacco shop—Corvin's bruises are fading fast, and he looks surprisingly striking, like the son of a nobleman, with his light windswept hair and silver buttons.

He catches me looking at him, and for a moment our eyes meet. My respiratory system apparently doesn't know what to do with this information, and my throat jerks into a cough. Fir throws me a puzzled look, and I swallow and fall into step as we make our way past a cluster of carts blooming with silk flowers.

I collect my senses. Of course it's exciting to have a handsome young man look at you. I can understand why Jey enjoys it so much. But seeing Fir and Corvin in their upper-class costumes only reminds me of someone else—a real aristocrat who wears stateliness and leisure with equal ease.

But that evening in the Feather & Scuttle took place in another lifetime. Before Jey left. Before I became a Fog Walker. Would things be different now if I had stayed, admitted everything to Zahi? Would he have protected me and my family from the Onyx Staff?

No. I've read enough penny pulps to know the redwing never gets the prince. She gets the sword, or the bullet, or the noose.

Fir stops outside a shop with large, clean windows. "Remember," she whispers fiercely, leaning into my ear, "do not reveal what you are." As if I needed to be reminded.

"Tell as much truth as you can," Corvin says gently. "That makes it easier."

I stare into the shop window, a rainbow of beads, lace, and feathers adorning carved heads.

Mr. MONTROSE HORRO, HATTER
Fine HATS to Suit Discerning LADIES and GENTLEMEN
For All Occasions

The sign, with its bulbous carvings and garish paint, is as pompous as the fellow who greets us as we step into the airy shop.

"My young friends! What a pleasant surprise." The shop owner bows low, his starched shirt crackling and the gold chain of his pocket watch dangling flagrantly from his silk waistcoat. The shop smells of leather and stritch feathers, and faintly of soot. Corvin removes his hat.

The dapper little man addresses me. "And what a charming young lady you've brought with you." His voice is wheezy and slippery at the same time. "Monty Horro. Delighted." He takes my hand and kisses it, lingering a bit long for my taste. Especially since he just referred to me as a "charming young lady," which feels like it should be a description reserved for children. Then he straightens up and winks theatrically at Corvin, who looks rather horrified.

I'm really going to have to get used to all this social interaction, because I have absolutely no idea what is going on.

"May I present . . . uh, our friend," Fir says, an introduction that started off with a touch of showmanship but ended up a bit pathetic.

"Lin," Corvin says quickly. "Our friend Lin." I give him a questioning look and he shrugs.

Monty Horro casts a skeptical eye. "Lin, 'the girl with the blond hair.' Hmm. I see you've left yours at home today."

Lin. Horro is right—Lins are usually named for their golden hair, the color of linstalks. But after seeing the painting of the lin fields in Nara and Elena's apartment, a blanket of purple-blue blossoms bending in the spring wind, I know why Corvin chose it for me. My chest tingles. I always thought my eyes were wrong, that they should be dark like Jey's. But she and I have never been the same on the inside. Maybe my outside isn't so wrong after all.

Is this . . . my *name,* then?

I have a name?

Corvin is looking at me uncertainly, and even as a lump fills my throat, I give him a smile: *I like it.* He looks away, color flooding his cheeks.

"So you're here to save the city." Monty Horro is a man who gets to the point. "It's time to close up shop anyway, if you'll excuse me." He bustles over to the door and throws the bolt, pausing at the window before pulling the shade. "Shame, it's a fine day, the last sun for a year. But we shall just have to manage, yes? Come with me."

We follow him into a back room, which is as chaotic as the front room is orderly. He pulls a trunk from below a shelf of half-finished men's hats and seats himself, gesturing for us to take our seats on the rickety metal folding chairs that seem to designate various workstations around the room. We slide together, and Monty Horro oozes a smile at me.

"So you're going to a ball tonight, Miss Lin? Straight out of a fairy tale. Does it make your heart flutter?"

"I don't know what you mean," I say.

He shrugs. "It doesn't matter. As long as you beautiful young people keep lining up to do these rascals' dirty work for them."

"I hardly think—" Fir starts, but Horro waves dismissively. Corvin is silent, but I see a pulse going at the side of his jaw.

Monty Horro leans forward, speaking to me in a low, raspy voice. "All right, Miss Lin, how much do you know?"

I blink. "I . . . uh—"

"She knows the basics," Fir cuts in. "We just need any new information you have regarding the mission."

Horro sits back and shrugs. "The mission is the mission. Mol's Heart is somewhere on Roet Island, and we need to find it and destroy it before Bet-Nef's melt-brained followers awaken the volcano and sizzle us all. That's it."

His manner indicates I should know exactly what I'm supposed to do. But I'm done with delicacy. "Mol's Heart?" I cross my arms. "I have no idea where Mol's Heart is, how to destroy it, or what in wet hell it looks like."

Monty Horro's eyes narrow. "Trust me, you'll know it when you see it, my girl. It's protected by something that has killed everyone else who's been sent to find it."

I stiffen, forcing myself not to react outwardly to his words. There is something familiar about his voice. Could I have met him before? Unlikely; I haven't met many people. Still, the way his breath wheezes like a bellows with a hole—it's distinct, and it tickles my memory.

Fir curls her head back. "Surely our contact there has learned *something*."

Horro's face darkens. "In my opinion, she's gotten too close to the situation. But apparently, she has made progress. I am to meet with her when we arrive."

My memory snaps into focus. The voices I overheard from under the dodder bush in the Empress's private garden—one of them was Monty Horro's. My spine sparks as I look at him, this round little hatmaker who exudes an almost comical self-importance. I remember the fear in the young woman's voice when he threatened her.

"What about the Black Thorn?" Corvin asks. "He'll be protecting the Heart, as well."

"I'll say it again," Horro snaps. "He doesn't exist. And if he does exist, he's a man. No more."

Corvin nods, but his expression is troubled. Who or what is the Black Thorn? I want to ask, but Horro's tone on the matter was quite final.

"Someone knows," Fir says. "Someone on that island knows where the Heart is." She sighs her frustration.

Monty Horro turns his attention to me. "You'll come with me, as my assistant. You'll have to wear what you have on, I suppose. Not very festive, really." He looks me up and down. "But you need to lose that scarf, my dear. Collars are being worn unbuttoned to the clavicle at present. You want that sensuous little neck of yours peeking through."

"Sorry," I say, putting a hand to my throat. "This has to stay on."

Horro frowns. "Well, can we at least change the color? Black makes you look like an assassin."

I give him what I hope is a mysterious look. "I could be an assassin."

He chuckles and taps my nose with a bejeweled finger. "So could I. And guess which one of us they won't see coming?"

I swallow, and the gash on my neck twinges.

"Lin isn't going after a target," Corvin says. "She's there for the Heart, nothing more."

Horro huffs. "She's there to do her job, whatever that entails." He looks at me again. "I think your best shot at this point is to hope either the Commandant or one of his sons has a penchant for brunettes, my dear."

"No." Corvin's voice is edged now. "We're not asking her to do anything she doesn't want to do."

"You've seen the Admirable Zahi Zan." Horro's tone is light, and he smirks. "Of course she wants to." He winks mischievously at me, which makes my stomach squirm.

"I thought Zahi Zan was studying at the Temple of Rasus?" I hope my face doesn't look as ashen as it feels.

"You see?" Horro waves a finger at Corvin. "She's very informed."

"He'll be at Crepuscule," Fir says. "All the nobility will be there."

Of course he will. "The plan won't work," I say. "I can't go to Crepuscule if Zahi Zan will be there. He—he knows me."

The other three turn to me, and I feel as if even the carved heads that dot the room are staring. "What in blazes do you mean?" Horro asks.

Corvin puts a hand on my forearm. *Tell as much truth as you can.* "I—I sometimes dust the peonies on Restlight. My father is one of the master gardeners on Roet Island."

Horro gives me a fiery look. "Is your father sympathetic to our cause?"

I pause. I hadn't thought about whether Papa would approve of my killing a god. A plant, no. But a god? I'm not sure. "He's away," I say. "Tending to the wheat blight in the east." I sense a subtle release of tension from Corvin and Fir.

"That's just as well," Horro says. "Now, what is this nonsense about knowing the Empress's son? Will he recognize you?"

I avoid the others' eyes. "Yes."

Horro frowns. "Are you absolutely—?"

"*Yes.*"

"It doesn't matter," Fir says. "Your identities will be concealed, after all."

Horro eyes her, but nods. "It's risky, but you're right. Although it would be much simpler to bring along an unknown. Or send that idiot layabout, Sunny."

"It must be Lin," Corvin says. "She has the training."

Horro shrugs. "I just do what Nara says." He rises, and we follow suit. "Let's do something extraordinarily foolish, shall we? I'll have my carriage brought around. I just need to collect our disguises." He turns to me. "I'll be back for you in a moment, my dear."

What? Go with *him*? And did he say "disguises"? I blink my reluctance at Fir, who ignores me. Monty Horro gives a neat, jerky bow, and we take our leave. I am shaken, wobbling on my high heels, and Corvin takes my arm and steers me gently out of the shop.

Back on the busy street, we wait for Horro to return with his carriage. Corvin leans against the shiny iron gate that guards a tidy alleyway. I turn to him. "I've had enough of disguises, I'll have you know."

Fir laughs. "Not real disguises, princess. Costumes."

"Costumes!"

Fir smirks. "It's a costume party."

"Mol's cursed firehole!" I lean next to Corvin, the metal warm through my clothes.

"I heard Monty say he got you a fetching little ensemble," Fir says. "Lady Pink Petals the Unclothed. Not much more than an elaborate wig, I understand. And some . . . foliage."

"Why, Fir," I say lightly, "you've acquired a sense of humor. Did you cut someone's throat for it?"

Fir snorts. "Anyway," she says, "I hope you've bathed recently."

"I haven't." Though I wish I had; the light fog is already dampening my clothes.

A carriage, gleaming yellow in the tilted beams of the low sun, clatters up outside the shop. In front, two cantankerous-looking stritches with festive red satin ribbons around their necks shuffle their clawed feet impatiently.

A carriage. I have read about them, certainly. I have seen them rolling by on the street. But why does this one seem so large and unstable? Fir goes to talk with the driver.

Corvin's face is grave. "Remember, Horro doesn't know about you."

"What I am."

"Who you are," he says. "He doesn't know to protect you from the bonescorch orchis." He looks into my eyes. "Keep away from it. It will reveal you."

I grunt in frustration. "I don't even know where it is!"

He leans against the gate. "Our spy says it is well protected, and will only be brought out to be unveiled by the Empress. Just stay away."

"I'll try."

"Remember what I said before," he murmurs. "It's your choice to do this."

I fold my arms. "Not much of a choice, is it? If it can only be done by a—me. A Lin."

"I love my sister," he says quietly, "but she is not always right."

I can't make sense of his grim expression. Surely this will be a dangerous undertaking, but there is something else simmering under his surface. "Do you believe in this cult of Bet-Nef?" I ask him. "I mean, are they really up to what Nara says they're up to?"

He nods. "Certainly they are. We have been spying on them for months. Thanks to you, now we know the executions that have been taking place are orchestrated by the Onyx Staff himself. He has sown fear of redwings into the priests of the Temple."

He studies me. "And you don't think it was your imagination that almost kicked the life out of me in that alley, do you?"

"No." I see Fir peering across the street, her shoulders rigid. Always vigilant. "And I'm—sorry about that."

Corvin gives me a half smile. "I feel more foolish about it than anything. You didn't need my protection. Not mine nor anyone else's."

"That's not true," I say softly.

"I just," he begins, "I feel there is something Nara isn't telling us."

I give him a hard look. "You think she's lying? And I'm going in there to risk my life?"

"No." I have his full attention now. "No, she's not lying. There's just so much we don't know. So much we can't know until it's done." He touches my arm. "Until it's done by a Lin."

I smile. "Thanks for my name, by the way."

He leans back against the fence, his gaze elsewhere. "You don't have to keep it."

"It's the only one I have," I say.

"Be careful." Corvin brings his attention back to me. "Zahi Zan is not to be trusted."

"Don't worry." I put my hands in my pockets. "I can handle Zahi Zan." The reality settles on my shoulders, and I shiver even in this warm mist. The Copper Palace. The grass. The peonies.

And . . . a heart?

Fir comes over. "Horro should be back any moment. You'd better get in. Best not stand in the street if you don't have to." She opens the door to the carriage, and a metal step unfolds. I peer into the shadowy compartment. After a moment, she asks, "What's the matter? Have you never ridden in one of these?"

"Not really."

"Not really?"

"No."

Corvin puts a hand on the door. "Are you all right?"

This is ridiculous. I'm fine. *I'm fine.* "I, uh . . . I guess I just don't like the idea of not having control over where I'm going." I'm doing this all backwards. I should be telling myself the truth and lying to them.

Corvin steps into the carriage, which creaks and rocks with his weight. "I understand," he says, extending a hand. "Look, it's not going anywhere yet. Come sit inside for a minute. You'll get used to it."

I inhale and entwine my fingers with his, and he gives me a reassuring nod. But just as I put a toe onto the metal step, Monty Horro's voice bark-wheezes through the street.

"Get in, get in! Rasus, we're running late." He reaches us, lugging a leather bag and wearing an outfit even more ridiculous than his last one. I have no idea who he is supposed to be dressed as—I can't imagine that anyone in history or literature has voluntarily sported such a violently golden duster coat and sky-high tendriled collar. "What do you think you're doing?" the vision says, pointing at Corvin inside the carriage. "Get out of there. This isn't a taxi service." He looks at Fir. "You two follow us in. Be aristocrats, all right? But don't make too much of yourselves. Those invitations were not easy to come by, and they won't hold up under scrutiny."

Fir backs out of Horro's way as Corvin swings open the little door on the other side of the carriage and jumps down. Before I can process what is happening, Monty Horro has pushed me and his bag inside, clambered onto the seat across from me, and called to the driver to get going. We lurch forward and I'm tossed against the backrest. By the time I've arranged myself enough to look out the window, we've bumped around a corner and Corvin and Fir are no longer in sight.

Nausea hits. I close my eyes. How do people do this on a regular basis?

"Here's your costume." Horro throws a bag my way. His gold satin duster gleams dully in the dirty light from the windows.

"Very well."

He taps his fingers on his knee. "Go on, then."

My guts wrench as we turn another corner. "Is it safe to change clothes in a moving carriage?"

Horro snorts. "Open the bag, you little fathead." I do so, and find only a glittering red mask. "We don't need to win the costume contest," he says. "We just need you not to be recognized."

"Ah. Of course." I slide the mask over my face, pulling the ribbon tight at the back. Stomach flipping, I attempt to smile. "How do I look?"

"Nondescript," he says, "which is just what we want." He leans forward. "Remember, this is our last chance. And if Nara says it has to be you, then it has to be you. I don't question her. She's all that stands between this city and destruction, so you sure as wet hell better make her proud or I'll gut you myself. Now, listen, the Onyx Staff will make his move when the star Bel rises. You have until then to find and destroy the Heart. If you fail—well, I happen to enjoy not having my home burned to the ground."

Having one's home burn to the ground is certainly not enjoyable, as I well know. But being burn-suffocated by lava is worse. Horro doesn't even mention the people of this city who wouldn't be able to get out in time should Mol erupt.

I turn my head. None of this seems real. I am caught up in mythology. But perhaps that is the only reason I exist. I would be impossible in the real world.

"As my assistant, you will accompany me to the salon when we arrive." Horro adjusts his lace cuffs as we rattle along. "I will be attending to Her Imperial Majesty, and I will send you off on some trivial errand. Follow the stritch path outside the gates to the Pool of the Long Angel. Sunny will meet you there—she assures me she has made progress." His eyes narrow. "Make sure you get her to open up. Someone at the palace knows where the Heart is. Honestly," he mutters, "we should just take the Empress's prettyboy son and *slice* the information out of him."

I watch the gray streets of Caldaras City shudder by, flashes of misty bricks and faceless people. It's difficult to envision something as fierce and bright as a wave of lava existing here. None of it— the Heart, the cult of Bet-Nef, Mol—even seems possible. The Deep Dark is years, eons away, not hours. But now, with Monty Horro's callous words still hissing in my ear, my chest burns with a new determination.

No one is going to put their hands on Zahi Zan.

The servants are dressed in glass-smooth white jumpsuits; there is no need for dusters here, since the ash is kept at bay. They wear their hair short, as their station demands, combed and stiff like dolls' hair. A man extends a white-gloved hand to assist Monty

Horro down from the carriage, which bumps and tosses with his every movement, and a woman pulls the leather bag from under the seat. No one assists me as I clamber awkwardly out of the compartment. It's just as well.

As I step into low sunlight, I am overwhelmed again by the crispness and color of Roet Island. Green lawns, decadent flowers, a sky more blue than anything real has the right to be. The extravagance of it all is dizzying. Blood blossoms through my heart again and again as I stare, the rhythm of it in my ears, the slosh of its movement buzzing my veins. *This is lust,* I realize. I lust after this place.

Even though Crepuscule isn't set to begin for a few hours, the aristocracy has come out to watch the sun set. The lawns, dotted with Zahi's friends the last time I was here, are already teeming with brightly colored guests of all ages, many of them hiding behind jeweled masks or flaunting feathered collars or wide, shimmering wings. I look down at my silk shirt . . . adequate.

"Bring my bag." Monty Horro tosses the order at me before being whisked away by the servants—or whisking the servants away—through an elegant doorway that arches two stories up the gleaming copper façade of the palace. Our driver barks the stritches to action, and they pull the yellow carriage away. I am not sad to see it go.

Horro's leather bag is cumbersome, but I manage to navigate the large doorway and totter after him.

Despite its age—two centuries at least, if one doesn't count the modernizations—the Copper Palace doesn't feel like a relic. The long entrance hall that greets me shimmers with life. The last of this year's naked sunlight unabashedly pushes itself in through the clear, high windows of the entrance hall, illuminating wide stone flower beds and little trees. In the central fountain, boiling water streams endlessly from the outstretched hands of a woman on the back of what is surely the world's most amiable-looking stritch. A landscape of fat lilies floats below, and hardy little hot-budges, who don't mind the steam, sit happily on the fountain's bulges and edges, tweeting and puffing their feathers.

Past the fountain, Monty Horro and the servants veer left, and I follow them into a high-ceilinged room filled with gilded furniture and a floor extravagantly decorated with pictures of animals, gardens, and stars. The walls are tall mirrors alternating with tall windows. Out of the corner of my eye, I can't quite tell if my reflection is standing in this room or amid the rainbow of flowers that cluster outside in the setting sun.

"Over here, over here," Horro says impatiently, beckoning me. I set the leather bag between the front legs of a purple lion painted on the floor next to him. He waves the two servants away and points. "I need my things. Get my things out. The Empress will be here any moment for her mask." I click open the bag and pull out a silk-wrapped box. "There, there!" Horro points to a delicate side table, and I set the box down and start removing the bag's other contents—sewing supplies, a pot of glue, a pair of sharp scissors.

A few minutes later, we are joined by a group of people who emerge from an elaborate mirrored doorway. The procession reminds me of the priest-at-the-altar flower that lords over a particularly splendid corner of the Dome. But instead of a brilliant, pollen-laden stalk, a woman rises at the center of this botanical tableau, the satin of her pale lavender sleeves lustrous in the mirrored sunset. Surrounding her, an assemblage of white-clad attendants has gathered, their bodies curved like the flower's broad ivory petals.

The lavender woman is tall, with thick dark eyebrows and a nose whose bridge juts out at the top and descends in a nearly vertical line. She walks with the casual confidence of the very powerful. The Empress.

Monty Horro bustles over to her, fingers steepled and lips jutting with self-importance.

"Welcome, Mr. Horro," the Empress says. "Thank you for attending to my disguise for the evening."

"Your Imperial Majesty," Horro wheezes. "It is an honor to see you again. I hope you will be pleased with the quality and appearance of the mask I have designed for this momentous event."

The Empress turns a bland smile; then her gaze finds me. I don't have to recall the chapters I've read on etiquette; under that authoritative gaze, my arms straighten and my body bends at the waist out of sheer instinct.

She is still watching me when I come out of my bow. "We haven't been introduced, have we?" she says. I shudder. *Eyes again, so many eyes out here in the world.*

Monty Horro gestures. "This is my assistant, Lin."

I smile politely, concentrating on appearing normal.

"I see you have already donned your disguise for the festivities," the Empress says, and I involuntarily put a hand to my glittering red mask. I sense Horro stiffen, but the Empress offers no further comment and turns her attention to the silk-covered box on the gilded end table.

"We have chosen a lustrous satin, as you will see," Monty

Horro starts, undoing the box's fussy ribbon. "And before we begin"—he shoots me a look—"perhaps I might ask my assistant to go and fetch—" He cuts off abruptly when the door from the entrance hall opens and a man strides into the salon. He is tall and worm thin, with reddish, curly hair that hangs from the bald dome of his head like water weeds clinging to a stone. His bearing is that of nobility, but he wears a shade of green that, if it were rolled in dirt and boiled, might resemble the utilitarian green the gardeners wear. This man, then, must be Master Fibbori, the Head Gardener of Roet Island.

Who knows Jey.

I turn away quickly, arranging the pincushion and scissors and measuring tape on a long side table. I keep my back to the Head Gardener, my eyes on the mirror in front of me.

"Ah, Master Fibbori," the Empress says evenly. "I was expecting you in the Tea Room half an hour ago. I trust nothing is amiss?"

Master Fibbori clears his throat. "I regret, Your Majesty, that . . ."

"That what?" the Empress asks. "My goodness, you're distressingly peaked."

"I apologize, Your Majesty," Fibbori says. "I— It's better if I show you." He turns to the door. "Onna!"

Onna, the girl I taught to dust the peonies. This just keeps getting better. I watch the mirror and keep still. Onna steps through the doorway, a good deal more drawn and miserable than when I last saw her. She clutches a pot containing what looks like a burning twig.

I lean forward, peering into the mirror as Onna moves into

the room. What she holds is not a burning twig after all, but the most extraordinary flower I've ever seen. Its stem is long and black, with the sheen and texture of coal. Its petals—I squint—its few petals, arranged mostly vertically, are wide and vibrantly orange with shredded edges, and they *glow,* dancing in the air like flames.

But the main stalk of the plant juts at a severe angle, twisted and unsettling as a broken leg.

I turn around, mesmerized. The structure and the shape of this plant's leaves are a bit like the common bluebird orchis I have at home, but this one is bigger and wilder, with more audacious curves and curls. The leaves perk up and glow a little more strongly as I look at them.

My muscles go rigid. *This is the bonescorch orchis.* Instinctively, I grab the scissors and hold them at my side.

"Is this my orchis?" The Empress's voice is even. I am not well enough acquainted with her to know whether this is dangerous.

"Yes, Your Majesty," Fibbori says, clasping his hands. "There has been an accident."

"That is plain. What do you plan to do about it?"

I hold my breath. The broken plant gleams weakly, the bulk of its body hanging from the shiny base of the black stalk by mere splinters. No one remarks on the glowing leaves—apparently, even if the legend is true, this bonescorch orchis is too damaged to respond to me much. I am safe, for now, from the plant that would betray me. It is an amazing stroke of luck.

And yet, when the beautiful flame leaves start to flicker as though they know they are dying, my heart grieves.

Onna adjusts the pot, pulling at a strip of burlap and rattling, "It's a simple matter of mending the stalk, Your Majesty—" She nearly drops the cloth. Master Fibbori's mouth hardens, but Onna continues blathering, her face flushed. "We apply a strip of quality binding cloth—thusly—and secure it, and—"

"Like a tomato plant," the Empress says with an undercurrent of disapproval.

Master Fibbori nods, a little muscle in his jaw pulsing. He helps Onna wind the burlap as the orchis crunches and flutters. The Empress watches, silent and expressionless, and Monty Horro looks delightfully scandalized.

But I feel sick. The flame leaves of this stunning plant are almost dark. The sound of the broken halves of the black stalk being ground against each other as the burlap forces them into place sets my nerves on edge. I may not know this bonescorch well, but I know orchises, and they are nothing like tomato plants.

I once vowed to find this orchis and pull it out by its traitorous roots. Now, it is dying, and all I need to do is let it. But everything in me cries out in protest. Every inch of my soul scratches under my skin; my legs and fingers ache to do something. My father wouldn't let them do this horrific, lethal surgery on an orchis as noble as this. And I can't stand by and watch, either.

Clutching the scissors, I slip past everyone and hurry to the fountain in the entryway. A good dip in the boiling water, and the blades come out shining and sanitary. No one notices me as I stride back. Master Fibbori and Onna are too busy wrestling with fear and dirty burlap, Monty Horro is too busy watching them with amusement, and Her Majesty and her flock of servants are too busy sitting in judgment.

I slide over to the pot, and in one quick movement, I thrust the shears forward and cut the plant off at its base. The two halves of black stem and a riot of curving, nearly dark leaves fall uncer-emoniously to the floor, leaving only a tiny nub protruding from the soil.

Silence descends. Horro and Onna gape at me. Fibbori says nothing, but his beady eyes flash.

The Empress turns to me, frowning. "*Who* did you say you were?"

There is something familiar about her regard—that serene self-assurance that emanates from those who have a great deal of power. I saw it in Zahi Zan, and in the Onyx Staff as well.

I drop my hands to my sides, the shears bumping my leg. "My name is Lin, Your Majesty." The people around me are hardly breathing. Through the eerie quiet, I can hear faint birdsong and moving water from the entrance hall.

The Empress looks at the tattered remains of the plant at my feet. "I would be interested in hearing, Miss Lin, why you have chosen to cut down, before my very eyes, a rare example of the most valuable botanical species in Caldaras, especially given the fact that the Commandant and I were expecting it to be the centerpiece of tonight's once-in-a-millennium celebration."

To his credit, Monty Horro steps forward. "Your Majesty, I take full responsibility for this. Lin is my apprentice. Her de-struction of the orchis is on my head." His voice drips danger.

The Empress regards him briefly, then returns her focus to me but doesn't speak.

An unconvincing throat clearing disturbs the atmosphere, and we all look at Master Fibbori, who is frowning at me. "Actually, Your Majesty"—he turns to her—"the orchis is not destroyed."

The Empress raises a dark eyebrow.

"Upon further consideration," Fibbori continues, "I believe cutting it off at the base may be its best hope of recovery." There is distaste in his tone. "You see, the bonescorch—all orchises—are susceptible to infection when they are damaged. If the injury is severe enough, a sterile severing as close to the roots as possible is the wisest course of action."

"I see." The Empress gives me a thoughtful look. "In that case—well done, Miss Lin. It is a shame not to have the orchis to unveil at Crepuscule, but at least we have not lost it altogether." She purses her lips. "You might consider employment working with plants instead of hats." She unbuttons a lavender fan from her waist, flips it open, and says, "Now, Mr. Horro, tell me about the new beading technique you mentioned."

"Certainly, Your Majesty," Horro says, giving her a quick, deferential nod. "Miss Lin, would you mind very much gathering just a few fresh bluelet blossoms? If you can find any, that is. Go on." He shoos me, and at last I am free to meet Sunny by the Long Angel Pool.

"Miss Lin," a commanding voice says as I reach the door. I turn around. "I wonder," the Empress goes on, "if, while you are out, you could let my son Zahi know that Mr. Horro has arrived with a disguise for him? I believe you will find him in the hedge maze. Thank you."

I nod and hurry from the room as my blood turns icy. *Damn.* I can't disobey the Empress. I can only hope the twilight and my mask will hide my identity from Zahi Zan. But what will I say if he recognizes me? What will I do if he doesn't?

The entrance hall is bustling now as guests make their way into what I suspect is some kind of grand ballroom at the other end. I catch a glimpse of it—bright, cavernous, draped in copper fabric and golden flowers.

A hand touches my shoulder. Master Fibbori has followed me from the room, and now stands in the shadow of a tall flower bed, holding the orchis pot. He gives me an inscrutable look. "Miss . . . Lin, is it? Funny, you remind me very strongly of one of my less talented undergardeners."

I stick out my chin. "You're not going to scold me for saving that plant, are you?"

He considers me for a moment. "No," he says. "But I must ask you a question. How certain were you that you were doing the right thing?"

I shrug. "I've got a bluebird orchis at home. That's what I would have done for it."

He nods. "Logical. Tell me, what do you know about the bone-scorch?" He gestures to the severed stalk and withered leaves like dead birds lying on the pot's soil.

"Truly, not very much."

"Well," he says, "the specimen you saved today is the only one that has ever been found. It is more valuable than the whole of the Copper Palace. More valuable than all the treasures of Rasus."

I inhale. "I . . . that makes sense, I suppose."

"Yes," Fibbori says. "And if you had dared harm it in front of Her Imperial Majesty, your punishment would have been instant death."

"Boiling?" I ask hopefully.

"Hanging," he says.

"Rasus's rotten teeth," I mutter before I can stop myself. "Well, it's a good thing I didn't kill it."

"Rasus's rotten teeth indeed." Master Fibbori's voice is stern, but there is a hint of a smile underneath.

I leave the entrance hall's smells of copper, water, and tidy blooms for the outdoor scents of grass and night flowers. The sun set quickly, though Crepuscule won't officially begin until the rise of Bel. The brightest object in the night sky, Bel is known as the Queen of the Stars because she will rule for the next year.

As I move away from the Copper Palace, there are few people left on the lawns. The moon is out, and by its light I see a charming hedge maze in a corner of the grounds. The Empress said Zahi would be there.

I've never really seen moonlight before—just the weak, diluted stuff that drizzles its way through the clouds Mol spits at us in the lower city. But this moonlight is unfiltered, potent. As I walk among the flowers, it changes the color of my skin and the palace walls and the petals. A little breeze sweeps over the grass and flower beds in playful waves. It strokes my hair, lifting and winding the strands, prickling my scalp.

I know why Mol left his heart here; already this place tugs at my own. I follow the sound of water to the maze. The dark, bluish leaves of the hedges are a deeper blue at night, the walls of a secret magical land straight out of a Mother May story. As I enter the corridors of the maze, the silty ground under my feet as soft as feathers, I half expect to find an Other prince waiting there.

I smile. *Maybe I am turning into Jey.* My smile fades quickly, however. Jey is done with fairy tales now. Done with me.

My fingers trace the contours of the living walls as I venture farther in. Nearby I hear voices intermingled with the sound of a fountain burbling. My first thought is to turn away. But I pause.

I was sent to fetch Zahi Zan. If I do not, it will cause suspicion. And my search for the Heart is more important than anything else; I can't jeopardize it.

I hold my breath and take a few careful steps closer until I turn a corner to find a large open space—the center of the maze.

Before me, tiny streams of water shoot upward and fall back into a pool ringed by wide stone ledges. The air is misty here, but with water vapor, not ash. Two people sit next to the pool with their backs to me, their shoulders touching, heads close together. Laughter. A young woman turns briefly to toss a flower—a delicate pearl avens, I think—into the pool behind her. Her smile is lovely, her features perfect.

She was wearing butter yellow the day I saw her with Zahi Zan on the lawn.

It is him again, next to her. I know him even from here. His hair is loose. He leans back, draped over the stone with the placid air of ownership, and says something I can't make out. The Butter Yellow Girl laughs again and rests her head on his shoulder.

I lean against the hedge. "Zahi Zan!"

Two faces turn to me. Zahi squints into the shadows. "Hello?"

"Your mother wants you in the salon! Your mask is here."

As I turn away, I hear the Butter Yellow Girl say, "Was that a servant?"

My stomach suddenly aching, I make my way back through the hedge maze. I run across the lawn, past a row of stone servants' huts that look like an enormous, sleeping caterpillar, and past the glass dome of the Empress's garden. Hope I didn't know I had gushes away in a torrent. I have lied to myself, haven't I? Despite the cult of Bet-Nef and the Fog Walkers and *knowing* that I must destroy Mol's Heart to save Caldaras City, as I crossed the Jade Bridge this evening in that awful carriage, there was a part of me that only wanted to see Zahi Zan again.

My guts knotted, I reach the curving wall that guards the grounds of the Copper Palace. Carriages arrive one after another down the sandstone road, aristocrats in flamboyant attire alighting, laughing, venturing inside. I look out over the lawns, where the light from the palace can't reach, and the once-bright memory of Zahi's face so close to mine, his arms around me, is merely another shadow in this ghostly landscape. Now, when I shut my eyes, I am met with a brighter memory, of rippling water and a wide stone ledge and two heads very close together. *I've seen him now, haven't I?*

What did I imagine would happen? I should have known as soon as I noticed him for the first time, cutting the grass in his rust-colored waistcoat, a prince disguised as a peasant. As beautiful and expensive as a bonescorch orchis.

I have been whipped, boiled, shot, isolated, and threatened. But it is only now, as I press my face into the carved jade arch that marks the edge of the grounds, that my eyebrows crinkle, the corners of my mouth tense, and tears slither down my cheeks in a ridiculous display of self-pity.

What disdain I used to have for Jey when she would come home with broken heart after broken heart, yet look at me now. I have to save the city from fiery annihilation, and I'm weeping for Zahi Zan.

Balderdash, I say to myself in my best Elena voice.

The air is wet and thick in the jungle outside the palace walls. Here everything is as messy and untamed as the Empress's gardens are orderly and manicured. Despite myself, I am swept up in the excitement this wild place carries, gawking at all the strange life—twisting vines in moonlit greens and blues, brazen, ragged flowers, and insects like jewels, engorged with nectar. While the Dome and Copper Palace boast species from all over Caldaras, the jungle of Roet Island is inhabited entirely by native specimens—plants and animals who belong here. It's strange, but part of me feels like I belong here, too.

I weave in and out of bent trees and broad, slick leaves, following the path Horro said would be there. It ends at a shadowy depression of lumpy black stone that contains stagnant water cool enough to drink. Next to the pool is a toppled, overgrown statue— the Long Angel, one clawed foot sticking out from a generous robe. I seat myself on its mossy hip and wait. All I know about my fellow infiltrator is that she will meet me here.

It's her footsteps I hear first. No wild creature would be so obvious, swishing its way along the path, rustling the underbrush. I rise, wiping condensation from my face. A cluster of big, rubbery leaves shudders, and my contact emerges.

I freeze.

"You must be Lin," the Butter Yellow Girl says. "I'm Sunny."

Of course you are. Up close, she is as beautiful as a wild stardrop, with flawless skin and shiny hair. She looks at me appraisingly as I stammer an unintelligible greeting.

"Where did Monty find you?" she asks, then narrows her eyes. "Have I seen you before?"

"Perhaps," I say, collecting myself. "And Nara found me, not Monty."

Her plucked eyebrows arch dramatically at me. "You're in thick, then." A conspiratorial smile. "Good for you."

I nod. "Just another Fog Walker, I guess."

"You are?" Sunny tilts her head in surprise. "I thought you were an agent. I don't think I've ever seen a Fog Walker. Except Fir, who set me up with a nobleman agent who passed me off as his daughter. That was my way onto the island, you see. Most of us are nobility or close to it." She doesn't say it with pride. The pride of generations of aristocracy is so thick in her bones, it doesn't need to creep into her voice.

I change my tune. "Oh, aren't we official Fog Walkers? I guess I'm confused. But yes, I'm posing as Monty Horro's assistant."

Sunny sits on the overturned statue of the Long Angel and I join her. "I know where the Heart is." She speaks in a low voice, as if the mossy trees might betray us. "But it is well hidden—and protected."

"So I would imagine," I say. Will I be able to protect myself? Nara thinks so; she knows what I did to the priests in the alley. She doesn't know I was utterly useless in the Temple, where my enemies were actually prepared to face me.

Sunny inches closer to me. "I've been talking to Zahi—Zahi Zan, you know, the Empress's second son"—*oh, I know*—"and it's taken me a while, but I finally got it out of him. He's, uh, he's less guarded when he's . . . drowsy."

She must be drugging him. I'm going to choose to believe she's drugging him.

"Anyway," Sunny continues, "I got him talking about the secrets of the island, and he let slip that there's a hidden underground passage in the Empress's personal garden. And he told me *never to go down there.* Quite telling, yes? The perfect hiding place!"

"How revealing," I say flatly. "Are you sure you weren't reading a penny pulp?"

Sunny crosses her arms. Roet Island's impossible moonlight drips green and gold through the leaves onto her face as she studies me. "Look, it's the best lead we've got. Nara's agents have thoroughly combed this island. We've been planted here for months, and nothing. Sometimes I think she should listen to the old legends, try to get help from one of those—*things.*" She hacks out a bitter laugh. "It's crazy, isn't it?"

"I— One of what things? You mean a redwing?" I force a laugh, but the hair on my arms tingles *danger.* "I'm still surprised people actually believe any exist. I mean, I don't know about you, but I haven't exactly seen any Others wandering the streets of Caldaras City."

Sunny nods, her shoulders relaxing. She flicks a green insect off her forearm. "But if we don't find the Heart . . . The Others do exist, you know. Of course you know. What am I saying? That's why you're here. I just— It's vital we find it."

I don't know what to do with the silence she wraps around the words that would come next. Her eyes are distant. Jey would prod and peel. But I'm not Jey, so I just wait.

After a few moments of stillness, Sunny says, "Horro doesn't realize it; he's bent as an old pipe and twice as mean. But I want you to know—I'm in this entirely." She takes my hand. "I won't let everyone down like the others have. You see, I'm—I'm a twin myself. Not an unmarked human twin. I'm one of *them.*"

Be careful. I grip every nerve in my face to show the correct amount of surprise. I mustn't appear overeager to talk about it, even though a bright pinprick in my brain screams for answers.

The first words out of my mouth are the wrong ones. "Where is your sister?"

She stiffens. "You mean the beast. It was destroyed, of course, shortly after it was born. By the Other creature who seduced my mother."

"Your father."

Sunny looks at me with a new hardness. "He was technically my father, just as that monster was technically my brother."

Another redwing. A boy who would have been my age. One who didn't get smuggled into the city in a raptor basket. One who spent most of his short life underwater, dying, rather than under glass. I turn my eyes skyward, focusing on the glittering canopy, willing the moisture in my lower lids to recede back into my body before Sunny notices it.

"It broke my mother's heart, you know," she says. "She thought she was prepared. But the damned thing looked so much like a *baby.*"

I stand, twisting my arms in front of me, behind me, in front of me. "So what is our next step?"

Sunny stands, as well, smoothing bits of bark and leaves from her satiny yellow pants. "I have a date for Crepuscule. I'll see if I can get anything else out of Zahi, but my suspicion is you're on your own from here." She extends a hand, which I take. "Death to Mol, sister," she says. "Find his burning Heart and squeeze it until it's black."

No *Save the city?* Or *Stop the Beautiful Ones?* Just—Death to Mol? I stare at her, with what expression I have no idea. Mol may be a god, or he may be only a volcano, but there is no burning heart in Caldaras I would relish extinguishing. I will do it only for the sake of my home and those who live here. As I look into Sunny's cruel eyes, I finally understand where Nara finds her "agents." They are from the darkest edges of society—not the garbage-strewn alleys of Caldaras City, but its gilded, curving towers, where hatred is cultivated and prized.

fifteen

A glistening green nightmare and a giant snake pull me aside as I step through the jade arch and onto the grounds of the Copper Palace.

"Did you choose that costume to complement your forked tongue?" I ask as Fir slides off her mask.

"I chose it because it's not bulky," she says, eyeing my mask. "Or sparkly. What did Sunny say?"

"Sunny is a bit scary." I follow them into the dark corner of a geometric hedge sculpture. "As is that thing that is accompanying us."

Fir reaches over and pulls off the green nightmare's face to reveal Corvin looking a little sweaty. "I'm supposed to be Ver," he says.

I consider him. "Maybe after a hard night in the forest."

"Or as a salad," Fir says, and I snicker.

"Yes, fine." Corvin tosses his mask onto the lawn. "So what's our next move?"

I lower my voice. "Sunny says there's a secret passageway in the Commandant's private garden. So we need to—"

" 'Snake,' I said, not 'lake'!" a voice croaks through the night air. "Sssssssnake! You know, your lonely mum's best friend!"

"Oh, sweet Ver," Corvin mutters, and I follow his gaze. In front of the palace, amid all the fine carriages, a small person wearing a horrible coat and a paper sack on its head is yelling at one of the palace servants. "How in blazes would you even *dress* as a lake? You're going to be *in* the lake in a minute, buddy—"

"Hey!" Corvin yells.

The sack turns toward us at the sound of his voice. "Oh, there they are. Have a nice evening, soldier." It shuffles over as we try to retreat farther into the shadows of the hedge sculpture.

"For the love of all that's on fire," Fir says. "Take that ridiculous bag off your head." She snatches the paper sack to reveal the filthy white hair and milky eyes of Teppa the Fowl.

Corvin sighs. "I thought Nara was going to sneak you in as a cook?"

Teppa shrugs. "They wouldn't buy it for some reason. But I found this bag and I improvised. That fathead guard at the gate gave me some lip, but I said, 'I'm clean, friend! Got my costume on and everything! I got no weapons! Nothing! Strip me down and search all my crevices!' I meant it, too, got my pants halfway off and everything, and I guess that was good enough for him, because he just escorted me through like a fine lady." She puts her hands on her hips. "So where are we headed?"

Teppa makes short work of the arched golden doors to the Empress's private garden. Corvin, Fir, and I stand strategically to hide her from view while she rattles the lock and grumbles, but there are enough people wandering the grounds to make us nervous. Luckily, after a few moments, a smooth click tells us our way is open.

"I'll keep watch out here," Teppa says, looking shifty.

"I'm sure you'll keep a close eye on all the free champagne, anyway," Fir says over her shoulder as we pass through the doors.

"Free champagne?"

I close the golden door behind me, and Teppa is already gone.

Corvin laughs. "We figured we might have to get into a part of the palace that isn't open to the public. It was always a possibility. So that's what we paid her for—to get us in."

"And now that we're in, we can just fend for ourselves, is that it?" I say.

"That's Teppa." He shrugs.

I step onto the path of brass stones, letting my mask fall to the ground. Even in shadow and silence, the Empress's garden is breathtaking. The colors are different at night. It still feels like a kaleidoscope, but instead of an array of jewel shards in all hues, it is set with a thousand subtly different pieces of one exquisite blue gemstone. I let my eyes travel the path, up the trunks of the slender trees, in and around the untidy shrubs.

"So where do we look?" Fir asks. Deduction isn't exactly her strong suit, unless she is solving the mystery of where the sharp end of her saber will go next.

Corvin takes a few steps and brushes the tip of a stone archer's arrow with his fingers. "If it's a secret the Commandant wants kept from the undergardeners and tourists, it won't be anywhere that requires maintenance or invites scrutiny."

I close my eyes. "It will be somewhere unchanging."

"Let's spread out," Corvin says, and Fir and I nod.

I follow the path of brass stones to the right, past a dodder bush whose flowers reach high into the air. Around a curve, a stone bench in the shape of a giant feather sits empty amid a riot of gangly morning wisp flowers. Then I head through a little grove of miniature evergreen trees no taller than my head, each one pruned to symmetrical perfection.

The garden, while magnificent, is not enormous, and I can hear the rustles and crunches of Corvin making his way around the other side and Fir cutting across the middle. I stop when I reach the waterfall that streams down the dome into a brass pool. The wide sheet of water against the glass forms vast, ever-changing images of light and dark that hold me spellbound.

I stare into the brass pool, where the water keeps pouring but never overflows, disappearing into a wide grate. Despite its simple appearance, with no complex carving or precious materials, this is perhaps the most impressive fountain in Caldaras City. Outside, on a wild, moonlit meadow behind the garden dome, I see a little stream that winds back into an old grove of trees. So much planning, so much effort, for this vision of beauty.

"Lovely," a voice at my shoulder says.

I spin around. "Nara?"

She stands, a hand on her hip, gazing at the waterfall. "Not so secret a passageway, is it?"

"I—" I start, and then I realize she is right. The grate at the bottom of the brass pool is more than big enough to allow a person to pass through.

"Nara!" Corvin hurries down the path. Fir appears a moment later.

"Now, how to turn off the water so we can get down?" Nara says.

Fir's expression is hard to read, but she seems a little more guarded than usual. "What are you doing here?"

Nara regards her from beneath perfectly curled eyelashes. "You didn't think I'd want to be there when the redwing saves us all?" She surveys the waterfall again. "So where's the switch?"

I lift my eyes, examining the top of the waterfall. An unassuming pipe fits invisibly into the seam between the large glass panels of the dome, and I follow it until it disappears behind the vegetation. "Is there a maintenance room below this one?" I ask.

"Not to my knowledge," Nara says. "Though I'm not very familiar with this garden."

"No," Fir says. "I've been all over this island. On bad tips from Nara's agents."

"Then I think"— I push aside the branches of some low, fat shrubs to find a valve set in the wall—"I think this is what we're looking for." The valve complains a bit, but I turn it until the waterfall trickles away to nothing.

Nara nods. "Well done!" She stands at the edge of the brass pool, watching the water recede.

"One of us should wait here and keep watch," Fir says, exchanging a look with Corvin.

"Fir, you stay." Nara waves a hand. "Corvin, help me get this grate up."

We step into the slick, empty pool. The bars of the grate are still hot when Corvin grabs them, and he recoils, cursing.

"Let me," I say. "I may bleed as easily as humans, but hot water doesn't bother me." I grasp the scalding bars and pull the grate up, revealing a black hole. "I'll go first."

"I'll put the grate back over you," Fir says as I dangle my feet over the edge of the hole. "I can kick it into place."

"Just don't turn the valve on," Corvin says. "I can't swim even in cool water."

I lower myself into the gloom, my feet brushing the slippery wall. I look up into the pleasant garden one more time. "Be careful, Fir. If the Onyx Staff and his followers come, let them. Don't take them on by yourself."

She skews her shoulders, combative. "What's that supposed to mean?"

I sigh. "Whatever you want it to, I suppose." And I drop down into darkness.

The drop is farther than I expect, although I have no reason to expect any specific distance. It could be a hundred feet, for all I know. Still, after a brief lurch in my belly, I land hard but safely. The moonlight drifts down from above, weakly illuminating a wide tunnel, its sloping walls sleek with algae.

"How far down is it?" the silhouette of Corvin's head calls from above.

"Maybe ten feet?" I hazard.

He lands with an "Oof!"

"Or fifteen?"

Nara drops silently next to us and rolls. Then she stands, wiping muck off her well-tailored suit. I hear the scratch of a matchstick, and a lantern flares to life. "Well," she says. "Let's see where this goes, shall we?"

The tunnel continues for some ways, sloping ever downward. I begin to suspect it may lead us to the shore of Lake Azure Wave, just another wastewater drain. After we have walked for several minutes, the tunnel begins to narrow, and another hundred yards or so later, we are forced to squeeze through the muck on our stomachs, one by one.

I take the lantern and go first, spilling out the other side of the opening into a wide, flat depression—it must be a pool, I realize, when the water is flowing here. I raise the lantern above my head, but turn its light down after a moment and peer into the large space beyond the pool. There is moonlight coming from above. We are not so far underground as I had imagined.

"This is where the water collects," Nara says, startling me once again. Corvin has emerged from the tunnel, as well, and makes his way along the edge of the empty pool. Nara lifts herself up. "What is this place?"

My eyes adjust while I stand at the edge of the depression, the slick wall as high as my chest. Round, black mouths of pipes dot the sides of the pool, waiting to carry water away to where it is needed. I look up, examining the shapes and shades of the darkness. "Water and light," I say.

I hoist myself out of the empty pool and turn up the lantern's light again. Corvin follows. "It's a garden," he says with astonishment.

It *is* a garden. I swing the lantern in an arc, entranced by all the strange plants, and move farther in among them. Tall and tiny, willowy and chunky, there is something familiar about some of them, but there is nothing growing in this odd underground room that I keep in the Dome. Still, these plants are not entirely unknown to me. I study the shapes of the leaves, the posture of the unusual flowers.

Then the realization hits me. I nearly drop the lantern.

Nara bends over to touch the fuzzy leaves of a squat little shrub.

"Nara, no!"

She retracts her hand and straightens up, looking at me quizzically.

"Don't touch anything!" I say. "Don't touch any of these plants!"

Corvin freezes. "What do you mean?"

I move among the plants, holding the lantern high. "This is a poison garden." Nara and Corvin step back toward the lip of the pool. The names are coming to me now, dusty and shadowed, plants I've held in my mind but never seen. Icevein, Ver's tears, and anydeath, the more potent cousin of Corvin's handy sleep powder. This garden is a maze of thorns, leaves, and flowers waiting to do harm. Or kill.

"Well, is it dangerous even to breathe?" Nara asks, gesturing impatiently. "Or should we just not be plucking our salad greens here?"

I survey the tangle of plants before us. "It's difficult to say." I point. "That spiky fellow over there, for instance, that's a jib jab. His thorns are deadly poison. Even just a scratch will paralyze your blood in minutes."

"Good to know," Corvin says grimly.

I look around. "But that one, that's known as raptorchoke—or raptorchoker. I don't remember. He looks just as scary as the jib jab, but his thorns are harmless, other than the fact that they'll prick you. No, the way he gets you is with his spores. They hang around him in a cloud, and if you breathe them, your bones will turn to liquid."

Nara nods. "A clever way to protect whatever is on the other side of this room, don't you think? I don't suppose we could get Fir to hack her way through?"

"No." I lower the lantern. "Some of these plants defend themselves by releasing poison into the air if they are cut."

"Bandannas," Corvin says. "Keep out the bad air."

"You couldn't," I explain. "You could wear a suit of iron from head to toe, cover your mouth with the finest linen, but if the smallest puff touched your skin, or if one spore made it through a joint in your armor . . ."

Corvin shakes his head. "So some plants are deadly to touch, some are deadly to breathe, and some are deadly to break."

Nara puts her fingers to her lips. "Which means," she says slowly, "that some are *not* deadly to touch, breathe, or break."

"Well, yes," I say.

"So there may very well be a safe path through, if we can only find it." Nara steps closer to the edge of the poison garden again. She turns to me, businesslike. "Can you lead us?"

Corvin has moved next to me, and places a warm hand on my back that I'm fairly certain Nara can't see in the gloom.

"I . . ." I start. I scan the wide snarl of a garden again. "The problem is I don't know all these plants. I know some of them, but in a garden like this, just one mistake could be deadly."

"Then it will also be deadly for the Beautiful Ones," Corvin says. "Nara, the Onyx Staff cannot navigate this poison garden any more than we can. The only way through is to kill the garden entirely—cut off its water and let it dry up—and that would take more time than they have. In a few short hours, Crepuscule will be over. I say we gather all the Fog Walkers here—send Fir after them—and stand guard."

"No!" Nara snaps. She marches over to us, leans into Corvin's face. "You would wager the whole of Caldaras City on our ability to fend off an army of cultists? The Fog Walkers are skilled, but we will be outnumbered."

"We have Lin," Corvin says.

"The redwing is not enough. We must be certain." Her expression is hard. But when I imagine that great wave of lava, unrelenting, swallowing Roet Island and Sweetrose Avenue and even our house on Saltball Street, I understand.

"Stand back, all right?" I step toward the edge of the garden. "I'll try to walk a safe path. I'll tell you when to follow." Heart thumping, I move along the first row of plants, trying to put a name to each one as I approach it.

When I have inched several paces, I notice a strange orange light. Feeble, but distinct. I extinguish the lantern.

"I trust you know what you're doing," Nara says stonily.

The orange light is coming from the edge of the garden, a few paces farther along. I move toward it. And as I get closer, the light grows stronger. When I finally reach it, the light is so bright, it stretches to the high ceiling.

"Ver's ass," Corvin says.

I stare at the source of the light—a broad-leafed bush, low and drab. If it weren't for the light, I would say this was a boat-leaf, a common scrubland bush whose roots cause the teeth of anyone who chews them to turn pink and fall out. I bend down—surely this *is* a boat-leaf? Holding my breath, I grasp one of the wide leaves to examine it more closely.

And underneath, hidden by the leaves of the bush, I see the real source of the strange orange light.

This bonescorch orchis is not broken or weak. It is not confined to a pot. It flourishes, its fiery, feathery leaves shining bright through the gaps between the leaves and stems of the plants around it. But if I had not moved the boat-leaf's branch, I would never have seen it.

I straighten my spine and see another orange glow several paces away to my left.

"What's happening?" Nara says. "What's that glow?"

I face them. "It's a bonescorch. It's glowing because I'm a— a—"

"A Lin," Corvin says, and I can't help a smile that prickles me to my toes.

"A redwing," Nara says without emotion. "So what does that mean?"

I inhale deeply. "I think there must be several bonescorches hidden in this garden. And that their purpose is to show us—me— the way through. That would explain why only a redwing can find the Heart." I bite my lip. "Of course, if I'm wrong, we could all die."

Nara shakes her head. "I don't think you're wrong. And it's our only shot, in any case."

"I'm in if you're in," Corvin says.

"Very well. Come and stand behind me. Move only where I move." I fix my gaze on the next faint orange glow. There is a straightish path between the two bonescorches, but it is crowded on both sides with plants of every size and description. As we move, we will brush them and breathe them. There is no avoiding it.

I take a step. A patch of tall, bony grass to my right scratches at my shoulders. Another step, and twisted shrub to my left slices my pants with its leaves. I keep moving.

"Ouch!" Corvin cries out. "That bush just cut me!"

"It's all right," I say over my shoulder. "That's razorwood. All it can do is cut you."

"Great," he mutters.

We soon reach the second bonescorch, now blazing vibrantly. This time it's Nara who spots the next orchis, closer this time, its feeble gleam about two dozen paces in front of us. Aside from a few minor pricks and bitter odors that burn our stomachs, we reach it without incident.

It must take us close to an hour to cross the entire poison garden. Some orchises are so far away, we can barely see them at first, while some are less than ten paces. Always the deadly plants crowd us, caressing us with hairy leaves, jabbing us with sharp sticks, or choking us with hostile pollen. But we don't die. We don't collapse. We reach the other side.

I hand the lantern to Corvin, who strikes a match and illuminates our new surroundings.

"Well done," Nara says, smoothing her jacket and looking critically at the root-lined walls. "We can't be far from the Heart now."

The only way forward is a low, dirt passageway on one side of the long room. Corvin goes first this time, arms outstretched, wriggling through behind the lantern like an earthworm. Nara follows, and I squeeze in behind her, feeling my way through almost total darkness.

The passage is not long, barely more than the length of my own body. It ends in a large dirt room, at the center of which is a mass of black tendrils streaked with brilliant red. They sit curled and spiraling, sprawling over the floor, piled in the middle of the room like discarded ribbons. I watch, fascinated. They do not move, but there is something alive about them.

At their center perches a faintly glowing egg-shaped object. No bigger than my hand, it pulses with life. Nara and Corvin stare at it, its clean yellow light reflected in their eyes.

I step toward it. "Is this . . . it?" I know the answer already. This small, bright thing is undoubtedly a heart. I look at Nara. "I—I don't know if we should harm this."

Her eyes flash. "Compose yourself, redwing. You know what this is. You know the danger it poses. Do what is right."

"I agree with Lin," Corvin says. "Something about this feels wrong. It's just sitting there. It's alive."

Nara grabs each of us by a shoulder. "Listen to yourselves. This is the Heart of Mol. You know what the Onyx Staff wants to do with this—what he can do *tonight* if we don't stop him. We've spent months looking for the Heart. Fog Walkers and agents have lost their lives in pursuit of it. And you're prepared to forget the whole thing because it's *pretty*?"

I look down. "I'm sorry, Nara. Of course you're right."

Corvin nods. "I lost my head for a moment."

"Now, pluck it from its perch, redwing," Nara says. "And smash the life out of it."

I reach toward the shining, pulsing heart, as small as the hot-budges with their puffed-out feathers.

"Death to Mol, sister," Nara whispers. "Death to the Others."

My fingers freeze. "Death to the Others?"

Nara jerks a sour smile. "What do you think will happen when we destroy their godforsaken Burning Lands? They will perish like the plague they are, cleansed from the world."

I don't recognize the voice that comes out of me now, small and low. *"All* of them?"

"Nara," Corvin says. "I thought destroying the Heart would put the volcano to sleep so it couldn't be used to harm the city."

"So it will," Nara says. "And it will ensure that no one will ever have to go through what we went through, Corvin. Never again." There is a look in her eyes, shiny and distant, that sets me on edge.

"Corvin?" I ask.

"This is not about revenge, Nara," he says quietly. "Sweet Rasus, there's no one left for revenge. They're gone. They're all gone."

"Do you know what Others are like, redwing?" Nara's grip on me grows tighter. "What kind of creature can drown its own child?" Her voice becomes ragged. "My father wouldn't let her do it. My sister, and then Corvin's brother, Ana and Birdy. For ten years, he wouldn't let her do it, the four of us believing more strongly each day that we would all get to grow up. But she couldn't live with the fear. She knew we were just children—all of us, just children—but her own skin was more important to her. So one night, she took a branch-lopper from the toolshed and killed Father in his sleep."

"That's enough, Nara." Corvin's face is streaked with tears.

Nara clutches my arm. "Then she beheaded Ana and Birdy in their beds. But you know what?" Her pupils are large. "A branch-lopper is an impressive blade. It carves Others up just as easily as it does humans." She smiles. "That was the first wrong I righted."

"I said, that's enough!" Corvin pulls her off me. "My god, Nara, think of Elena!"

"Elena knows this is necessary," Nara spits. "Oh, Rasus, just finish it!" She thrusts a hand forward, grasping at the beating heart.

And screams.

I look down. Blood pours from the end of her arm. Her severed hand rests on the dirt floor like a fallen red bloom.

A voice speaks from the shadows. "Touch the Heart again, and it will be your head."

Nara falls to her knees. Corvin and I turn in alarm as a figure steps into the light. He is masked, dressed in shadow from head to foot, except for one long blade that gleams in his hand and another that hangs at his hip. "The Black Thorn," Corvin whispers. "They say he is the right hand of the Salt Throne, that he has killed many Fog Walkers, but there has never been any proof."

"If the Black Thorn exists, he is just a man," I say, remembering the words. "Who are you?"

The figure approaches. "I am the one who protects the Heart from those who would do it harm." He raises a gloved hand to his mouth and blows. Glittering powder billows around us, a sweet, biting scent. Nara collapses onto her side. Corvin falls.

My skin shivers as my eyelids grow heavy. I gaze blearily at the shadowy man in front of me. "Your voice . . . I know you."

The Black Thorn pulls off his mask and throws it to the ground in one savage motion. "And I thought I knew you," Zahi says.

sixteen

Grimy walls, low candlelight, the overpowering scent of mold and oil—I awaken to sickeningly familiar surroundings.

I can't say I've missed the dungeon in the Temple of Rasus. Still groggy, I swing my legs off the bare metal bench someone thought would pass as a bed and pad over to the wall of bars in front of me. Grit crunches under my now bare feet. They've taken all my clothing except my sleeveless undershirt and the uncomfortable tweed pants from the Under House lost-and-found. Which, I suspect, they probably couldn't peel off my body.

I have no idea how many hours have passed or what is going on in the outside world. Caldaras City may not have been a bastion of comfort and safety for me, but it is my home. And if there is a chance I can still save it, I will try.

Closing my eyes, I call on the power below me. It finds me even here, snaking up through the soles of my feet, filling my veins.

It's my most impressive fireball to date. The stones on the far wall glow red. But the bars of my cell remain solid.

Damn.

"Hey!" I call into the dim space beyond the bars. "Anyone! I have information for the Empress! Hey!" I rattle the bars.

I keep shouting for a few minutes. Finally, a vertical shaft of light appears in the darkness beyond my cage. It widens, a door opening, and three figures step through.

"We don't have time to waste," I say. "I need to speak to the Empress. And the Commandant."

"You will do no such thing." One of the figures detaches and approaches the bars; two hooded guards flank the door.

"Zahi," I say. "Listen to me. The cult of Bet-Nef is alive and well in this Temple. They mean to awaken—"

"I know what the Beautiful Ones mean to do," he says. "Why do you think I watch them from within their own Temple? The Heart of Mol is precious and powerful. Many would use it for their own ends. That is why, after the War of the Burning Land, the Salt Throne created the first Black Thorn from the second child of the King. I guard the Heart as my predecessors have done for a thousand years. I guard it from the cult of Bet-Nef. And from creatures like you."

"You don't understand," I say.

"Who is Jey Fairweather?" His voice cracks at the edges. "Is she even real?"

My chest burns. "She's my sister," I whisper. "She's real. She's as real as Sunny."

"Sunny!" he exclaims. "I had to spoon-feed her the location of the tunnel just to find out what she was up to. I followed her around for an hour this evening before I realized she must have passed the information off."

"Zahi, listen—"

"I've listened to enough of your lies," he says bitterly.

This is too much. I grip the bars. "What would you have had me do? Don't you see? Even you've locked me in a cage."

The light from the doorway ripples across his face as he looks at me, searching. "We always think we will know evil when it comes," he says quietly. "And we rarely do."

"Stop," I plead.

He raises a hand tentatively, but lowers it after a moment. "Evil does not always conquer with wings of flame." *He's going to leave me here.* "I've saved the Others, haven't I?" His voice is low, dull. "An entire society. It's the right thing to do. Isn't it?"

I feel my face heating up. I do not answer him.

Now he flashes a crooked smile with no mirth behind it. "But you've won anyway. You've won because despite everything, all the secrecy, the killing . . . right now, this—" His voice breaks and he looks away. "This is the hardest thing I've ever done."

"I thought you cared for me." The heat in my face stings tears into the corners of my eyes. I look for understanding in his face, for resolve. For regret. But I find nothing but stillness.

"I do," he says. "But that doesn't mean I'm not your enemy."

I lean my forehead against the grimy bars. "Please don't do this."

"I'm sorry, redwing." He turns from me, curved by sadness, and I watch his silhouette move through the doorway, the inhuman shadow he casts on the walls of the stairwell growing as he ascends. The guards follow, phantoms in the torchlight, and I turn away.

A tingle starts in my chest and sparks outward—sharp heat that makes my heart race. At first, I cannot name it. But then I remember the alley—Corvin's face, bloodied, a pistol at his throat—and I recognize the feeling for what it is. Anger.

Still, I will not let Zahi Zan die in a cascade of lava. The way forward is clear. *Out.*

There must be a weakness to this dungeon. I slide my palms across the rough surface of the wall behind me. I scrape my nails and drag my knuckles across the stone. I push threads of flame into the corners of the cell but find no hope of freedom. The penny pulp redwings sneer from my memory: eyes like embers, muscles like stone. The world looks at me and sees them. Yet I can't picture a real redwing trapped in a pen like a baby stritch.

A real redwing. What does that even mean? I sit on the metal bench, letting my head fall into my hands.

"All right, enough. We've got work to do." A voice bounces off the dank walls. I look up, startled. One of Zahi's guards has stayed behind, and detaches himself from a black corner of the room.

I sigh. "Look, I have no secrets anymore, so before you torture me, why don't you just try asking me what you want to know?"

The guard lowers his hood. "Very well. Do you intend on wearing those painful-looking old pants until they have completely shredded themselves off your body?"

"Corvin!" I run to the bars. "How—?"

He cocks his head. "You don't think I can really be knocked out by anysleep, do you? Do you have any idea how much of that stuff I've inhaled over my lifetime? It was just a matter of finding the right opportunity to slip away." He bends, and I hear a key clunking into the lock.

"Where's Nara?"

"To his credit, your young man had her bandaged up and sent to the private hospital on Roet Island. Under heavy guard, of course." He gives the key a shake, and the rusty mechanism thunks into place.

I step out of the cage. "He's not my young man."

"I told you not to trust him." Corvin pulls a pair of shoes from his pocket. Ver knows where he found them; they are little more than leather wraps. Still, I am grateful to get something on my feet.

"He is not untrustworthy," I say. "He is a good man, and who's to say he's wrong? I still don't truly know what we ought to have done with the Heart when we had the chance. Do you?"

"No. But that's not what I meant," Corvin says with an expression I cannot read. "I just knew he would break your heart."

I look away. "My heart is of no concern to you." I finish tying the leather shoes.

He gives a sharp nod. "Very well. Let's go. The Salt Throne's procession has just left for Roet Island, and we still have to collect Fir."

I groan. "Do we have to?"

Fir, it turns out, does not have the high tolerance for anysleep that Corvin does. She's curled in a nest of dirty burlap at the bottom of the little boat we have commandeered to take us across Lake Azure Wave. The lake is not meant for boating, though the temple keeps one or two of these impractical craft for emergencies. Certainly the potential inferno-death of the city constitutes an emergency.

Corvin rows quickly as we try to reach the shore of Roet Island before the boat becomes too hot to sit in. Already his gloveless hands are slipping on the metal oars. Every once in a while, Fir raises her groggy head and I push her down again before an oar can smack her in the face. This is easily my favorite part of Crepuscule so far.

We approach the island out of sight of the Jade Bridge, skimming through the shining water and dark sky. Corvin wraps shreds of burlap around the oar handles, but still grimaces as he pulls. When we reach the island, I jump over the side and haul the boat on shore as quickly as I can, the scalding lake water lapping at my shins.

Once the boat is on land, Corvin rolls Fir over the side, where she lands in a heap on the fragrant earth. "Fir!" he hisses, swatting her cheek. "Hey!"

"Let me try," I whisper, and give her a good smack.

"Ow!" she whines.

"Get up," I say. "We're on Roet Island, and the Onyx Staff is probably already here."

She squints up at me. "Wha?"

Corvin puts a hand to his forehead. "All right. Leave her." He bends down and speaks into her ear. "Don't wander off! And don't go into the lake!"

She spits—or perhaps drools—and takes a groggy swing at him, which he dodges. "Don' tell me whatta do, you fedderless son of a . . . You're not my . . ." And she falls back onto the dirt, eyes closed.

Corvin looks at her. "She's fine." I raise an eyebrow at him. "No, she's fine," he says. "Let's go. Wait, I'm taking her saber."

After much painful negotiating with a tree, Corvin and I perch on the wall that surrounds the Copper Palace. From here, we have a good view of the main lawn, where all the Empress's guests are gathering to watch the ascendance of Bel, the Queen of the Stars.

FOOOOOOO! The unmistakable sound of an official olimu-horn is a clear, mellow disturbance in the night air. I turn my head toward the long note. At the edge of the lawn is a small raised tent hung with bright flags. After a moment, a cheer goes up as a woman waves from under the flags—the Empress, tall and distinguished even from this distance. The Commandant, all medals, stands to one side, and the Admirable Zahi Zan stands on the other next to a plain young man I take to be his older brother.

He's not protecting the Heart now, is he? I think sourly. I watch the doors to the Empress's private garden dome, but there is no sign of activity.

The Empress addresses the crowd. She is a model politician, speaking calmly—but with a commanding edge—about the value of coming together as a society to flourish in the Deep Dark. It is an eloquent and confident address, but my mind is focused on the monstrous sleeping mountain that looms over all of us, just out of sight beyond the black mist.

Corvin fidgets, tapping his fingers on the flat surface of the wall. But when the Salt Throne rises to speak, he becomes utterly still, tensed for action.

"Beloved," the Salt Throne says. I have to strain my ears to hear him. "We embark now on a journey together. A journey into the darkness that Caldaras has not seen for a thousand years. But we do not go without Rasus." Several people in the crowd make the open-palmed gesture of acknowledgment. "In the sky, our sun may give way to lovely Queen Bel for a time, but he lives on in the life he has made possible here. In the food that we have grown. In our very flesh."

From my perch, I look up and down the length of the Copper Palace. All is still. I see Corvin's eyes searching the crowd on the lawn, but nothing seems out of place.

Until the hedge maze explodes.

Screams shoot out from the throng of aristocrats; people scramble over and around each other in an attempt to escape the debris. Corvin is on his feet. I try to take in as much as possible— the Commandant and the Empress with their arms protectively around the Salt Throne, Zahi Zan with his long blades unsheathed, running toward the site of the explosion, the Onyx Staff . . . where?

I scan the grounds. Corvin looks, too. And at the same moment, we find him. Serene in shining white, he stands near the gaping hole where the hedge maze once was, his onyx staff raised high above his head. And from the hole, a star rises. But it is not Queen Bel in ascendence.

"The Heart," I whisper.

"He didn't have to find it," Corvin murmurs. "He's calling it."

"Well, he's going to stop calling it." I jump down from the wall, my blood roiling.

Corvin and I run for the Onyx Staff, knocking through priests and temple guards that have detached from the swirling crowd to protect him. Corvin efficiently hacks and threatens his way forward with Fir's saber—I'm surprised he really does know how to use it—and I lash out with blazing abandon, no weapons necessary. Zahi advances from the other side of the lawn, and we descend on the Onyx Staff at almost the same moment. But when we get close, the Onyx Staff strikes out and knocks us all backwards onto the grass.

Or does he?

I scramble to my feet and watch Zahi swing at him again. I'm not quite sure what I see; there is a strange duality to the Onyx Staff now. The man I remember stands placidly with the staff raised, calling forth Mol's Heart from its nest in the earth. But when others advance on him—Zahi, Corvin, the palace guards—a bright, *different* version of himself lashes out, as though the Onyx Staff is two beings at once.

And the second being begins to grow. The bigger it gets, the more fiercely it defends itself, a shimmering, translucent man with broad shoulders and a sword whose every flourish leaves a trail of sparks in the air.

"What in wet hell are you doing here?" Zahi grabs my

shoulder. I jerk away as a purple priest thumps a palace guard off his feet between us.

"What is going on?" I point to the giant defending the Onyx Staff. *I have seen him before, but where?* "What is the Onyx Staff doing?" I back up, my feet sliding on the grass. Zahi pulls me behind a stone flower bed.

"He's meditating," he says, out of breath.

I poke my head out. The huge, glowing warrior swings his translucent sword, lopping off the top of an ornamental tree and causing the heavy branches to fly at a knot of palace guards. "Huh," I say. "I thought meditation was less . . . exciting."

Zahi's eyes meet mine for just a moment. "Sometimes," he says.

Corvin rolls to a stop next to us. "Hello, kids," he says as Zahi shoots him a venomous look. "So, Lord Zan, any thoughts about taking on an enormous, slightly invisible soldier from what looks to be roughly"—he cranes his neck over the top of the flower bed—"a thousand years ago?"

"I certainly have some thoughts about beefing up security in the Temple dungeon," Zahi says sardonically.

A thousand years ago. I peer through the flowers at the giant soldier. And then I know him—he is the warrior from the fountain in High Ra Square. "That's Dal Roet," I say. "Why?"

"Advanced meditation can produce visions of the past, as you know," Zahi says.

"That vision just tossed a man ten yards," Corvin says.

"The Onyx Staff is a powerful priest." Zahi risks a glance over the top of the flower bed and ducks as a piece of twisted metal zings by his head. "His vision is—well, it's *real.* Sort of. I think this Dal Roet is fighting the War of the Burning Land, right here. He's enormous, I'd guess, because he's so legendary. Or something." He stands. "Look, redwing, I need to stop this one way or another." And he is off into the confusion of moonlit bodies.

I look at the towering warrior, then at Corvin. "But why? Why would the Onyx Staff summon—or meditate on, or whatever it is—why would he call forth Dal Roet?"

Corvin wipes Fir's saber on the grass. "I don't know. The Onyx Staff isn't known for making logical decisions."

I shake my head. "They're logical to him. And he wouldn't call forth Dal Roet." My stomach lurches. "He would call forth Bet-Nef."

And then it makes sense. But can it really be true? Is the striking warrior whose elegant marble face gazes dispassionately over the most powerful temple in Caldaras not the hero Dal Roet— but the monster Bet-Nef?

Suddenly, the warrior turns his massive head toward me and fixes me with a burning gaze. The adrenaline surging through my body numbed my awareness of everything else, but now I start to feel again. Not only the sparking at my center, but a terrible burning throughout the scars on my back. It's all I can do not to curl up on the ground.

Corvin leans in. "No one can fight this thing. We should help get people to safety, figure out what to do next. Start to evacuate the city."

"Go," I say, craning my neck to make out the features of the now towering man. "I have to talk to him."

"You have to *talk to him*?" Corvin's eyes widen.

"Go!" I snap, and I start to run. Most of the guards have fled. I see Zahi—a prostrate shape, unmoving in a bed of trampled flowers.

My breath stops for a moment. But I can do nothing for him, so I keep running.

"Bet-Nef!" I shout to the enormous warrior. "Monster that you are! Over here!"

The Onyx Staff turns to me from inside Bet-Nef's glowing boot. He clutches Mol's Heart, which glows red between his fingers. He frowns at me. "I remember you. Did I not have you put down?"

"Not quite," I say. Now his expression turns to one of horror, as a searing pain rips through my back and forces me to my knees.

"Sweet Rasus," he murmurs. "A redwing."

My vision is hazy with agony, but I manage to snort at him. "Yes. A *goddamn redwing*. The lies you told my sister? Turns out they were all true. Surprise, you bastard." And all at once, the pain is gone. The Onyx Staff takes a step backwards, and Bet-Nef finally looks down at me.

"Surrender, Dal Roet." His voice booms through the grounds, rattling windows and bending flower stalks.

I look up. "What? Me?"

"Surrender, Dal Roet. I shall not be merciful."

"Get away," the Onyx Staff barks. "I'll give you one chance, you uncrushable flea. Run away before I bestow this heart upon Bet-Nef, and you may be granted a third life."

"Give him Mol's Heart?" I say. "He is only a memory!"

The Onyx Staff smiles. "For now. But when I give him the

beating heart of a god, he will live again." And he throws his hands into the air and releases the Heart, which starts to float upward.

I gape at him. Nara was wrong. The Beautiful Ones didn't just want to bring back Bet-Nef's ideals. They wanted to bring back Bet-Nef himself. And it's happening.

The giant warrior has me in his gaze still, and for a moment, all I can do is stare. As Mol's Heart rises, it glows more fiercely with each passing second.

"Lin!" A hand finds my shoulder. I turn. Corvin remains after all, and is staring at me with wide, shimmering eyes. "Look at you!"

I stare back at him. My chemise hangs from my body by threads, and I'm suddenly off balance. Corvin steadies me with his hand. I twist my neck, and freeze in shock. Behind me, I can just see a glimmering curve, a spiderweb of red that illuminates Corvin's face and everything around me, shuddering in the light breeze.

"Lin," Corvin says. "They're—"

But I know what they are. Four of them, just like the redwing in High Ra Square. I know the pattern of those glowing red spiderwebs; I have known it my entire life. Not scars after all. Lying dormant. Just waiting to peel away from my back.

So redwings have wings after all.

Inhaling, I flex these new muscles. The night breeze lifts me, slides over my skin like silk, as the humans on the lawn watch in astonishment. I tilt and ride and ascend, the insect wings that reach into the sky from my raw back bathing the grounds of the Copper Palace in vivid red light.

Bet-Nef gives a roar and swings his fiery sword, but I dance away from it, propelling myself over his shoulder with little effort. I do not feel like the raptors, gliding with the air currents, negotiating. Nor am I reminded of the thick weightlessness of water. I ride the light, the red radiance from my own wings.

I am free.

"Redwing!" the Onyx Staff bellows from below, pointing. "See it there, you who did not heed my warnings!"

The crowd watches, rapt. But I keep my focus on the giant Bet-Nef, who lunges at me again, the rush of air from his translucent sword swirling my ragged clothes. He becomes more solid with each second.

I fix my gaze on the pulsing Heart within him. If only I had destroyed it when I had the chance . . . but my own heart wouldn't let me.

I dive behind a copper tower, Bet-Nef's blade nicking my arm with cold fire. I have no weapons, only the blaze at the center of my body that longs to lash out in lightning fury. But maybe that will be enough against a memory?

He coils his muscles again, ready to swing. I have to time it right. Too early and his first slice will connect. Too late, and his second will. I hover at the edge of his reach. He draws back his enormous blade, its white glimmer making the walls of the Copper Palace gleam against the night.

He swings and I dive, shooting straight for his chest. The ancient sword misses me by inches, singeing the cuff of my pant leg, and he draws it back for another go. But I am through him, arms outstretched. I am through his glowing armor, his translucent flesh. The cold memory of his blood surrounds me, suffocating, and I push through until I feel the small warmth of Mol's Heart at my fingers. I grasp it and clutch it to my chest as my body keeps going, shattering through the massive, glistening spine and back out into the balmy air.

The warrior drops his sword, pressing his hands to his chest. With a force that makes Roet Island tremble, he falls. The Onyx Staff falls with him.

Bet-Nef follows my progress with great, luminous eyes, until I alight. I stare at my hands, now empty. Where is the Heart? Did I drop it? Destroy it?

And then I know. I *feel*. A tiny pulsing in my chest, a new glow to my skin.

Mol's Heart is mine.

"I would speak with you," the echoing voice of Bet-Nef calls to me across the grass.

"And I would speak with you," I say. "This city is under my protection."

"You fight well, Dal Roet." Bet-Nef's voice is becoming fainter.

"Why do you call me by that name?" I ask. Beyond the palace walls, the looming summit of Mol gleams soft orange in the darkness.

Bet-Nef regards me. "You do not know me, brother?"

Brother. I remain still, casting my red light onto the wide lawn. I sense the people around me watching, holding their breath. "I know you only as a monster," I say.

The vision of Bet-Nef blinks slowly. "Humans are many things, brother. Monsters all. Angels all." He surveys the grounds. I can't tell if his gaze is with us or in the past. "You have the best of me this day. My army is in ruins. The city is yours. And yet . . ." He smiles.

"Out with it," I say. Mol's Heart thrums lightly in my chest, sending tingles through my veins.

Bet-Nef breathes deeply. "And yet, I will have the best of you. My name may be hated henceforth and yours will be glorified. But even now, my followers burrow into this city. They come not with swords, but words. Tales. Legends." He closes his shining eyes. "In a century, no one will remember what you were, my brother. I have sown the seeds of history, and the harvest will bring nothing but misery for your kind." He laughs. "Enjoy your victory, redwing."

And then he is gone, the light of memory faded once again into the gray wash of time.

seventeen

Caldaras City at night always carried with it a unique combination of gloom and menace. But now that the Deep Dark is upon us, the citizenry has embraced the black fog and strange noises. We prod the night with glittering candles and bright fabrics. We walk the streets at all hours.

With the poultry living out what will probably be the most confusing year of their lives, we awaken each day to bells instead of crowing. Ornate old things, the bells' dusty voices sing over the city from forgotten cupolas and bell towers, with the most resonant, imposing song coming from the highest dome of the Temple of Rasus.

It is fitting that when we learned the true nature of our

storied heroes, day became night. So many hearts and words were turned upside down the evening of Crepuscule. Bet-Nef, both a monster and a human. Dal Roet, his twin brother and our savior, a redwing. Yet now a rightness pervades the city that wasn't there before. At least for me.

As soon as Master Fibbori's team had made the Copper Palace grounds beautiful again, it was time for official words to be spoken. When the Empress declared me a hero, Papa fell to his knees in the middle of the crowd on the Copper Palace lawn. And when the Salt Throne pardoned all redwings, past and future, he wept for three days. I had so much fear and guilt bottled up in my veins, I never realized how much my father had been keeping in his own heart.

"It's damned chilly," Fir says, her hair a dark tangle against the night sky. "Can't you set something on fire with those crazy spark-fingers of yours?"

I rest my chin on the aviary's metal railing. Below us in High Ra Square, the priests are just finishing their morning meditations. Without the sunlight interfering, we can see the muted rainbow of the glowing visions much more distinctly. "I could melt this railing," I say, "but I'd probably burn your face off in the process."

"Cute," she says, shivering so intensely in the breeze that it borders on theatrical.

"Some Fog Walker you are, Fir," Corvin pipes up from my other side. "Ten degrees' difference, and your blood turns to ice water."

"More like twenty," Fir grumbles, rubbing her hands together. "Thirty, even."

"It's only a year," I say. "Then we can steam like vegetables all we want."

The priests begin to disperse, but the three of us remain. Is it comfort or simply inertia? Or something else?

"How's your garden taking to the darkness?" Corvin asks me.

"Better than expected." I watch a few storefronts and offices flicker to life in the streets below. "My father constructed a spectacularly odd arrangement of mirrors and lamps that seems to be doing the trick. It's based on some Roet Island designs."

Corvin smiles in the dimness. Then he asks quietly, "Still no word from your sister?"

"Tactful," Fir says.

I laugh over the pang in my heart, and both the pain and the joy are real. "That's all right. If you can't ask awkward personal questions of your friends, who can you?"

Corvin looks out across the twinkling square. "She should have come for your ceremony."

"She'll come eventually," I say.

The railing clangs as Fir gets to her feet. "Can't waste the day up here." She leans over, her hair streaming in the dark breeze. "It'll take us until lunchtime just to climb down." Now she looks over at me. "Those of us who can't fly."

I rest back on my elbows. "I'm not just going to fly everywhere, you know."

"Not even for our enjoyment?" Corvin gives me a cheeky smile. Then he says softly, "I'll never forget the way those wings peeled away from your back and sent you dancing into the air. They were there the whole time, and nobody knew."

Fir takes an echoey step toward the little window we climbed out of. "Oh, keep it together, will you? Ver's green ass, Corvin. Come on, Lin. The Empress will be expecting us."

I get lazily to my feet. "The Heart is fine. I can feel it inside me, humming along." I gesture to the volcano that watches over us from beyond Lake Azure Wave, still glowing faintly from the inside. "Mol doesn't seem to be complaining, at any rate."

"She wants reassurance," Fir says. "You can't begrudge her that."

"If we must." I stretch down a hand and pull Corvin to his feet.

Fir pulls open the creaking window frame. "You'll be fine. *He* won't even be there. They say he left before the mess was even cleared up. Won't even help his brother hunt down the Beautiful Ones."

In truth, I still don't know which of us betrayed the other. Zahi is gone, and I can hardly blame him. But all I say to Fir is, "I don't know who you mean."

Fir laughs, but Corvin is silent. We crawl through the window one by one, descend into the quiet shadows of the old aviary. In some ways, I have traveled this path many times, as my sister and I came together to watch the morning meditations, or separated afterwards, she to her life and me to mine. But today, in the new darkness, I am no longer Jey with the wrong eyes and the wrong blood. I am me. A redwing. With all as it should be. I am Lin.

acknowledgments

Thanks to my mum and dad, Mr. K, Ammi-Joan Paquette, Vicki Lame, Katie Bayerl, Liz Cook, Alicia Potter, Erin O'Halloran, the Thunder Badgers, and the wonderful communities of the Tanglewood Festival Chorus and the Vermont College of Fine Arts.

Discover a world of dark secrets, music,
and romance in Adi Rule's

Strange Sweet Song

Read on for more.

Available now from St. Martin's Griffin.

one

If you had been there that night, the night it happened, you might not have even noticed. The strings and woodwinds shone fat and glossy in the concert hall's perfect humidity, and the brass instruments sparkled in the gentle light of the chandeliers. The music itself shimmered as well, lighting up dark places people hadn't even known were there.

You might not have noticed the small movement. It fluttered the fading sunlight stretching in through one of the high, arched windows that encircled the room like a crown. You would have been staring at the orchestra, or at the polished floor, or at the blackness inside your closed eyelids, as the music swirled around you. Had you opened your eyes or broken your fuzzy-glass gaze and looked up at the fluttering light, you would have seen the silhouette of the crow. But you wouldn't have heard it, because the crow didn't make a sound.

At least, not at first. It alighted on the ledge of the little window and folded its wings, flexing its toes as though it meant to be there awhile. Some of the windows still held their colorful panels, but the crow had chosen one through which tendrils of ivy had pushed their way, dislodging the glass with a long-forgotten drop and shatter.

The crow seemed comfortable, somehow, and not just because it was a crow adorning a remote Gothic hall surrounded by dark pine trees; not just because St. Augustine's was a natural place for a crow to be. It seemed to be *listening,* cocking its head and stretching its black neck as far into the room as it could.

At intermission, the grand piano was wheeled onto the stage, black and sleek and curvy. The crow looked at the piano with one eye and then the other and ruffled its wings. As the audience applauded, a middle-aged woman lowered herself onto the bench and placed her hands on the gleaming keys, stretching and bending her fingers. The crow twitched its own knobbly gray feet experimentally.

Then the conductor waved the orchestra to life again—a romantic piano concerto well known to the concertgoers, who settled in their seats and breathed.

When the woman at the piano began to play, when the first smooth, icy notes reached the small, broken window in the ceiling, the crow froze. It stared, its dingy feathers raised just a little. It was listening again, but now it listened with its whole body. As the concerto progressed, the crow remained utterly still. It might have been a stone gargoyle, except there was something too bright about its eyes. They were fixed on the woman's hands.

If you had looked, then, into the crow's eyes, if you had been a ghost or a puff of smoke and had floated up to the ceiling to look deeply into those shiny black eyes where the brilliant white keys were reflected, you would have seen a despair bigger than those eyes could hold, bigger than the hall itself.

And you would have heard the faintest hiss—an ugly, crackling hiss, as different from the pure, clear tones of the piano as it could possibly be. You might then have noticed the grubby beak was open very slightly. And you might have realized with a start that the crow was trying to *sing*.

But perhaps you *were* there. Perhaps you already know this story.

two

Sing da Navelli stares across the moonlit quadrangle and up the snowy mountain that watches over the campus. A porter unloads baggage from her father's Mercedes. Just inside the doorway to the dormitory, a haggard young man in gray academic robes speaks to one of her father's secretaries. She is finally here, counted among the select few.

Dunhammond Conservatory. European prestige tucked away in New World mountain wilderness, surrounded by its own black forest. A scattering of mismatched buildings huddle in the shadow of St. Augustine's, the famous Gothic church synonymous with musical greatness. Until her first visit, this spring, Sing had seen St. Augustine's only in magazines. Now she is here to sing, in the place that has produced the brightest stars in classical music for a century and a half.

She drifts away from the yellow lights of campus toward the chilly northern woods. Not too far, not too deep, just the shadowy, crackling edge. The mountain snow tingles her nose as she peers into the twisted darkness. *Quand il se trouvera dans la forêt sombre* . . . She finds herself humming an all-too-familiar aria. *When he finds himself in the dark forest* . . .

When she was little, music was her nanny when her parents were gone, which was most of the time. Sure, various starched, soap-smelling women bustled around, but it was music that raised her, folding around her like a blanket—fuzzy or spiky or cold or sweet and warm. It sparked her, calmed her, made her want to get off the velvety floor and look out the window. Sing da Navelli is more music than words, inside.

Chatter from the campus drowns out the song in her mind. People are taking care of her registration, checking in, all those little details she has never had to worry about. Then it will be official. No more mediocre high school ensembles. She will spend the last of her teen years with her peers—those young musicians destined to attend the best universities and build careers like fireworks, explosive and brilliant. She is finally going to sing for real.

How can something so wonderful fill her with dread?

It would be better if Zhin were here. Zhin, Sing's first almost best friend, who loves the violin almost as much as the soap opera world of classical music. She looked out for Sing at Stone Hill Youth Music Retreat this past summer—can it have been only a few weeks ago? They even got to do the opera together, *Osiris and Seth.* Sing loved the elaborate set with the big lotus pillars. Zhin loved the battle scene with all the shirtless baritones.

If Zhin were here, she would tell Sing what she can't quite tell herself: *You are good enough. You belong at Dunhammond Conservatory. You deserve this.*

The voice in Sing's head won't say these things. It says, *Not yet. Something is missing.* But it offers no insight when she tries, every day at the piano, to perfect her imperfect voice.

She heard some of the other singers through the wall at the spring auditions; they were good. Very good, but not out of her league. Now, across the gravel driveway, Sing hears her father speaking. *He* wouldn't let her come to DC if he didn't think she could be good enough.

It's just that, in her family, "good enough" means "the best."

Her parents could have named her Aria, or Harmonia, or Tessitura, or a hundred other clever names that would have alluded to her ancestry. But they weren't for her, these names that roll or sparkle or play or simply proclaim, *I am normal!*

No, it was Sing. A name and a command.

"Sing, must you wander off? It is time to go in." Her father is suddenly there, speaking in that calm, unwavering voice, more used to command than leisure. Instead of his native Italian, he speaks to her in English, her language. Her mother's language. "You must get to bed as soon as possible, but do not sleep too long tomorrow. When is your placement audition?"

It is a quiz. He knows the answer already. "One o'clock." Her voice feels small here, at the edge of this great forest.

"So you must be awake and singing by when?"

"Nine o'clock."

"Exactly. Eat a good breakfast. Go over your piece tonight, but don't overdo it. It is there, eh?" He taps her head lightly. "You know it very well. I have heard you sing this vocalize one hundred times, eh?" Sing nods. Her father looks back toward campus. "It is a shame we are so late in arriving. I would like to see Maestro Keppler—I so much enjoyed his interpretation of the *Little Night Music* last spring. He has not aged one day since I last saw him! And I have not the opportunity to speak with my old friend Martin."

It's just as well he won't get to speak with DC's president. Sing already feels her father tugging on the invisible marionette strings of her budding career. The conservatory's brand-new theater is evidence of his sudden interest in philanthropy toward his alma mater.

"I hope they have chosen a suitable opera for the Autumn Festival." He puts an arm around her shoulders. "Something Baroque, eh, *carina*? That would be lovely in your voice. I would like to hear it."

Something Baroque, she thinks. *Something safe. Something technical and stylized.* But in her mind she keeps hearing a different melody, a sweeping, wailing one that was born of this very forest almost one hundred fifty years ago. *Quand il se trouvera dans la forêt sombre . . .*

"This is where Durand wrote *Angelique*," she whispers, and is surprised to have said it out loud.

Her father's arm stiffens. "Yes, certainly it is. This is a beautiful place to write an opera. *Vieni*, it is time to go in."

Sing hesitates, gazing into the dark forest, Durand's dark forest. Angelique's dark forest. She is unable to turn away.

After a moment, her father speaks in a heavy, quiet voice and calls her by a name she hasn't heard in years. *"Farfallina,"* he says, "I leave tonight. But please promise me to stay always on the campus. They say this forest is dangerous."

Sing tilts her head. "That sounds almost superstitious of you, *Papà*."

He smiles. "I am just being your father, my dear."

If he wanted to, Sing's father could conduct *Angelique* as well as anyone in the world. But Sing couldn't imagine him doing something as impractical as wandering around the very forest that inspired it. Her mother, perhaps. But she didn't attend Dunhammond Conservatory and would never see it now. Who knows if she would have answered the forest's call—or if she would have even heard it.

She shrugs. "I'm not afraid of ghosts."

Her father continues to smile, but his eyes are grave. "That is good to hear."